When I'm 64

The Lovesong Encore Series

LESLIE J. WYATT

Sibylline Press

Copyright © 2025 by Leslie Wyatt
All Rights Reserved.

Published in the United States by Sibylline Press,
an imprint of All Things Book LLC, California.

Sibylline Press is dedicated to publishing the
brilliant work of women authors ages 50 and older.
www.sibyllinepress.com

Sibylline Digital First Edition
eBook ISBN: 9781960573315
Print ISBN: 9798897409631

Cover Design: Alicia Feltman
Book Production: Aaron Laughlin

Sibylline
Press

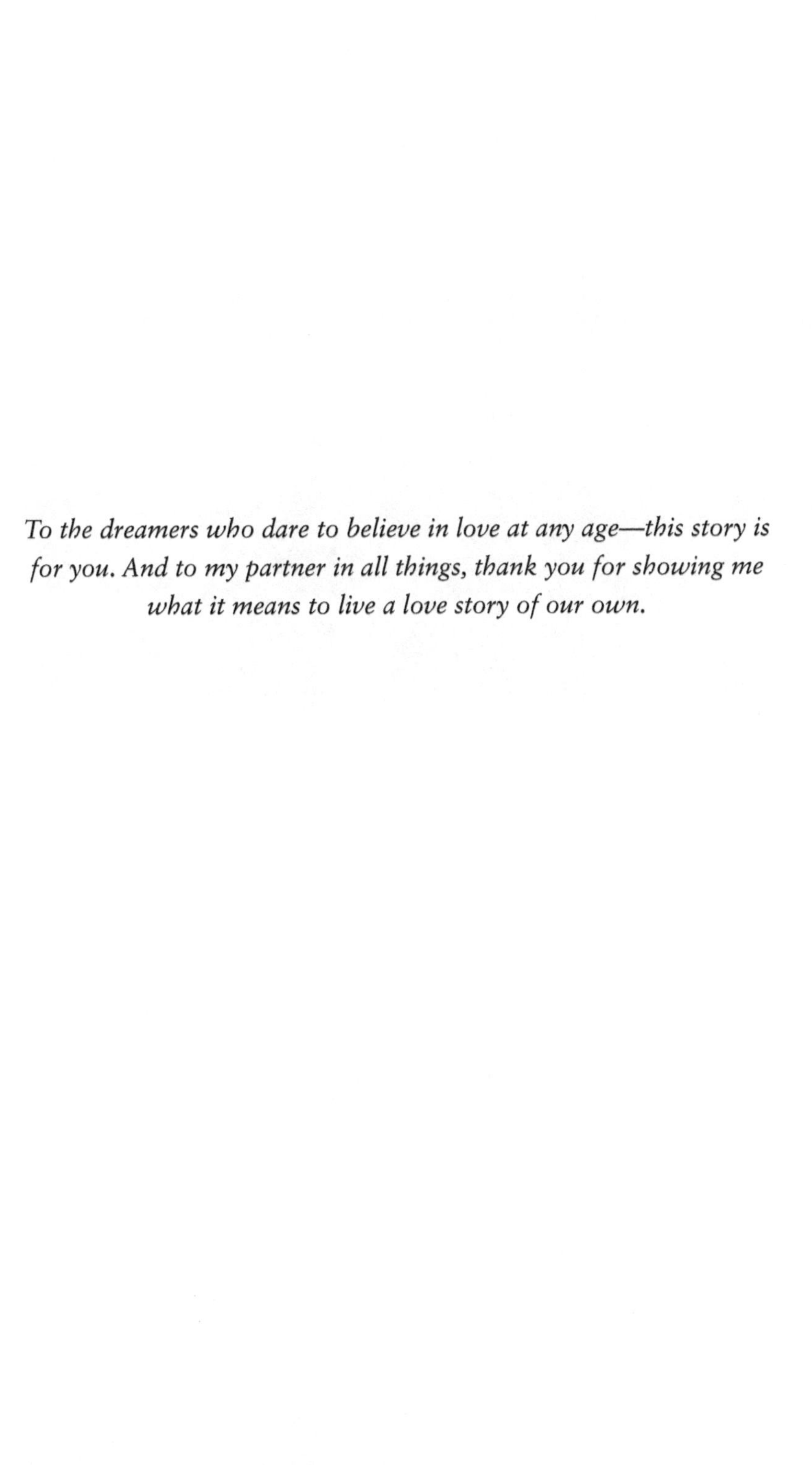

To the dreamers who dare to believe in love at any age—this story is for you. And to my partner in all things, thank you for showing me what it means to live a love story of our own.

CHAPTER 1

Until the point when the Universe swept me up in the air, threw me against the kitchen wall, and left me to pick up whatever pieces remained, I would have told you I liked my life quite well, thank you very much. I just turned sixty-four, and the most troublesome blip on my horizon was signing up for Medicare before I turn sixty-five and which of the plans—A, B, D, or G (whatever happened to C, E, and F?) did I need to apply for to avoid being penalized for the rest of my days?

That morning, the sun reached long, bright fingers through our kitchen window, turning Jimmy's gray hair gold. I know he's no angel, but I had no idea what was about to land on me from this golden-haloed guy I'd been married to for forty-three years. "The time has come, Eisel. I'm going to Peru."

Please. Not this conversation again. Peru is not my favorite subject, especially first thing in the morning, and he can talk about it for hours. I take another sip of the brew that is true. "Ah." Believe me, it's a very non-committal ah.

Jimmy turns, and I see a look in his warm brown eyes that cues me to set my cup down and brace myself. "I mean now." he says. "I'm going to Peru *now*."

"Now?"

"Now. Next Tuesday now, anyway." He rushes into his next sentence before I question his sanity. "You know how I majored in archeology in college and spent the summers in Lima help-ing excavate historical sites? The college obtained a three-year archeological grant this year and contacted me to be part of the team they're taking down to help on a dig. This is a chance of a lifetime for me to be involved in the field again."

He sits down across from me, fixing me with those earnest eyes I thought I knew completely. Suddenly, I'm not so sure I do. "Here's the thing, honey. I felt incredibly alive when I was working on those archeological sites back in the day. Now here I am at sixty-nine, and the long and short of it is I want to spend this next year of my life feeling that alive again. They accepted me on the team, I bought my ticket, and I'm going. Isn't that amazing?"

I'm sure I display a classic deer-in-the-headlights look. "You know what's amazing?" I ask, trying to keep my voice regulated. "That you did all that without even discussing it with me or asking me to go along."

He rolls his eyes. "You don't want to go, and you know it, Eisel. I've been talking about doing something like this ever since I retired. Every time I do, you give me reasons why it can't happen and why you don't want to go. What's the point of even asking you?"

Gripping the countertop to steady myself, I clear my throat. "Jimmy—it's not that I want to go—it's that I want to be included in the decision process. It scares me to think you're making plans and buying tickets—living your own life, but without me." In all honesty, he's been doing that in smaller ways for a quite a few years, and I feel left out every time. This, however, is a whole other league.

"What's the point of asking you if you always say no?"

"Like I just said, inclusion. I'd love to feel wanted, you know? Desired. To be with you in the process. Otherwise, it feels like we're merely roommates. I want—"

"Here's the thing, honey. You can't talk me out of this. I'm doing it. Besides, I think it will be good for both of us. I hope it will, anyway. We're so dug into our routines around here and with each other it feels as if nothing ever changes. If I do this, our worlds will expand." He gives me a hopeful glance.

"I'm not sure I want that, Jim." Actually, I'm quite sure I don't or at least not the way this is stacking up, though it sounds a bit stodgy to say that right out loud.

"I do. Call it a late life crisis, but I feel like I'm dying on the vine. I'm trapped in that Beatles song, 'When I'm Sixty-four'—you know, where they sing about asking nothing more from life than tending the garden and digging the weeds?" He snorts. "I'm not satisfied with that. In fact. I want a whole lot more. If all my final years hold is you knitting sweaters and us going on Sunday drives, I'll shrivel up and finish dying of boredom."

"Hey, I like that song," I protest. "Especially now that I'm sixty-four, because we made it this far. I also like the part about you still needing and still feeding me, you know?"

He smiles, but his answer isn't the one I'm looking for. "I think I'll always need you, Eisel. However, that's not enough for me anymore."

"Wait. What's that supposed to mean?"

"I mean that I've spent my entire life doing mundane stuff while dreaming about joining another archeological expedition, and never actually doing anything about it. Nothing. Except for my time on the digs in Peru, I slogged away at the post office. Forty-four years, for God's sake—which you must admit is about as tame a job as you'll ever find—then I retired. Face it, honey. That's not exactly the embodiment of doing something extraordinary with this one precious life and all that jazz." He grimaces. "I've decided to launch out before I'm too old to travel down my own hallway. You're free to do the same should you desire. I mean, not Peru, you know, but to follow your dreams."

As I said, no inclusion. Heart riding somewhere below my sternum now, I frown. "I see. In other words, forty-three years of marriage erased as irrelevant. Are you divorcing me?"

He huffs. "Don't be ridiculous, Eisel. I'm not saying that. I'm only saying that for a year or so—unless I decide to stay longer (I like how he adds a disclaimer, as if I could make him come back earlier than he desires)—I'll be embedded with the archeological team. Please try to understand. I don't have many years left in the bigger scheme of things; I don't want to waste any of them."

"Waste them," I repeat. "Do I take that to mean living here with me in the life we've created is a waste of your last years? Nice to know."

"I did not say that, and you know it," he clips, mouth tight, eyes narrowing. "I'm simply saying I want to do this. I'm not asking you to do it also."

"I noticed. That being the case, I guess I need to decide what I want to do and whether I want to stay married to you while you're off living your dream without me for the foreseeable future." Holding my coffee cup to my chest like a shield, I stand up, shake my head, and stalk out.

This can't be happening to me. To my marriage. I feel like I did when my second-grade classmate, Shawn, announced that Santa Claus is not real and only babies believe in him. Crushed. Dumbfounded. Completely without a clue how the world can go on like it was doing a mere sip of coffee ago. Maybe Jimmy doesn't include me in his day-to-day all that often, but we don't act independently of each other. Not on the big stuff. Not usually.

I walk back into the kitchen. "You're kidding, right?"

"No. I'm not kidding. I'm going to Peru next Tuesday." He lifts his chin like he's inviting me to challenge him.

I stalk back out.

I stalk back in. "Really? You made this decision that alters everything in our known existence—in *my* known existence—and you're only now telling me about it? Don't I have a say in it, or are you singlehandedly dismantling life as we know it?" My voice breaks at the end.

He throws up his hands like I'm beyond a basket case. "I knew this would happen. That's exactly why I didn't discuss it with you. You always manage to make things turn out the way you want them to. I'm sorry. You're not going to do that this time, Eisel. Not with Peru. I'm going, and there's nothing you can say to stop me."

This is actually happening.

Jimmy really is leaving. I see that in his eyes, read it on his face, and my heart is now a tight, burning lump in my chest. If we have one more verbal exchange, I might end up in a fetal position right here on the kitchen floor. I can't comprehend how this man I love who I would have sworn loved me in return can be leaving. Leaving me, moving forward with his life solo, and what I cannot wrap my mind around is how he has apparently planned it all before letting me know. I walk away.

Stuffing my feet into my shoes, I set my coffee down on the hall table, and head for my favorite walking trail. The morning seems like any other in Ranger Falls. The sky is as blue as a baby's eyes. Birds are tuning up as if the world is completely normal. So normal, in fact that this could be one of those dreams that happens just before you wake up—the ones where you're trying to convince someone that they shouldn't be unloading their truck full of belongings onto your porch and setting up shop. Or in this case, that they're not actually heading to Peru.

But this is not a dream. I really am hiking along with tears leaking out my eyes, heart imploding. I process Jimmy's news as best I can and manage to talk myself back from the emotional cliff I teetered over by the time I return home.

Jimmy meets me at the door with a fresh cup of coffee and a hug. "Eisel, honey, I'm sorry I lost it earlier. Of course, it would be a shock to you. I didn't include you in the planning because I want this so badly, and I was afraid you'd somehow keep it from happening. I should have been braver, I guess."

Ya think? Of course, I don't actually say this nor can I look him in the eyes, though I do manage to mumble, "Thanks. Sorry—" Words fail, especially since I didn't do anything wrong, but "sorry" really does encapsulate it all, since this is certainly a sorry state of affairs.

Despite what could only be described as a tentative peace between us, Jimmy is like a kid on the first day of summer vacation. Me? It feels more like the first day of a life sentence for a crime I didn't commit. I want to meet him halfway and be happy that his dream is coming true. Instead, it's all I can do to not follow him around like a puppy dog trying to persuade him to stay.

Speaking of puppy dogs, along about Monday, I deliver the one thing I'm certain about. "Jimmy, I will not take care of your dog while you are gone."

"What?"

"Exactly what I said. My dream life does not include dogs."

"You love Trencher, though."

He's shocked, but you know what? In view of what he dropped on me, I can't seem to find it in me to care overly much. "No, I don't. I don't like dogs, and you know it. Never have. You also know that."

"But—"

"*You* love dogs, and I love you, and you wanted one so much I decided I shouldn't be responsible for depriving you. However, I will not keep him for you while you're gone. If you won't find a home for him, I will." I experience the first blip of joy since his announcement to be laying down this clear boundary. Granted, I do feel like Cruella de Vil later that day when Jimmy cries as his cousin loads Trencher—bed, bowls, and chew toys—and drives away.

Of note, those are the first tears I've seen him cry since he made his big announcement, though I've cried enough tears for both of us, I suppose.

"Would you drop me off at the airport tomorrow, Eisel?" he asks that evening. Our last evening.

I almost say yes. I pretty much always say yes to Jimmy if I can because I tend to avoid conflict like week-old liver and onions. This time, though? No way I'm going to assist in my own funeral. "No, Jim. You want to go? You figure out how to get there."

I know. Not the most gracious or loving response, but it really burns my bacon that he can make an announcement that flips my world into an alternate universe and then ask me to drive him to his leaping off place. I imagine a more mature person would suck it up and help her spouse live his dream even if it doesn't include her. I can't quite make myself embody that role. Nope. Not this time. I mean, if forty-three years of being helpful, empowering, and supportive has not been sufficient to keep our marriage intact, then I'm sorry—I'm apparently not mature enough to take this last episode and act like I'm fine.

I am not fine.

I do assist him with laundry and packing, though, and I'm glad I manage these tasks at least, because when Jimmy's in the air somewhere over Central America, I'll be left here with only myself for company along with all sorts of guilt and regrets for being too hasty in my words, too harsh in my thinking, and too stubborn to apologize for any of that. Might as well not add "refused to fold his laundry" to the list.

Tuesday morning rolls around as if the universe decided to facilitate his plans while ignoring any preference I may have to the contrary—no hurricane to ground the plane, no torrential rains or airline strikes. Just blue, blue skies and light wind out of the southwest.

Jimmy parks his roller bags at the front door, beaming non-stop. "Well, can you believe it, sweetheart? I'm actually going to Peru after all these years!"

I don't have the heart to douse his brightness, though it's touch and go for a moment there. Not trusting my voice, I just nod and open the door for him. Down the suddenly endless sidewalk, I drag my heart along behind me like a feral cat on a leash; Jimmy walks like a man in a dream—which when I think about it, is probably exactly what's going on.

I think my emotions have gone comatose. Eyes swollen, sinuses plugged like a full-blown case of Covid, yet inside? Nothing. In fact, it's all I can do to kiss Jimmy goodbye. I want to, because there he is, smiling like a kid on Christmas Eve, and I love everything about him—his sweet brown eyes, his hair gone gray, every line, every wrinkle. The way his body is made and all the years we've shared together.

Goodbye? How do you say what feels like a forever farewell to your love, your partner, your life-as-we-know-it guy while standing on the sidewalk outside of your house with barely three days' notice. And the neighbors watching?

But I do. Somehow, and very poorly actually. Still, A+ for trying, I suppose. I give him a peck on the lips and a little hug, so afraid of last-minute dream killing I haven't a word I dare say past "have a good trip," and "stay safe."

Not fazed in the least, Jimmy pulls me close, which about does me in. He smells so familiar. So good. A mix of spice and soap, and I want to hold onto him forever, as if my heart needs his beating next to it to keep it going and without that, it might go offline indefinitely. How can this be the last time for possibly ever?

He hugs me longer and even stronger, then bending down, kisses me on the lips like a man going off to war. Stirred in spite of myself, I respond, kissing him back as deeply and desperately as I ever have in my life, as if he and I here together are the sum total of the universe and somehow, as long as we're kissing, my world will hold together.

Except he steps away as his buddy pulls up to the curb. Luggage loaded, he smiles into my eyes, which are awash with tears for the hundred and eleventh time since his announcement. "I'll miss you, and I wish you all the best in your adventures, too, my dear."

His dear?

I question the accuracy of those words. You don't exclude your dear from your life and leave her behind you, do you? I watch their brake lights flicker at the end of the street and fade into the distance. Just like my marriage. Jimmy assures me it's not over, that he'll be back sooner or later. Yet as I turn to go inside, I'm not at all sure about either of those things. All I really know is that I cannot live with my heart in two places, and it seems very clear in all of this that he's not leaving his here in Ranger Falls with me. When it all shakes out, I guess I'm not as important as his archeological dreams.

Among my various talents and accomplishments, I can throw a pity party with the best of them. Setting that activity aside , however, (which I suppose I will feel able to do after copious tears and punching of pillows), I must face it: if he can fly off to parts unknown without actually asking me if I would please, please go with him or without reassuring me that he can't live without me and that our relationship is top priority for him even in his absence—if he can move forward without me, then what do I have left?

Maybe I should follow suit, living my life as if he's not part of it. Not because I want to, necessarily, but because danged if I'm going to spend the rest of my life on this earth waiting for Jimmy to touch bases with me in between archeological finds.

In fact, maybe the best way to find my way through this uncharted territory is to figure out what I want moving forward, then simply do that. What if from here on out, I make all my decisions without considering him, exactly as he has done with me? Not by choice—I didn't ask to be in this position—but because apparently that's where we've landed.

I have no real idea what making my own decisions would even look like. I went from doing what my parent's thought I should to doing what Jimmy thinks is good, and to be honest, it isn't either of their faults. Or I should say, despite the fact that Jimmy apparently views me as powerful enough to prevent him from going to Peru, I rarely push back (for the record, if whining, complaining, and arguing about it would have prevented him from going, then yes. I guess I'm that powerful, because I know I would have done all those things if given the chance).

All that is now irrelevant. The question I need to answer is who am I outside of the construct of our marriage? Maybe all I have left of my original self is my name, and even that has changed. Eisel Jane McCord currently, I used to be a Wellington eons ago. I'm certainly not saying that the Wellington family is any better (read that as more functional) than the family I married into. My point is that I don't remember who I used to be, and come to think about it, I'm not sure I ever knew. Nor do I know what I want.

As much as I hate to acknowledge it, some of what Jimmy said may be right, or at least a silver lining may emerge from this unexpected, unwanted, uncalled for event—that "something good" he referenced. Perhaps it's time for me to dust off a few dreams of my own and see where they take me. Rediscover myself. Because I am not about to wait around here to pick up where we left off once archeology loses its appeal, if that's even possible, which I doubt.

I suppose some women might hang in there, waiting and hoping for that day, but I'm not wired that way. I refuse to spend the rest of my life as a nonessential. This much I do know. Sometimes you hit these spots where between one blink and the next, the whole world shifts. I just collided with one of those like a crash test vehicle impacting a concrete wall.

Sliding my wedding ring off—easier said than done—dislodging it from the groove it's worn into my finger. I vaguely recognize this as symbolic. Also, as painful as an amputation without anesthetic by the time I succeed, and stand there staring at my finger, naked for the first time in forty-three years.

Am I angry with this turn of events I did not create? You bet I'm angry. I also have no idea how to deal with the fact that my lifetime of trying to be a good wife and partner—doing what I felt was more than my fair share of the relational and emotional heavy lifting to maintain a modicum of connection—was all for nothing. In the end, here I am, alone.

I wallow. You better believe it. I hold pity party after pity party and in between engage in cathartic screams —first into pillows, and then heck. Since no one can hear me, I scream at the walls and the ceiling and the floor. It feels healing in a strange way, though of course it doesn't bring Jimmy back. It also leaves me with a ravaged throat.

"Fine, Jimbo," I croak, tossing back a gulp of licorice root tea (good for vocal cords). "You're off on your adventure that you didn't bother to even discuss with me? Okay then. I'm about to launch on mine."

CHAPTER 2

Brave words. In reality, that's not what I do. I spend the better part of the next three months hiding out in the house like a hibernating prairie dog. However, before I go to ground, I rally long enough to call our daughter, Maggie, which I've studiously avoided doing while Jimmy was still here in the vague notion that not talking about his Peru expedition would prevent it from happening.

"Hi Mags."

"Finally decided to call, huh?"

"Affirmative. I take that to mean you know your father has left me."

"Mother. He did not leave you. He went to Peru."

I love this daughter of mine to pieces. She's my alter-ego, sounding board, and a needed cold-water to-the-face at strategic moments. That does not mean she's always correct in her perspectives.

"Wrong. He's gone to Peru, *and* he's left me, having moved out of my life to pursue his own, thus demonstrating that his love of things archeological outranks me and our marriage. I suppose you have all the details because he actually talked it over with you, which he did not do with me."

"I'm sorry, Mom. I told him that was a tacky way to handle it."

"Ya think? There I was babbling about cleaning out the flowerbeds to usher in spring, him nodding like it's priority one on his agenda, too. Until Saturday, when he informs me that contrary to the famous Beatles song, he feels trapped by digging in said garden, and is leaving for the foreseeable future. Without me." Snort. "I think 'tacky' is a bit too tame of a word for that. How about inconsiderate, selfish, and plain ole cowardly with some betrayal and abandonment thrown in for good measure?"

Silence. She knows that if she continues to listen, I'll move past griping and victimhood to the real meat of what I called about. She never takes sides because she loves us both, which I do appreciate, though I will say she plays a mean devil's advocate sometimes, which I do *not* appreciate.

I clear my throat. "Here's the thing. Your father said, and I quote, 'I've decided to go, and I do think it's going to be good for both of us.' I'm not included in his dream. He made that clear."

"Mother. You've made it equally clear if not more so that you wouldn't go to Peru unless you were bound, gagged, and mind wiped. Why would you want him to include you?"

"I'm not saying I wanted to go. I'm saying that a wife of forty-three years deserves to be included in the decision-making process, especially considering that I'm half of our given equation. On what planet do you completely bypass an equal partner to make an executive decision the way he just did? If our marriage was a business, that would be illegal."

"I do agree on that point, Mom." I can feel her choosing her next words with the precision of a surgeon and brace myself. "I'm not saying it was mature, but I think he was afraid you would keep it from happening somehow if he let you in on his plans until they were a done deal."

"Be that as it may, it was still a chicken-hearted thing to do. I am not that powerful. If he really wanted to do it, a little opposition shouldn't stop him."

She scoffs.

"Anyway, that's not my point. I called to tell you that starting today, I'm going to do exactly what he did."

"Which is?"

"I will make every decision moving forward as if there is no one to consider except myself. I've never done that in my entire life, and I think it's high time I did. Your dad is spending the foreseeable future doing exactly what he wants to regardless of how it affects me. He's made it clear he doesn't need or want me in his picture. That being the case, I'm going to take this year before I turn sixty-five to figure out exactly what I want to do with the rest of *my* life. A reset on all circuits."

Silence again. She could either be gathering ammunition or waiting for further targets before launching her arguments. It doesn't matter. I'm not required to consider anyone except myself. That's my new sorting rule, and while I know it sounds selfish as heck, from what I've observed, selfish people aren't thinking about anyone else, so it's a moot point.

"That's all I called to say. Also to let you know I'm not able to carry on with regular life right now. Please keep texting, though, and I'll answer as I feel able. It's going to take me a while. Please send daily pictures of Portia. I'm always up for Facetiming her, of course."

"Okay. Will do." There's a longish pause before Maggie adds, "I'm very sorry this is happening, Mom. Are you alright? Is there anything I can do to make this time easier for you?"

"That's sweet of you, honey. I think I'm doing okay (if you call hanging on by your toenails okay). I expect it will take me a bit of time to regroup."

"Understandable. I don't want to bug you, but please let me know if I can do anything to help. You know I love you past the moon and Mars, right?"

"I do, my dear, and I love you the same."

★ ★ ★ ★

These are the basic activities I manage to accomplish:

Texting (occasionally).
Crying (often and loudly).
Wallowing (with a generous lacing of self-pity).
Angrifying (I'm becoming more comfortable with this,
    which I hope is a good thing, though it doesn't feel
    amazing).
Grieving (which never becomes any less painful).
Making bold declarations I don't follow through on. (No
    explanation needed).

The dig site Jimmy spends his days on has very poor internet reception, which turns out to be both therapeutic and devastating. It means I don't need to adult with him and can squeak by with a periodic text along the lines of "hope you're doing well," and several days later, he'll respond that yes, he is, and how am I. It also means that right now when I need him the most, he's unavailable. Unreliable. Unreachable.

I say I'm okay when he asks. The actual truth is I'm not okay, yet not only is he the cause of that, he's not here to help with the situation nor does he want to be, so no point of going into it. He does send a picture every so often when a periodic blip of internet comes available. Thus far, he's not been able to call because the coverage doesn't hang in there long enough to hold onto the connection (metaphor, anyone?). For the record, not once since he left Ranger Falls has he said he wishes I was there with him or he was here with me. That's telling, I think.

I punctuate my seclusion by periodic bursts of verbal processing with my friend, Kate, who stops by periodically with an almond bear claw or an apple fritter along with a cup of coffee from one of our favorite shops. She also insists I go walking with her at least once a week. I suspect it's her way of ensuring I breathe a little fresh air and absorb a dash of vitamin D, because she knows I've gone full-on couch potato mode. This is made possible by Instacart, Door Dash, and Amazon, who have me to thank for helping pay their overhead lately, as I use them for a supply line.

I have no doubt others in my situation would conduct themselves with much more functionality and grace, but I'm sorry. For me, it feels like walking barefoot over gravel day after day after day, with very few smooth patches. My feet are raw, my heart is raw, and frankly, I'm still very much upset by the fact that I didn't have a say about this new route I find myself on. Instead, dumped out by the side of the road, I'm left to find my way home as best I can. I'm not yet convinced I'll make it out alive, either, seeing that I spend the bulk of my time listening to old love songs and crying at least several times a day.

Then one morning as I'm grinding coffee beans for my first cup, pondering whether to take a long soaking bath while reading or zone in front of the TV watching some love story or another and whimpering while blotting tears, I look out on the lovely breezy morning. Little white clouds scud across a royal blue expanse. On a day like today, pre-Peru, if you will, I would be hiking, staring up at the blueness of the sky, and smelling the trees around me. Then, like a returning heartbeat, I remember my bold declaration to the living room ceiling the Tuesday Jimmy left. "I'm going to launch on my own adventure."

Well, girl, about time to start on that little item, don't you think?

Yes, I answer myself. What it should look like, though, I have no clue. My bucket list of dreams dates back to high school, and

I haven't read it in probably fifteen years, because the last time I did, I saw it had taken me forty-five years to complete a total of three items. I felt depressed for weeks afterwards.

I do happen to know where said list is, however, so I fetch it from my underwear drawer. It's strange to see the schoolgirl version of my handwriting. Who was I when I wrote those entries down? Can I find that teen-age version of myself again, or do I even want to? Maybe I should simply set forth here and discover who I am now, having lived the life I have, and learned so many things the hard way.

Eisel's Bucket List
1. Go sky diving
2. Hike the Appalachian Trail
3. Experience a great romance
4. Get married
5. Have children
6. Own a house
7. Go snorkeling on a pacific island reef
8. Go to college
9. Write a book
10. Visit the cliff dwellings at Mesa Verde, Colorado
11. Discover something remarkable
12. Help other humans

Yup. As suspected, I've made zero progress on these entries since last I checked. I can only truthfully cross out items four, five, and six: Get married, have children (child, really, though I think that suffices), and own a house. One might assume I've also accomplished number three in the process: "Experience a great romance." However, one would be incorrect because I can vouch for the fact that that's not really what happened with Jimmy and me.

We met in a church singles' group. I'd just turned twenty. He was tall, cute, and twenty-five, newly returned from Peru, and tanned to an even delicious brown. What's not to love? We married a year later, and I, for one, never looked back. A great romance, though? I don't even know what one would look like. Or feel like, for that matter. I only know I didn't have one, and I still want one, and by a strange twist of fate, Jimmy excusing himself from the picture has paved my way to explore possibilities, should I be interested in checking out other masculine prospects.

Whoa. Also, yikes.

Some people may wonder how a mere three months after Jimmy's departure I could so suddenly be thinking about exploring romance with someone not him. However, as previously mentioned, if you remove the "suddenly," replacing it with days and weeks and years of not including me in decisions he either didn't think I would be interested in or in which he didn't want the hassle of discussion or resistance, you'd discover not only a clear trail between him leaving and me considering my options, you'd find a dang paved highway linking the two. All that lack of consideration, all that being left out of the equation as if I'm simply a friend or roommate rather than integrally part of his life—that leaves a mark.

This is all I will say about that, and I hope it lays to rest any speculations about whether I'm the philandering type. I'm not. Neither am I the type to wither away waiting for someone to check off all the exciting things on their to-do list until they arrive at my name somewhere down the roster. As far as I'm concerned, Jimmy's leaving technically qualifies as spousal abandonment, and I have never dealt with abandonment well, I will admit.

The thought of replacing these more painful long-term emotions with a great romance is both scary and attractive. Sipping my coffee, I ponder this new and unexpected relational frontier. Call me clueless (and you'd be correct on that) but how does this thing called romance even work? The only thing I know for sure is that in my current marital context, experiencing a great romance is bound to be complicated.

I suppose the simplest possibility would be that Jimmy would hop a plane back to Ranger Falls, declare he can't live without me after all, and then proceed to romance me off my feet for the duration of our years. However, considering not only has that not happened in the last forty or so years if not more, we're three months in from Departure Day, and no hint of romance from Jimmy has so much as blipped on the radar. Clearly, he's abdicating his first position by default if not by declaration.

The thought of meeting a man I'd want to spend time with who sees me as valuable, wants me in every part of his life, and treats me accordingly sends a surprising jolt through my mid-section. How do I go about meeting someone of who fits that description? Online dating apps abound, which I think is a good thing considering a lot of very nice people surely live beyond Ranger Falls, though arguably, some nice men must live here as well.

How I'd meet one of them is less certain, since my haunts include home, the grocery as seldom as possible, maybe the library, and solitary trails. The prospect of meeting an eligible, attractive, desirable match here or afield feels daunting given that romance is a closed book to me at this point.

Maybe I'll give this thought a rest and simply sit down with my journal in hand to define what, exactly, would be included in a romantic relationship. However, after staring at the blank page for half an hour, I still have nothing. Zilch. Nada. So, I do what everyone does these days (though part of me still thinks it's like using Cliff Notes on doing life in general)—I ask AI. "What are the elements of a great romance?"

The helpful bot generates "what to include in a great romance story" instead.

I don't want a story. I want a reality. With a body and a mind and a smile that wraps me in safety (hypothesizing here). I try again. "What are the elements of a great romantic relationship?"

Bingo. "A great romantic relationship is built on a foundation of love, trust, and mutual respect. While specific dynamics can vary, several key elements are generally important for a successful and fulfilling romantic relationship." Words like "intentional," "unmistakable" and "deeply affectionate" come up under what it means to be romantic.

That makes sense, sounds lovely, and isn't totally overwhelming, though quite wordy, I will say. On the other hand, what can you expect from AI? After I read through the eighteen-point list going into more detail, I realize I have my work cut out for me for any future relationship. Conclusion (and no surprise): it looks as if experiencing a great romance is going to take a container ship load of intentionality.

It could be argued that I have nothing more important to do and plenty of time. In fact, that's all I have, since my husband is gone. Still, I could decide to invest my efforts in finding a fresh romantic space with him since he's a known quantity. and the pursuit wouldn't take me into murky territory marriage-wise.

On the other hand, breaking out of our relational patterns seems a task on par with leveling the Grand Tetons one shovelful at a time. If forty-three years has yielded so little romance, I must look up what it is and how to have it, it may be time to turn my efforts elsewhere, since according to my new sorting rule, I call the shots now.

Before I lose courage, I decide to text Kate, who I know I can depend on to jump aboard my romance train and shovel on the coal. *I'm looking at my high school bucket list, and it's pitiful—only three items checked off. Get married. Have a child. Buy a house.*

Her reply: *Don't beat yourself up too badly, friend. Mine doesn't edge yours out by much.*

About then I realize I need to hear someone's voice, so I call her. "Have a minute?"

"I do. Especially for you. How's it going?"

"Still a bit rough. I might have turned a bit of a corner today, though."

"Good for you. What's the most interesting thing on your bucket list—the thing you want to tackle first?"

"It's rather pathetic, really. I listed 'experience a great romance' preliminary to being married, yet that didn't happen. I don't even know what it would feel like to be romanced, to have a man think about me that way."

"What way?"

"This is how pathetic it is: I don't really know what 'that way' would be, only that I don't think I've experienced it. It's like having the title of a recipe and no ingredients. I drew such a blank I resorted to AI, which tells you how far out of my zone of experience romance is at this point."

She laughs. "You called the right person, E."

"Yeah?" I mean, we both know she's had a couple of bummer relationships after a painful divorce twenty-five years ago, so I wouldn't exactly call her an expert resource. Even so, I'm sure she at least has more experience with romance than I do.

"Yes, because I think Eric is a keeper. He treats me as if I matter to him and values me above other things like his job, motorcycle buddies, and such."

"Now you're talking. I'm pondering whether to stop hoping Jimmy is going to level up in that area, since he's now left me for a greater love, Peru."

"That's so rough, babe." Her words hang between us in the friendly silence we've cultivated over the years. "How about dipping your toe into the shallow end while you figure that out?

If you're interested in meeting a nice single guy in your age range to start on that bucket list item, I might know one."

Am I interested? Yikes. "Maybe?"

"Have you ever met my friend Dan?"

"Nope. Or I can't remember if I did, being with Jimmy and all, so I probably need to start over. Tell me about him."

She sends a picture instead. It feels surreal to be sitting in the living room with my husband in South America doing his own thing while I'm checking out possible competition. I wait to feel guilty, but I don't. I just feel irritated at Jim for leaving me without warning and apparently without regret, both of which still hurt pretty much all my waking hours. However, I'm not about to spend the rest of my life in that heart space.

I stare at this man's face. Dan. Who are you, Dan? "I'm not used to blue eyes," I say. "Although maybe that's a good thing?"

"Absolutely it's a good thing." Kate, the inveterate optimist. "Hey, how about we do a foursome?"

"Yikes, girlfriend. I've hardly left the house for three months."

"I know, and it's high time you did."

"Do you really think some man would think that above all things, I'm the most wondrous treasure, the most intriguing person he's ever met, and would want to spend his days with me?" (I silently add 'and nights'). How wild that I, Eisel McCord, am considering a blind date as if I'm twenty again.

"Absolutely. Don't sell yourself short, babe. You're the world's best kept secret, and I'm sorry—what was Jim thinking to leave you behind to enter the dating scene?"

"I don't think the idea of me dating while he excavates Peru remotely occurred to him."

"Oops, my boss just walked in. I'll call you back in a few. Bye now."

While I'm waiting for Kate, I wonder whether Jimmy ever felt as if I was the most desirable and fascinating person in his universe. If he did, surely, I'd remember it. I think he married me because I was a good, wholesome, likable girl, not bad-looking, and he was ready to settle down. It's what kids our age did in the late seventies, early eighties. Anyway, if he ever did think I was a treasure, he lost touch with those feelings sometime during our last four decades, or else he'd have at least telegraphed a detectable modicum of agonizing over leaving me.

At the same time, it also raises the question of whether I ever felt that way about him. I remember having the usual butterflies in my stomach early on, and there was no shortage of sexual attraction (we've enjoyed some mighty good years in that way). My point is, to have a great romance, adoration must be reciprocal.

I take another gander at the photo Kate sent. Silver gray hair. Nice smile. I can't tell how tall Dan is or how he's built. Does he have a sense of humor, monologue about his hobbies, or have a dog and want me to love it (shudder)?

My cell rings. "Okay, girlfriend. Let's lock this in. How about El Camino Real this Thursday night? I'll text Dan, and if he's in, I'll text Eric, and we'll make it a foursome."

Am I really going to do this?

"Esiel?"

"Er—yes? Yes. I'm in."

CHAPTER 3

Who is this woman making dates with unknown men? No, wait a minute—let's de-escalate that a bit—making one (double) date with one unknown man. Point being, it doesn't fit my norm. On the other hand, I've never really been alone with only myself and my own thoughts and desires, so who says my norm is more me than this version making a solid move toward what she wants in life? Maybe in reality, I'm merely uncovering aspects of myself I've not been aware of or needed before. Either way, I've taken my first step toward tackling what to me is the single most important item on my bucket list, and the euphoria from that action carries all the way to dinner time.

Then, as happens pretty much every evening since Jimmy's departure, when six o'clock rolls around and the sun begins its path to the horizon, my heart follows it to the ground. This is when Jimmy and I used to look at each other and one of us would say, "Any ideas for dinner?" (I turned in my cook's apron when Jimmy retired). Then one or the other of us suggests something, narrowing it down until we hit on a tasty choice, and we take turns more or less on who prepares it. If it's grilled cheese, we assume Jimmy makes them. If it's tostados, I take over the kitchen.

Tonight? I find grilled cheese sandwiches are the only possible choice, all hot and crispy, drooling cheese like a teething toddler, with a generous pool of ketchup for dipping. However, the grilled cheese master left me to fend for myself, and that feels like a fresh stab to my heart.

Three months later, I'm still processing how he could do that to me, the woman who has given him my last forty-three years. On the heels of this thought, I armor up with a bit of anger. I know how to make grilled cheese, too, Jimmy, I tell him in my head as I jerk open the freezer to dig out the sourdough bread, yank the griddle from its storage space, and slice up some cheese.

If he comes back (and if I let him back into my life, which is feeling like a pretty big if at this exact moment), I will never admit my grilled cheese sandwiches could possibly be as good as his, because I like not having to make them myself. I carry my plate of said comparable sandwiches to the couch, open my current read (*Eleven Stolen Horses* by Robin Somers) and move into sensory heaven.

Enjoyment lasts basically as long as I have food on my plate. It's now seven pm, and the house is too quiet. Along about now, I suppose some well-meaning person might be thinking, why did you banish the dog? He would have given you company plus a bodyguard. They'd be wrong on both counts. Trencher? He's a Basset hound. Fat as they come, and not only does he think every human is a chance to glean some adoration or a morsel of food, I'd much rather spend my evenings dealing with The Great Silence than irritation plus guilt for being irritated, which is what I always feel with that dog (dogs in general and Trencher in particular).

I make a cup of chamomile tea, tell Alexa to play my love song playlist, and sit there listening to Patsy Cline singing "Crazy," which seems quite apropos. I can't say that all the words fit my situation—I mean, unless you count archeology in Peru as the "somebody new," and I wager Jimmy never actually intended to replace me. It happened by default as he moved toward his rediscovered love. Yet the rest of song fits how I'm feeling: I love him. I miss him, and in light of everything, I do feel crazy for trying, for crying, and for still loving him when he's clearly doing what he really wants to do.

To think that my love is the one thing that could have held him here in Ranger Falls, though? No. Love doesn't work that way. Love is a two-way street where each person must curate their own heart's affections, isn't it? While it's true that I've not been perfect nor easy to live with, and I won't even try to pretend I was, the one thing I do know is that the power to make Jimmy do anything he doesn't already want to do does not lie with me and never has.

Oof. Introspection and grilled cheese sandwiches are making quite a lump in my stomach, despite the tea. Yet as the next song begins—John Denver's "Rocky Mountain High," I relax a bit. I've always loved the picture it paints of a young man finding himself in a way he hadn't before. Maybe it's a picture for my life now. Coming home to myself, discovering what *I* want.

On that note, I do enjoy some aspects about being the only one here: playing my music of choice, watching my pick of movies, or reading the night away. Not needing to field another person's wishes or expectations is at least a bit of compensation for the loneliness, I suppose.

Tonight, I'm still acclimating to this level of non-responsibility, my time completely at my own disposal. I can leave the dishes for tomorrow if I want (I usually want). I can rummage through the pantry for the package of Oreos I bought in a moment of hunger at the grocery last week and eat as many as I desire (which I do, losing count after five). Being able to do whatever I choose is both terrifying and gratifying in equal proportions, since I have no idea what I desire long term besides experiencing a great romance. Time to analyze my list. I'll cross off those three items I managed to accomplish, reorder the ones I'm still interested in, and maybe add a few new entries.

Number on my old list is skydiving.

What was I thinking?

Actually, I remember exactly what I was thinking when I wrote that item down. At seventeen, I'd broken up with my first ever boyfriend, a charmer named Archer Stevens, and my life was over. Capital O Over. After I wallowed for weeks and talked it over with my BFF, Vicki, until she threatened to un-BFF me, I decided it was time to prove I had moved on from my break-up, and in the process, become the girl who dared.

The most daring thing I could think of was to go skydiving. Vicki approved, and when word leaked out (she was good at this) that Eisel Wellington was going skydiving, my street cred finally went from flatline to slightly visible, at least in my own mind. I lived on that for the rest of the year, graduated high school, and as my class dissipated to the four winds as high schoolers will, with them went any impetus or necessity to cross item number one off my list. I kept it as the top entry, though, because I enjoyed thinking I'm the type of person who does life-defying feats like that.

I still like to see myself this way, though nothing I've done in my life has validated this identity unless you count sticking with the same marriage partner for more than four decades. It may not be as dramatic, yet I posit it takes all the elements I assume skydivers possess—daring, determination, and a bit of a death wish. I move Sky Diving to my Maybe/Not sure category.

2. Hike the Appalachian Trail.

I chew on my pencil and let myself ponder. I still like this item a lot. I also realize I needn't limit it the Appalachian Trail specifically. The Pacific Crest Trail would suffice, or a section of it, even. What draws me is the freedom, the autonomy of hiking a long trail. To carry my entire world on my back, answering to no one, with only myself and my own thoughts under the wide blue sky beckons to me. I could stop when I want. Cook my meals over a campfire and roll out my sleeping bag with the starry heavens as my ceiling.

This item stays on my list. For the ultimate long hike, logistics are myriad, and I'll figure them out later. Meanwhile, I will dig out my hiking boots and start going on day hikes to condition. Who knows? Maybe this Dan person I'm going to meet likes to hike, and wouldn't that be fortuitous? That is also when I realize that company on a day hike is fine, yet when I go for that bucket list item, I'm doing it solo, because that is the whole point of it for me.

Granted, I do find it rather ironic that the key element of this particular adventure is going it alone, while I'm currently struggling with being by myself and am about to engage in the process of finding someone to fill my relationship gap. Still, theoretically, you should be able to be in a meaningful relationship and also have time alone to be with yourself and hear your own thoughts. It's a lost art and a basic human right (or should be). That said, I'm also living proof that being alone and being lonely are two different things, yet they often occur simultaneously.

Next item: Experience a great romance

Feeling quite proud that I'm already taking steps toward this one, I transfer it over to the top entry on my new list. If Dan doesn't pan out, it doesn't matter, really. I'm just starting out. I may have to meet multiple candidates before something clicks, and I'm okay with that. I mean, I've had two boyfriends in my whole sixty-four years—Archer and Jimmy—so I say why rush through this potentially sweet and exciting season. I pause to enjoy the little electric tingle that flicks through me at the possibilities).

The next three I cross off boom, boom, boom.

4. *Get married*
5. *Have children*
6. *Own a house*

It strikes me as both ironic and bittersweet that I can dismiss forty-three years of life by checking off these items in two seconds flat, as if they were lived so succinctly. Housed in those words are the sweetest and the most difficult moments of my life, encompassing my twenties, full of enthusiasm and trying on adulthood as if it was an option rather than an inevitability. Feeling proud I was doing what adults do yet feeling like an imposter at the same time because inside I was still Eisel Wellington, maker (not doer) of lists, who was not at all certain how to live life well. I merely put on a good front and followed in the footsteps of my parents and their parents and so on.

Birthing Maggie was simultaneously the most painful and joyous thing I'd done up to that point and arguably since. Looking down at her tiny face, her perfection, meeting Jimmy's wondering gaze as we wrapped our minds and hearts around the fact that this tiny human was now our responsibility was transcendent. I remember locking eyes with him and how we linked souls through in that moment. I was swept by such wonder and love and fear that my only anchor was his steady brown gaze and familiar face.

Owning a house—not this one I'm in right now, but our first modest purchase—felt like a cakewalk compared to parenting our then two-year-old. Sign away a significant portion of our monthly income for the next thirty years? No biggie. The fact that Maggie was systematically exfoliating the fig tree in the banker's office and taking any attempt to distract her as a screaming offense felt much more impactful than owning a house. Three houses in now, it no longer feels like an accomplishment at all.

However, on second glance, I look at this item with suddenly single eyes (a confusing image, granted, but hang in with me here). I myself have never owned a house. Only *co-owned*, and in my current state of mind that is an entirely different thing. What if I bought a property of my very own, using my new sorting rule of considering only what *I* want?

I flat out love this idea. The fun of the search. Envisioning myself in this place or that. Mentally redecorating and remodeling space after space, and then the actual doing of it all lights me up inside. If it weren't nearly nine pm, I'd call a realtor right now. Once I have my own little home, I can rent this house of Jimmy's and mine out, and then when (or face it, *if*) Jimmy comes back, he can evict the tenants and collect Trencher from his cousin, while I'll be already settled in my new space. I write "Own a house," on my updated list right under "Experience a great romance," add "Make a long solo hike," and then do a happy little dance.

Eisel's When I'm Sixty-Four List
1. *Experience a great romance*
2. *Own my own house*
3. *Make a long solo hike*

I'll tackle the other items later. Meanwhile, carried by this trifecta of bucket list items, mind full of planning and pictures, I slide under the blankets, and by force of habit, stretch out a foot to contact Jimmy's leg. Once again, my world screeches to a halt. I'm not sure I'll ever become used to this. No warm body next to mine. No goodnight kiss and sleep tight wish. Just me, marooned on my side of a suddenly huge, cold bed.

I thought I'd cried every tear available to me over the last few months. I find more. "Jiiiimmmmyyyyyy," I sob into his pillow, which used to smell like him. Now that's faded, and this realization makes the ache worse. "I miss youuuuuu. Also, I'm still so mad at you. How could you go away and leave me here all alone?" At this time of night, this fact feels especially cruel.

I love him, but right now? If he suddenly walked through the doorway, I'd take my pillow and my favorite plush blanket and stomp my way down the hall to the guest room. In addition, I would still find a house of my own and hike (by myself), and darned if I also wouldn't continue my search for a great romance that he could participate in or not, because I have no doubt in my mind at this moment that I want to experience one, whether he does or not.

Ping. As if my thinking of him triggered a message, it's from Jimmy. My heart does a little pirouette though I do try not to apply it to a "he loves me, he loves me not" roster, because that's crazy making. Sure enough, clicking on it, my momentary joy takes a head dive.

Headed to Machu Picchu. Can you believe I'm finally seeing it after sixty years of wishing?

I'm excited for you, I text. I notice he didn't add "Wish you were here," or that sort of thing. Like maybe I wouldn't mind seeing one of the seven great wonders of the ancient world, too, and thanks for asking. Ugh. I wonder when I'll accept the fact that he's having a great time without me. *Happy Machu Picchu to you, Jimbo.* I add a clapping hands emoji and a heart so that any undertones of angst remain incognito on my end.

Sniff. I'm so tired of crying. Maybe I should see how long I can go without thinking of Jimmy and what I no longer have. Not exactly a bucket list item, though essential to survival, I do believe.

Kate rescues me from this spiral by her phone call. "Hi E, me again. Sorry for the late call. The guys say Thursday is great, and Dan is looking forward to meeting you."

My heart rebounds a little at that (although it could just be nerves). At least *someone* is interested in my company. "He is?"

"Yes, he is. Let's talk about what you'll wear."

"Clothes. I plan on wearing clothes, Kate."

"I'm serious. The venue is a Mexican restaurant, so informal is fine, but really Eisel, your informal can be a bit too casual, shall I say?"

I groan. I hadn't actually thought about trying to impress Dan. I mean, think about it—if I pretend to be someone I'm not by dressing up in something not my norm, that's who he'll think I am. I can bank on the fact I'll resent that layer of inauthenticity sooner or later. I guess Jimmy had the advantage of having my twenty-one-year-old version. However, my body at sixty-four is a whole 'nother animal, as they say.

Once I hit my late thirties, I went from having a metabolism that worked with me to having one oppose me twenty-four seven. I fought that battle for twenty-five years until a few years ago, I hit critical mass, no pun intended. Wearied to exhaustion from restricting myself to 800 calories a day by cutting out anything remotely tasty in an effort to keep a tenuous hold on 150 pounds, I quit. Quit counting macros, micros, protein, carbs. Why was I letting society dictate what makes me acceptable and valuable anyway? As if they even know I exist. These days, that fact is a comfort since I'm losing physical assets faster than Trencher sheds hair while gaining wrinkle after wrinkle as my eyebrows fade into wiry, pale shadows of their former selves.

Dye them, you say? To that I reply, have you ever tried dying wire? Let's just say, pomade is my friend. I could, of course, color my hair. However, I've never taken the plunge, since silver and faded brown are mingling okay. So far. Anyway, while it's true I would rather be myself as I am and deal with the fallout than live under the pressure to look a certain way, a blind date looming over me for tomorrow night has me running the whole gamut of insecurities about my appearance.

"Esiel, are you still there?"

"Kate, I don't know if I can do this dating thing after all. What if he's expecting a thin, older fashion model type?" I stop short of saying "like you." I think it, though.

"Stop, girl. You're cute as a bug." I know she means well, but that's pretty lame as a compliment, because have you examined any bugs lately? "Besides, it's blank slate time," she adds. "If Dan is hung up on that stuff, you don't need him, right? He's not, though. He's a really nice guy. I say give him a chance."

"Thanks, friend. You keep reminding me of that."

"Will do. Anyway, you could wear your black slacks and black boat neck tunic with that lovely yellow silk blouse you found the last time we went shopping. Truth: she dragged me there, bribed with coffee. I do not normally go shopping except online. "While you're at it, add that agate necklace you have that goes with everything."

"I can do that. However, I'm absolutely not wearing heels."

"Eisel, I know. You say that every time we dress up for anything."

I grin. "Good. At least that's established. I'll wear my black sandals."

"Puh-lease. They look like you used them to beat the rugs with."

I neither confirm nor deny. "Whatever. I'll wear my black boots."

"Fine. Maybe a touch of makeup, just for fun?'

"Maybe."

She laughs, knowing precisely how far to push me before I go all passive-aggressive on her. "I'll pick you up on my way."

"I can drive."

"My car's newer, though, so let's take mine."

"Who's keeping up appearances now?"

"Oops, gotta go, Eisel. See you at five tomorrow evening."

CHAPTER 4

I sit across the table from a stranger who is actively trying to move that status from the starting line. All I need to do is play along, and that's what I'm here for, so by golly, I'm going to show up as myself, and at the very least, I'll have no regrets about that.

"So Eisel—nice name, by the way," he says, clinking his glass against mine after we're seated—me directly across from him hence no escaping a face-to-face. "As Kate undoubtedly told you, my name's Dan. Dan Baker. I'm a general contractor in the area, mostly residential. How about you?"

Good question. I endeavor not to be distracted by his very blue eyes which are a bit disconcerting, since I'm used to staring into brown ones. Still, maybe Kate's right. Different is good. After all, if I want someone like Jimmy, I could simply expend effort to win the original back. Yeah, but no. "That's what I'm actively trying to discover," I answer with a grimace. "I'm sure Kate filled you in that after forty-three years together, my husband left me for an archeological dig in the Peruvian Andes. I decided that rather than hibernating and hoping he comes back, I'll focus on having my own adventure. So, I decided to unearth my old bucket list."

"Sounds intriguing. What's on it?"

I give a one-sided grin. "Skydiving is what seventeen-year-old me wrote down as number one, though if I remember correctly— and I do—that was more for shock value and wanting to feel like I was the kind of person that Does Things."

He laughs like I said something clever, which is surprisingly exhilarating, coming as it does from a six-foot-plus hunk of masculinity who smells nice and seems comfortable with maintaining eye contact. I grin at him across the table. "I have now relegated that to the probably not list."

"If you change your mind, I know a guy. My buddy, Hilton Bradshaw, does tandem jumping. Say the word, and I'll set you up."

"I see it pays to know the right people," I say, and can't believe I actually flutter my eyelashes at him as if by instinct. Maybe I'm better at this romance thing than I thought? (Although on second thought, I think use of eyelashes falls under the flirting category, which isn't really the same thing as romance. However, it's a useful skill in the pursuit thereof, I'm pretty sure).

He laughs again. "You better believe it. What's your top item now that skydiving is taking a lower seat?"

You better believe "experiencing a great romance" is not coming out of my mouth right now to this possible prospect of said endeavor. Blushing, I shake my head and take a gulp of my drink. "Your turn. Tell me about yourself."

"Nothing earth shaking. When I'm not on the job, I like to play golf. Jog. Read. Putter around in my garage fixing things, and once in a while I tear myself away from such exciting activities as those to do a bit of grilling." He laughs. "Saying that out loud makes me think maybe I should dust off my old bucket list, too." He was nice looking before he grins, but wow, that smile takes him into the category of ruggedly handsome and then some.

I nod, focusing on not showing how that observation has me all fluttery in the heart region. "Married?" This comes out sounding more abrupt than I mean to. Then again, Jimmy always did call me his "cut-to-the-chase" girl, and I must admit, it fits. I don't see any point wasting time pretending these larger questions aren't circling like piranhas just below the surface.

Dan's smile fades. "Was married. My wife died four years ago. Breast cancer."

"Oh, Dan." I lay a hand on his forearm, which I shouldn't have done because it is extremely distracting to feel the warmth of his skin and the silk of the hair there. I remove my hand. "I'm sorry for your loss. What was her name?"

"Rosalie."

"How beautiful. What do you love the most about her and what were some of her quirks?"

That opens the floodgates for sure. But I don't mind. I'm only a few months out from losing my husband. Even though he's not dead, I navigate around a bottomless hole in my life that wasn't there before. How much worse must it be when the person you love is irrevocably gone from the earth.

By the time our dinners arrive, I love his former wife to pieces, and I can see that Dan is a very kind and faithful human. Not only that, but I also now feel quite at ease with him, chatting about my next bucket list idea of buying a house and doing a bit of remodeling. What impression he has of me I have no idea, but hopefully he's enjoying this double date as much as I am.

Will I be interesting enough for him to want to hang out with me again? I can be funny on occasion if I'm not trying (I'm better at seeing a joke than telling one, though I do have a great laugh, so there is that). If the way his eyes twinkle and the number of times he smiles or laughs at what I say are any indication, he seems to be enjoying me quite a bit whatever the reason.

Eating my steak fajitas (yum), I make a mental list of Dan's qualities to jot them down later.

1. *Socially easy (not awkward).*
2. *Listens as much as he talks /doesn't dominate the conversation or make it all about him (starred item for me).*
3. *Has a great smile (I find I want to keep him smiling).*

> *4. Helpful (not that I'm asking, yet it's clear he's not afraid to offer).*
> *5. Has the ability to commit (married to the same woman for 35 years).*
> *6. Enjoys life (at least it seems that way from all he talks about).*
> *7. Enjoyable to be with (needs further exploration).*

On the way home, Kate grills me. "So, what do you think?"

"I had fun."

'Good. However, you know what I mean. What do you think about Dan?"

I picture his face, how his eyes light up when he's engaged, and the way he tips his head when he smiles. "He's cute."

She squeals. "Right? I think he likes you, too."

"I don't know about that."

"Eisel, C'mon. Guys do not lock eyes with you and tell you their life story and laugh at everything you say, funny or not, unless they're attracted to you."

"Hey." I poke her with my elbow. "I am funny (which we both know is a definite overstatement of the facts). Maybe he's just a lonely heart longing for someone to listen to him."

"Wrong. Dan Baker is on Ranger Falls' list of top five desirable bachelors over sixty. Believe me, he can have his pick of ladies any time he wants. I think you could move to the front of the pack if you wanted to."

Do I want to? The thought terrifies while also sending a shot of adrenaline through me and stirring a bit of warmth in my belly. This surprises me, and I blush, thankful the nighttime dimness hides that fact.

"I say strike while the iron is hot. Maybe you can hire him to take a look at your screen door, ask him to stay for dinner, and see where it leads."

I laugh while shrinking inside. Call me oblivious to the obvious, but when I brushed off my objective of experiencing a great romance, I didn't spend two seconds on the sexual aspect. I mean, seriously, after forty-three years of marriage and having finally achieved menopause after twelve years of hot flashes and waning sex drive—for both Jimmy and me—physical intimacy is not the major player it once was. I find this both a sadness and a relief. I can drift off to sleep at my leisure, no longer laying there deciphering if Jimmy's touching me with his foot to initiate a romp or merely to warm his toes. Of course, now that he's gone, all that is irrelevant anyway. I'm thinking about it, though, as I once again slip into my empty bed.

Nights are the worst. I should be used to spending them alone after more than three months, but so far, I have yet to figure out how to escape the loneliness of an empty bed. Tonight, I lay here remembering sweet, shared moments Jimmy and I had over the years. The special bonded feeling making love with someone you love brings. Could I have that with a different man?

According to AI, it's an aspect of a great romantic relationship, and I agree. I'd love to be swept off my feet that way again, to feel the surge of hunger, the flirting, feeling pursued and pursuing, and the ease of afterwards, the silly grins, the shared smiles, the knowing glances. There's a reason they include those scenes in movies. People are dying for intimacy, not merely a sexual encounter. I can empathize.

Lying in the dark, I text Jimmy. *How are you doing? Still at Machu Picchu?*

I wait and wait, yet no scrolling dots indicate he's seen my message. By now, I don't take this personally, or at least I try not to. Peru is two hours ahead of my own time zone, so it's twelve a.m. there, not a time when he'd be up even if the internet decided to cooperate. However, it does feel rather symbolic. How often have I sent him messages over the years, emotional, relational, and sexual, and he neglected to respond? Did he not see those, or did he just not want to answer?

Because it's nighttime and the house lies dark and quiet, inviting introspection, I also wonder if Jimmy used to send me those messages, too, and I didn't see them as the invitations they were to connect. Did he ever lie there wondering if we might do more than sleep together tonight, or if I was too tired?

I now regret I didn't expend more effort toward physical intimacy once our sex drives started to decline. In reality, while our bodies take more time and focus in our sixties than in earlier years, they do still function just fine, and the connection, the sweet bond between us, is a reward I long to experience with Jimmy again. Will we ever share that silken oneness I took for granted? I don't know what to do with that thought nor the tears it summons.

Jimmy John McCord, when did we lose our easy intimacy? Do you miss it, too? Could we regain what we used to have, or should I cut my losses and see if I can experience that with someone else, since you've taken yourself to Peru?

Or should I simply live without?

The night offers no answers beyond the wind in the trees, so I'll need to answer those questions myself. Not tonight, though. I fumble for my phone again and select my love songs playlist to sing me to sleep. It feels more than a little pointed and poignant that the first song is Ray Orbison's "Only the Lonely." Letting the words roll over me, I add my tears to the soundtrack.

Jimmy, I hate what has happened between us. We're so far apart now, and not in miles only. Are you lonely as well? Are you also feeling this way? I know better than to think that there'd be no sorrow in a new romance, as per the lyrics of the song. Still, maybe I should cut my losses. Take the chance, because laying here crying every night, wishing you wanted to be here with me or that you wanted me there with you—I can't keep doing this. Too many tears. Too much heartache.

CHAPTER 5

Jimmy's text comes in while I brew morning coffee, along with one from Maggie, Kate, and of all things, Dan. We exchanged numbers last night, and the fact he texted already encourages me. I always feel more hopeful in the mornings, though. The nights are when I drift on an endless dark ocean over depths holding things I'm terrified to see.

Taking the texts in order of appearance as I wait for my coffee to drip through, Jimmy says, *Good morning, Sunshine. I'm doing well, thanks. You'd love Machu Picchu. I'll be on the site for the rest of today, then head back to the dig up in Lima. Miss you.*

He includes a selfie with magnificent ruins all around him and misty mountains rolling on forever in the background. Staring at his face smiling out at me, every scar, every wrinkle is as familiar as my own despite the four-day scruff (which gives him an unfamiliar devil-may-care persona I've got to admit is rather dashing in a Harrison Ford sort of way). I smile. He misses me. I'm stoked to hear that, probably more than is good for me considering all things. I text back, *You look great, and Machu Picchu is gorgeous, too. I'm making coffee and missing your brewing skills.*

Too flippant? Too needy? I grimace. I don't want to come across as a grieving, paralyzed dependent dragging him back from his dream. That's what I realize as I add cream to my cup, also noting that someone should go to the grocery soon, because I have maybe one more cup's worth in that carton. Since Jimmy's gone, that someone is always me now, and that causes me to miss him even more. Or is missing what someone does the same thing as missing them?

No, I answer myself. Of course it's not.

I slam into the question behind that question: do I miss Jimmy, the person, or do I miss the way he padded all the corners in my world so I could live "needed and fed" with very little effort? Last night I would have said I mourn him as a person. This morning with my emotions less in the ascendancy, I'm sure only that it's too deep a question for my brain to process before coffee, so I let go of it. Instead, I take a picture of my coffee cup in a beam of sunlight like the one that put a halo over Jimmy's head on that Saturday before life as I knew it hit the fan. *Coffee time,* I text. *If you were here, I'd brew you a cup, too.*

Too much? Too leading? I don't know any more what is off limits, what would feel as if I'm trying to pull him back to Ranger Falls and me. I can only make sure that isn't my motive, I guess. What he does with it is on him. However, it does highlight to me the need to move him toward the friend zone when texting, so I don't send lonely, pitiful, I'm-not-okay-without-you subliminals.

I click on Maggie's text next. *Are you up for coffee sometime soon? Daisy says she'll take Portia for a playdate with Adam on Saturday—shall we meet at Sierra Roasters at ten?* She also sends a video of the most darling child ever, bedhead and all. "Say hi to Grammie, Porsh," Maggie prompts, and Portia blinks into the phone like "who's Grammie," and manages a tiny wave.

Funny how delighted I am with her lackluster efforts to connect. If it was Jimmy, I'd be feeling a dagger to the heart right about now for his lack of engagement. Sipping my coffee, I ponder the fact that I love my grandchild without expectations and without need, yet clearly, I don't extend that same level of unconditionality and delight to my marriage partner of four-plus decades.

Why not?

Did I ever? I want to defend myself, argue that of course I did. However, coming from the Wellington family as I do, I seriously doubt it just on principle. The reality is I needed to escape that household ASAP, and Jimmy met this need of mine. All these years later, I have so far distanced myself from the dysfunction I grew up with that I'm confident I don't need rescuing any more.

I've lamented his not needing me in his life as evidenced by his absconding to Peru without bringing me in on his process and preparation. However, the sword cuts both ways according to the old adage. Maybe I don't need Jimmy the way I used to either.

I know needing someone is not the same as loving them, and marriage is not about needing so much as a deep interdependence. More times than I want to recall, Jimmy and I slid through that sweet spot in between power struggles, loving those moments yet never quite figuring out how to stay in the safe and sacred interconnected space between us.

Taking a deep breath, I scrabble back from that yawning fissure of regret and text Maggie. *Perfect. See you there* ;-) and send a short clip of Grammie saying good morning to Portia aka Preshiness (like precious to the ness degree).

Next, Kate. Her text reads, *I have good feelings about you and Dan. [Winky face, kissy mouth emojis].*

Time will tell, I suppose. [Crooked smile, loony face, heart], I text back.

Opening Dan's message, I wonder if it will be a "Dear Jane" communication and what I will feel if it is (answer: pretty even levels of disappointment and relief).

Hello, Eisel. Your bucket list inspired me to dig mine out. I wonder if we have any overlaps that would be fun to achieve together. Would you like to come over Sunday afternoon for steak and sides and a bucket list discussion?

Would I? Yikes. Yes? No? Maybe I should simply go for it like Jimmy went for Peru. After all, you can't really do items on a bucket list without doing them, right? So, though I've mostly been a list maker, not a fulfiller, I text back. *I'd like that. I'll bring something for dessert. Do you like chocolate?*

Do squirrels climb trees? he sends back right away.

Grinning, I highlight his text and add *haha.*

After spending the next few hours stewing in my own circular thoughts, I decide to research houses for sale. After all, why drag my feet? I am fully capable of doing several bucket list items at once, seeing as experiencing a great romance is sure to be a long-term project anyway. Grabbing my notebook and a pencil, I start another page.

Wish List for My Own House
1. *Outside the city limits (I always wanted to live in the country).*
2. *Historic (I'd love a little farmhouse with Victorian leanings and a wraparound porch).*
3. *On the smaller side (I don't want to take care of a huge place).*
4. *A spot for flowers and herbs, and maybe a tomato plant or two (digging in the dirt is therapeutic for me).*
5. *Close access to a place I can take walks (nature keeps me sane).*
6. *Not so remote that it takes forever to make a trip to the grocery or visit grandchild (I need my weekly Portia fix)*
7. *Doesn't need extensive repairs (as in "isn't a complete disaster or money sink").*

Seven items should be doable. I type in historic country farmhouses for sale within ten miles of Ranger Falls, and bingo. The more I scroll through pictures, the more excited I become. I find a darling house about eight miles out on Maggie's side of town that goes top of my list. Another cute property, also with a porch plus a picket fence (admittedly quite the classic combo) I add as number two.

A third listing looks interesting as well, with a bit of gingerbread on the eves, and again a porch, though not a wraparound. No worries. I suddenly know a contractor who might be able to add on another section or two. Grinning, I write down the address. I'll drive by these first three, find a realtor if any of them interest me, and if not, peruse further listings.

Can this really be me making headway on a bucket list I forgot I even made? I like this version of myself. This woman doesn't let spousal abandonment, habit, and comfort zones dictate how she experiences life. Instead, she pursues romance, digs out her hiking boots, and looks into owning a house of her very own. On the relationship front, I know it's much too early to assume I found my great romance two days into trying, though I suppose stranger things have happened. All I know at this point is that I showed up as myself on Thursday evening, and now Dan has initiated a twosome, so apparently me being me didn't scare him off.

What if he wants to hold my hand or kiss me goodnight on Sunday? I picture him reaching across the table, inviting me to lay my hand in his. Will I? I mean, intentional contact is, how shall I describe it—so intentional. Am I ready to move to that level? Tossing the possibility back and forth, I ultimately decide that if he reaches for my hand, I'll meet him halfway. After all, we're adults. I can always let him know later if it's not working for me."

What about the kissing question?

I opt to leave that decision for later. In fact, contrary to my usual overthinking ways, I may even choose to go all spur of the moment and wing it if Dan offers me his lips. What I do know for sure is that I will not be initiating, because if romance is a recipe, surely one vital ingredient to me personally is that of being pursued.

Don't get me wrong. I'm not big on gender roles. It's completely fine if a woman pursues a man. However, this is me I'm talking about, Eisel Jane McCord, who has not been pursued since before my engagement forty-four years ago. Even then, I think Jimmy simply responded to my cues, because he had a bad experience with a previous girlfriend who accused him of being pushy. I'm not saying I'd appreciate pushy. At the same time, I certainly would be open to someone besides myself leading the chase. I grin at this picture. What am I wanting here—to have Dan or some other dream guy playing tag around the dining room table?

Could be fun.

Grinning, I wash my coffee cup then check on my hair before setting out on my exploratory foray toward owning my own house. My eyes sparkle back at me in the mirror, more green than gray in this moment as I rescue my eyebrows from obscurity so that in case I have a face-to-face conversation with someone, the other person will be able to read my facial cues better. As an aside, I think I would've been a good cave dweller. I doubt they gave three shakes of a club about the changes aging and lack of estrogen bring about in women's bodies. Then again, maybe they didn't live long enough for those things to transpire, so now that I think about it, maybe that's not an advantage.

★ ★ ★

Before I know it, I'm dusting down a gravel road headed out of town. I figure I'll drive by number three first to give it a fighting chance, check out number two, and finish off with the list leader. If I like any of them, I'll call the number on the corresponding realty sign, and we'll be off to the races.

The first house I drive by (read that to mean park, unlatch the gate, and spy in every window, since the place is clearly vacant) is cute as they come despite it being number three on my list and in need of some paint. Also, a porch extension wouldn't go amiss, as previously noted. I take copious notes of what I see through the original window glass on the tall, double-hung sashes. Transom windows glimmer over the doors (including the front and back). A jewel of a newel post in the entryway leads up to a second story. The ceilings are tall as are most of that era's architecture—ten feet? Eleven? The more I see, the more I like it.

I'm standing there taking it all in when a stench rolls in from across the road that literally takes my breath away. A dairy. Complete with a herd of black and white Holsteins, a milking parlor, and all the accompanying odors. I'm sorry. I cannot live this close to that much smell. I adore cows, but no way I can count on the prevailing wind to protect me from their less pleasant aspects. Nope. I'd be at the mercy of the breezes. I draw an X through number three. "Sorry, old house," I say. "You really are lovely. It's your neighbor I can't stomach."

House number two. Wiser now, I hold my heart in reserve until I take a cold hard look at the landscape. Thankfully, no neighbors appear closer than a quarter mile, and this house sits inside its white picket fence like a perfect lady dolled up for an afternoon tea party, complete with gingerbread trim. I know I'm mixing my descriptors, but my point is, cute house.

This house is in better repair than the one I ruled out due to the dairy situation. However, if I decide to take it, it also needs more porch space. What it has now is hardly big enough to fit a rocker, much less the porch swing and wicker furniture I envision. Noting the realtor's number, I head for the last one of the day.

May I just say, I now know how Goldilocks must have felt upon stumbling into the house of the three bears. That "coming home" sense sweeps over me in all its perfection. I do a frantic double take for the surroundings (you've got to admit it, I'm a quick learner) and believe it or not. It. Is. Perfect. No neighboring houses in sight, the land around has a touch of hill, creek, and farmland combined. It nestles right up against a greenbelt that I'm guessing belongs to the Army Corp of Engineers (code for will not be built on or cleared for time everlasting, and perfect for long walks under the trees). Wraparound porch. Check. Original window glass, transoms, and gingerbread trim, also check.

"Down, girl," I chide myself. "Why would someone sell this perfect gem for the listing price? Something must be wrong with it." Despite this possibility, I cannot simply drive home without at least finding out why this house is not right for me, so before I chicken out, I dial the number on the realtor's sign nailed to the gatepost.

"Hello, Robinson Realty, Calvin Robinson speaking."

I kid you not, for a moment I think I accidentally dialed heaven or the world's most beautiful voice. If caramel has a sound, it would be his, for sure. As if none of that is bombarding my brain, I say, "This is Eisel Jane McCord. I'm calling about a house you have listed, a little turn of the century farmhouse with a wraparound porch, eight-ish miles west of town on county road NE 510."

"The old Millsbaugh place. Cute, isn't it?"

Struggling to focus on his words rather than the music of them, I manage to reply. "It is, and that's why I'm calling. Forgive me if this sounds blunt, but what's wrong with it? Outside of a faded paint job and a dead lawn, of course."

His chuckle is a revelation of how velvety a voice can be. "Excellent question, Ms. McCord. May we meet for a walk through? I can point out the areas requiring attention and fill you in on the history to give you a fuller answer to your question."

May we? Absolutely. I must meet this voice. I mean man. What a pity it will be if he is not somewhere around my age. I may be wanting to experience a great romance, but I draw the line at robbing a cradle, no matter how plush his tones.

"I'm out here right now, sizing it up," I say. "I can wait here for you to come if you're available, or if not, name your time." I want to add, "Please don't sell it until I've had a chance to view it, though" Only the fear that doing so might undermine any bargaining power I might have restrains me.

"Excellent. I'm about to head home right now and don't mind at all to swing on by. You just sit tight and maybe make a list of questions you'd like to ask me. I'll be there in two jiffies and a fistful of popcorn."

I'm thankful for those two jiffies and however long a fistful of popcorn lasts, because it's going to take at least that much time for me to recuperate from how his voice affected me and locate my grown-up face so I'll feel prepared to meet this Mr. Robinson.

CHAPTER 6

You know those times when you try not to have expectations because the real situation rarely delivers? Well, this is not that. The man who steps out of the black Lincoln SUV, Mr. Calvin Robinson in the flesh, (I presume), is as dreamy as his voice.

"Howdy, ma'am," he says, taking my hand and bowing over it. Yes, you read that right. Bowing over it. Maybe a tad shorter than Dan Baker, about Jimmy's height, six feet of masculinity with broad shoulders, short-cropped salt-and-pepper curls, a skim of circle beard, and a white-toothed grin that melts whatever was left of my insides now that this rich, brown-skinned perfection stands in front of me. Oh, and did I mention he smells good, too?

I don't know what to focus on—his twinkling dark eyes are surrounded by enough wrinkles I feel eighty-seven percent certain I'm looking at someone in his sixties. Perfect. His body (no, don't go there) and his smile have me staring. Reeling myself in, I smile back, hoping I don't show how completely mesmerized I currently am. "Howdy. I mean, hello. Thanks so much for meeting me at short notice."

He nods, grinning. "My pleasure. May I call you Eisel?

Is this what attraction feels like? I like him so much already, and I don't even know him. Maybe my trial planning this morning about 'winging it" with Dan is in play. Something is, anyway, as I actually feel myself leaning infinitesimally toward him. Going, going—I break free of the spell and nod. "Please do."

"I'll start with your previous question, then, Eisel. What's wrong with the house."

"Exactly." I toddle after him, bombarded with a flood of thoughts and emotions, and what the heck, a heavy lacing of tingling in my midsection.

I do my best to pretend otherwise.

"Here's the deal: Miss Millsbaugh turned one hundred last month and called me the day after. 'Calvin,' she said. 'I have decided to move into an assisted living facility. I'm too old to want to keep up the place. Would you sell it for me?' Of course I said yes, because not only am I a realtor, I also grew up down the road from this place a few miles. My mom would send me to bring eggs to Miss Millsbaugh every other week. I guess you'd say we go way back."

"That's amazing." Really, I don't care what he's saying. Could I please spend the whole afternoon listening to this voice tell stories?

Oblivious to my fascination (I hope), he continues. "Miss Millsbaugh is one tough old bird, and anyone going toe to toe with her will naturally be the first to back down, which leads me to the reason this little gem wasn't snatched up and pushed into escrow the first day I listed it. She also said, 'Now boy, you know I don't like nor trust people in general and don't want any developers or folks looking to let it out to some no-account renters who won't take care of it. I want it to be loved like I've loved it, so I don't want you selling my place to someone you don't like.'" He laughs, a sound so infectious I join in.

Fighting the desire to step closer to this Calvin Robinson, I steady my voice. "She does sound like a character."

"She is, and that's not all the only stipulation. 'You screen 'em, Calvin,' she said, 'then if you like 'em, you bring 'em to meet me. If I like 'em, I'll give you the nod, and you can draw up the papers.'"

"May I conclude that so far, no one's come along she approves of?"

"That's about the size of it." He rolls his eyes and chuckles all deep and rumbly.

I manage not to let on how magnetizing that chuckle is, though I do hold onto the porch railing to steady myself, turning the gesture into an ill-concealed inspection of the paint.

"With those caveats, do you still want to view the premises?"

"Of course." I squeak. "The fact she loves her home makes it even more special to me. I would adore to meet her and hear all its history. Her history here. I always wanted to live in an old house in the country, and this one is so charming."

"Then, by all means, let us proceed."

He shows me the good, the bad, and the ugly, and it appears the old beauty requires little beyond what a healthy application of elbow grease and a paint upgrade can't address. He points out that the roof needs to be replaced. Check. I'll ask Dan about it. There are a couple of rotten windowsills. I jot that on my "Ask Dan" list as well, briefly hoping he won't feel taken advantage of. Of course, I'll pay him, and besides, it's his job, so we're probably fine there.

"The well yields good, clean water. Miss Millsbaugh has it tested every year. Says she hasn't lived this long to be poisoned by her own water."

I laugh. "I second that."

"I do think the water heater could stand to be replaced, and unless you're fond of cranky old appliances that go on strike as often as they function, you'd have to lay out some money for those types of things. I also need to tell you that Miss Millsbaugh says it goes as is. She fixed her price and won't budge."

"The listing says $150,000 firm. I know as a buyer, I probably shouldn't say this, but the price seems a little low for the house and property, which is why I thought something might be wrong with it." I bite my lip. "However, now that I hear Miss

Millsbaugh's story, I'm concerned that she ends up with a fair price so she has enough to last—last until."

"That's very neighborly of you, Eisel, and I appreciate it. Don't you worry about me taking leveraging your question. You're safe with me. I never take advantage of ladies." He smiles down at me with deep brown eyes.

That's a killer of a pick-up line, and quite affective, may I add. "I appreciate that, Mr. Robinson."

"Please. Call me Calvin."

"Calvin." I smile, all fluttery inside for more reasons than house alone. "Understanding those stipulations, if I meet your approval, and Miss Millsbaugh decides I pass muster, I'd like to buy this old beauty as is if you really feel it's a fair price for her to receive. I'll one hundred percent live here myself. No selling to other parties."

Slapping his notebook shut, he locks eyes with me, and I can only hope he doesn't detect I'm as enthralled as Mowgli under the spell of Kaa as I gaze up at him. "I don't mind saying that so far, I'm liking you just fine, Miss Eisel." He touches my elbow for a moment as we step down from the porch, grinning as he opens my car door for me. "However, I do like to be thorough in my process, so before I advance you to meeting Miss Millsbaugh, I think I should take you out to dinner and get to know you a bit better."

Is this really happening to me? I suppose he sees the shock on my face because he gives that warm rumbly chuckle I believe would disarm a grizzly bear. "Now don't you worry. As I said, you're safe with me. I've simply enjoyed meeting you and showing you around, remembered a nice Italian restaurant with authentic food and live music, and had the idea I'd like to take you there. Would you be available Saturday evening?"

I manage to accept the invitation and also not run off the road as I drive away, though when I recount it all to Kate that evening, I'm still in shock. Was it only this morning I pondered being pursued as a vital ingredient for romance? Because dang, Calvin Robinson, you know how to make a lady feel desirable. Then I remind myself that it's only dinner and only so he can make a decision for Miss Millsbaugh. Okay, right. Don't read into things, Eisel, I tell myself, but who am I kidding? Part of me is not interested in listening to that sound counsel.

★ ★ ★

When I wake up the next morning, I tumble into my usual introspectiveness. Through no arranging or intention on my part, I have met two very nice men, and setting aside the fact that I'm merely abandoned, not divorced at this point, is it ethical to accept a date from two different men two nights running as if I'm a serial dater? This is not a realm I'm familiar with, and I would never want to treat anyone's heart lightly.

On the other hand, I could be getting way ahead of myself with thinking that either one is anything more than a meal with company. No one has said anything about hearts. That's all in my own head. That is a disappointing thought, I discover, because the tiny taste I had of Dan enjoying me and then yesterday at the old house with Calvin—both were definitely fun.

Don't overthink it, Eisel, I tell myself. Let things play out. If anything develops in either direction, you can figure it out then. I think this is good advice, even if I say so myself, so I quest about for something else to ponder. Of course, I want to start mentally renovating and redecorating the Millsbaugh place, but I hesitate to invest too much of my heart before I'm cleared for purchase.

However, I do think unless Calvin Velvet-voice Robinson is a consummate lady's man (a possibility because wow, is he smooth or what?), he's quite likely to give me his stamp of approval. I hope Miss Millsbaugh will as well. All I can do is be myself in both cases and hope that is enough.

To take my mind off the house, I text Jimmy. *Are you back from Machu Picchu yet?*

Wonder of wonders, he responds right away. *Yes. Rode the train.*

I'm meeting Maggie for coffee this morning and making myself go to the grocery afterwards. I don't think I quite appreciated how much of that chore you've taken off my plate since you retired. So, thank you for your many grocery trips.

You're very welcome. How are you doing?

I'm tempted to stay on the surface. After all, he's the one who jettisoned me like outmoded baggage, so I'd be completely justified in doing that. Still, when you share life with someone for as long as we have, not being forthcoming feels disingenuous, so I throw him a crumb. After all, I was never the one who left him out of *my* planning. *I decided to dust off my old bucket list.*

That's great. What's on it?

Nervous now, part of me definitely wants to play cagey. However, I broached the subject, and besides, I have nothing to hide. In fact, it might be easier for us both in the long run for him to have time to adjust to changes I'm making in my world while he's thousands of miles away. *I'm focusing on three entries right now: a long solo hike, buying a house of my own, and experiencing a great romance.*

My heart does a 360 in my chest as I hit send. I know Jimmy won't find it easy to hear those last two goals, and the longer the dots scroll, the more on edge I feel.

Right about the time I'm ready to chew my fingernails off, his text pings in. *Not to discourage you from following your dreams or anything, but we do have a house you know, and I thought we surely experienced a great romance?*

He does, does he? Well, maybe he feels he has, and I'd be interested to hear about that, but I have not. *I figured. However, here's the thing,* I text back, tackling the less emotional one first. *As you know, I always wanted to live out of town. Also, this house we own together is nice, but it's not mine. It's ours. I want something all my own in its entirety. I have Granny's money to spend on it, which is part of what's going to make it truly mine.*

I do not tell him I'll be living in said house of mine when or if he ever returns. That's another text, another time.

Before he responds, I address the other item. *I'm not as sure as I used to be that you still love me, since leaving me seemed pretty effortless on your part—but I do still love you. However, the honest truth is that I, Eisel Jane, never experienced a great romance before or during our marriage.*

I gulp, picturing how his jaw will clench as he reads this. *I'm not faulting you. I'm saying I want more than mutually meeting each other's needs and living in the same house. Sorry to drop that bomb and run.* I refrain from referring to the nuclear device he detonated in the kitchen not all that long ago. *However, I need to meet Maggie. Chat soon.*

Send.

I'm shaking as I step out the door. It feels as if I just severed the cord that connects Jimmy and me. Or did he do that already, and I only now released my end of a limp strand? Honestly, I don't know. I'm not ruling him out of the running in my great romance. I'd be perfectly happy to have him pursue me if he will. However, I've never had that from him. Even when we dated, I met him more than halfway. He'd say, "Would you like…" and I'd start nodding before he finished his sentence. I was so eager to please, so desperately needing to be acceptable to him.

I won't do that with him or anyone else anymore. They're going to need to be very obvious in their intentionality, because

I won't read into things this time around. I want to be wanted, enjoyed, prioritized—the list goes on. I think everyone wants to feel these things, (beside the point, though it bolsters my sagging courage), and until I do, I will not be reciprocating. This includes Jimmy. If he wants a romantic relationship with me, he will need to pursue me. Woo me. Treat me like a treasure and an unceasing delightful discovery. I want a chance to respond to that kind of treatment instead of filling in the gaps so I don't have to face the fact he may not want to. There it is, flat and simple.

All this is still on my mind as I hug my daughter and order my coffee. "Vanilla cappuccino, whole milk, for here, please," and settle into the comfy leather chair opposite her. "How's it going, my dear?" I ask after we toast each other and take our first sips.

"Mom, I don't want to talk about that. I want to talk about what Dad just texted me."

Gazing off over the top of my cup to the busy sidewalk outside the window, I inhale the rich fragrance to settle my emotions. After Jimmy's track record, I should have seen that coming.

"He said your bucket list includes experiencing a great romance."

"It does."

"Wait, Mom. You had a great romance. With Dad."

"No. Dad and I have had a good marriage overall. However, I, Eisel Jane, McCord, have never (I feel myself ramping up to defend this suddenly dear objective)—I repeat, *never* actually experienced romance."

"How can you say that?"

"Because it's true. Your dad and I, we've had forty-three mostly good years together, created a comfortable, pleasant life, had a beautiful, wonderful daughter who has given us so much joy, and also a grandchild we love to pieces plus the son we never had. But be honest with me—can you tell me of even one time you can think of when your dad pursued me? Romanced me? Prioritized me?"

She wants to. I see that in her eyes as she scrolls back through her thirty-nine years for a qualifying event. Long moments go by, and finally she lights up. "He brings you flowers."

I take that in. True. He does, and has many times over the years, and I've enjoyed it so much every single time. Flowers brighten a corner and are so intricate. I'm always thrilled when he brings them, and I miss that now that he's gone. Why it never registered as romantic, I don't know, because trust me, if Dan or Calvin ever have occasion to show up with a bouquet, I will definitely register it as a romantic act.

"You're right," I answer. "He does. Or did, anyway. Yet it never seemed romantic to me. Why do you think that is? Am I'm blind to romantic gestures coming from him?" I certainly don't like that thought.

I know Maggie so well. She's struggling with whether to read me the riot act about my relationship with her father or soften into an authentic conversation. I see the moment she opts for the latter.

"I'm not sure, Mom. I see myself doing the same with Jared, to be honest. Maybe we've become so used to how much goodness they bring to our world, we start taking such things in stride, sort of like part and parcel of the life we're creating together. It's not only us, either." She sighs. "I see our guys doing the same thing. I mean for you, the way you stood at the door every morning of my growing up years when Dad drove off to work, and how you flashed the porch light for him as he backed out the driveway. It was you saying, 'have a great day, and I love you.' Yet he never seemed to notice."

I blink back tears, amazed at how good it feels to have that act seen and acknowledged after all this time. I moved away from doing it, and I know why: one day in a rare but epic fight, Jimmy said it meant nothing to him.

Nothing.

All those heart messages I sent toward him with the flickering of the lights and assumed he received them meant nothing? All the times I watched him drive away and wished for him a wonderful, peaceful day and sent my love after him—they hadn't mattered to him? At least that's what he said that day. Granted, he was full-on triggered, and I really shouldn't trust anything coming out of his mouth during those moments. Yet the words lodged like shrapnel in my heart. I couldn't seem to leave them behind me and go on unchanged.

Though I did continue flipping the light for him for a few years longer, it felt less and less joyful, because if it meant nothing to him, why continue doing it? Until finally one day, I just didn't. And you know what? He never mentioned that ceasing, and I was afraid to bring it up in case I would find that precisely as he said, it never mattered to him at all.

We humans are so complex and so fragile, aren't we? I see now that it would have been braver and way more functional (as opposed to dysfunctional) to have chatted about it. To risk finding out the worst, risk Jimmy growing angry, in order to be more emotionally healthy and know what I was really dealing with. Instead, I spent all the years since then pushing those anxious thoughts away.

"Mom?"

"Sorry honey. Processing that last item," I say, taking another sip of my coffee and following my thought all the way to the painful end. When I started out, I flipped the lights for Jimmy as a gift, unconditionally, out of the affection in my heart. Why then, upon finding it didn't mean anything to him, did I stop? I know on the surface it's obvious. However, at this moment, I see something new. I see that somewhere after our big fight about that, I began viewing the efforts I made toward Jimmy conditional upon acceptance—I'd continue doing them *if* he appreciated them.

That's a transactional exchange, which is not the same thing as unconditional love, of course. Unconditional is me giving one hundred percent regardless of how he receives my gift or what he gives in return. Conditional, transactional love (can you really call that love?) is at best fifty-fifty. We spent a lot of years locked in that later category, and this realization makes me sad.

I don't say any of that. Instead, I squeeze Maggie's hand. "I know the thought of your dad's and my relationship being less than stable must be super stressful for you. Please don't worry, honey. No matter what happens between him and me, you'll always be our completely loved daughter. We'll always agree about that and you, and all the time we had together as you grew up will always be completely valid and valuable. We feel about you like you and Jared feel about Portia."

She squeezes my hand back. "Thanks for that, Mom, and thanks for being brave and honest. If I may say it, I think your counseling and EMDR therapy is helping." She grins.

I raise my eyebrows. "That, at least, is a relief." We laugh and transition into talking about Little Miss P, who is arguably our most favorite common subject, and of course, Grammie must watch all the videos of her cuteness and exclaim over her latest brilliancy.

CHAPTER 7

I'm on my way out to the car from the coffee shop when I catch a glimpse of movement in the store window. It requires a couple of blinks before I recognize my own eyes staring back at me. First thought: I need to stand up straighter and hold my shoulders back (the voice of my mother harping on my posture, which according to her always needed improvement). Second thought: OMG. Kate is right. My casual look is *too* casual. If I'm going on dates, I need an upgrade. Nothing fake or not me, but more like shedding the layers of habit to uncover who I am and what I might enjoy wearing in this season. Something more authentically Eisel.

Being comfortable with status quo and used to functionality over "fashionability" as I tend to be (also hating to shop, as aforementioned), I usually check back on my Amazon orders and literally order the same clothing items I already have, just in different colors, necklines and lengths. The figure facing me in the window illustrates how complacent I've become about my appearance. That needs to change. So instead of heading to the grocery for cream for my coffee and a few other items and straight back home, I find myself parking in front of Wilda's Boutique.

Dangerously, right next door to Wilda's is Fresh Looks Hair Salon. I hesitate, then push the door open and present myself. "I'd like something less grandma-like," I say, plunking myself down in the indicated chair. "Maybe an asymmetrical cut?" I poke and prod my hair a bit then give myself up to fingers more skillful than my own. When the stylist finishes, I love it. I'm not sure if it's the cut, my upcoming dates with two very nice men who initiated said occasions, or what, but when I walk out of there and then out of Wilda's about an hour and a sizable chunk of change later, I feel like a teenager on prom night; every bit as stoked and easily as nervous, a welcome change from how I've dragged around since Jimmy left.

After I stow my groceries and display my new outfits to figure out all the combinations that these core pieces can perform, I buckle down to the challenge of figuring out what to wear for tonight with Mr. Calvin Robinson. Even thinking about it sends a shiver down my core. He mentioned an Italian restaurant with live music indicating semi-formal at the very least. That will be a stretch, since as I mentioned before, I lean toward a mix of comfort and again, comfort. Thankfully, today at Wilda's, and with Maggie and Kate as consultants via text, I ended up with a doable alternative.

Offhand, since I'm used to sharing the everyday bits of my life with him, I send Jimmy a selfie of my haircut. *New style.*

Too late, I realize that coming as it does on the heels of my announcement this morning of "experiencing a great romance" (which clearly upset him, as evidenced by the fact that he immediately texted Maggie), my words may not come across as the I-want-to-share-this-new-thing-with-you message I meant it as.

I am terrible at subterfuge, though. Besides, it will be better in the long run to keep everything out in the open. Secret keeping and misleading statements may build tension in movies and books, but in real life, who wants that? Jimmy knows this about me, and I like to think that's why he trusts me. I want to keep that trust. Opening the photo he sent yesterday, I gaze into those warm brown eyes of his. I can trust him as well, and I love that about him.

Studying his picture, I contemplate sending Maggie a text to let Jimmy know that if he cares to, he can pursue me, because I see no reason he can't be in the running if he wants to be. He could romance me. Sweep me off my feet and win my heart in a fresh way. I'd love that sort of a storybook ending. Ultimately though, I don't text her because firstly, I grew up with triangulation—you want someone to know something or do something and you don't want to tell them directly, so you ask someone else to. I refuse to engage in that level of relational dysfunction. Secondly, the decision, indeed, the idea of kindling a romance with me, needs to come from within him, not from without. He must want that himself with no prompting from me or anyone else, and believe me, I'll know the difference.

Enough. I want to enjoy this date with Calvin that has me as giddy as a fourteen-year-old, not obsess over the man who left me for a life in Peru. A quick google search shows the restaurant Calvin mentioned to be a white tablecloth, crystal, and silver establishment with waiters in swallowtail coats and a menu with prices that steal my breath. Consequently, I lay out the classic black dress I bought today as the only acceptable choice.

I was on the fence about it because it hugs my middle a little more closely than I like and is longer than I'm used to. However, the neckline is lovely. I pair it with low-slung black wedges, and a copper and stone creation of a necklace Wilda convinced me to add to my pile because, and I quote, "It goes with everything." Thanks to my outfit and my new haircut, I think I look slightly classy and maybe a bit mysterious.

I'm double checking my eyebrows and applying a bit of last-minute lip color when the doorbell rings. Calvin's right on time, definitely a point on the right side of the ledger in my books. Tucking my pocketbook under my arm along with a soft black shawl hardly thicker than an eyelash, I open the door.

If I thought he was dashing yesterday, tonight he is devastating in a suit and tie and a faint scent of some aftershave that may become my new favorite—a mix of sea, spice, and forest. My middle turns to water, the kind of rush that takes your breath for a moment, and I blush as I hold out my hand in greeting. "Hello."

Holding it rather than shaking it, he looks me over just a moment. "Eisel, you look lovely. Thank you for coming with me. I believe I need to thank Miss Millsbaugh for this assignment," he says with a slow wink.

I laugh as if I receive these kinds of comments every day, mentally adding a new item to my Ingredients of Romance list. Genuine appreciation and compliments (I guess that's two). Then, and I kid you not, he holds out a lovely corsage, and the fragrance of lavender and rose intermingle as I take it out of the box and pin it to my shoulder. "It's gorgeous, Calvin. Thank you so much."

"Merely gilding the lily, as it were," he says, wiggling his eyebrows at me. "Shall we go?"

Touching my elbow going down the steps as he did at the old house yesterday, this time he keeps it there, light as a bird's wing, as if to ensure I reach the car in safety. Partly to distract myself from that touch, I add a couple more components to my romance ingredients: meaningful gifts (sorry, Jimmy—your flowers should have counted) and care, if that's what you call this gallant attention to my well-being, even though I'm a perfectly healthy and capable adult who could totally make it to the curb under my own steam, last time I checked.

Clearly Calvin Robinson has developed the art of making a woman feel special into a science. He opens the door on my side of his big SUV that gleams like a raven in the golden light of the fading sun. Taking my hand to help me up on the running board of the behemoth vehicle, he tucks my dress in so it won't be shut in the door and locates my seatbelt, pulling it down and handing it to me with a smile and eye contact while his aftershave romances me all on its own. A whole evening of this? I better not have any alcohol to drink because I'm losing my bearings already, and we haven't even left my driveway.

Yet—and this is an important distinction I add to my mental list—he is not pushy. Pushy would be assuming he could pin on my corsage, fingers under my collar, face close to mine, or fasten my seatbelt for me, leaning over my body to do so. I would be uncomfortable with that, and this would be our last date. Men treating women as a physical target for their own pleasure angers me quicker than about anything else. No worries. He's a perfect gentleman. I don't know when I've felt more valued and seen, and that's just on the drive to dinner. I need to get ahead of the euphoria his attention produces lest I lose all perspective.

"Tell me something about yourself, Calvin," I blurt out before his caramel-toned voice begins weaving its spell. "Are you married? Have any kids or grandkids?" Maybe it's a bit too straight and to the point, but I prefer to know what I'm dealing with, because I'm way too attracted to him already to find out later that he's taken and merely being nice to me.

His velvety chuckle sends a tingle up my spine. "I like how you cut to the chase, Eisel. Just like you did about the Millsbaugh place. It's refreshing. None of that tiptoeing around the basic issues like they don't matter."

I nod, hoping he continues to view it as a good thing.

"I'll tell you right off since you asked. I was married. I have two kids, a boy and a girl who are grown and starting families of their own, and I'm divorced—have been for the past twenty or so years. Now your turn. Same questions."

"Yes, yes, and yes, but it's complicated."

I swear, the more he laughs, the more I want to say clever things, simply to hear it and see him smile as he's doing now. "Complicated how?"

"Out of the blue, or at least it feels like that to me, a little over three months ago now, my husband, Jimmy, announced he was going join the excavation crew on an archeological dig in Peru for the foreseeable future. Without me."

"Why without you?"

"Do you want the long or the short answer?"

He grins. "The long one, of course. I'm very interested to see why a perfectly sane man would not want you to go with him on an adventure." He smiles over at me, one eyebrow raised, necessitating a deep breath to settle myself.

"I think it boils down to him wanting to have a great adventure before he grows too old to do so. He always loved archeology and dreamed of going on another dig, plus he turns seventy this year, a rough milestone for him. Also, I guess—" I pause, needing to own my part yet hating what it will sound like. "I guess I didn't take him seriously when he'd talk about wanting to join an archeological team, and I'm afraid I also made it clear I saw no reason for him to go, nor did I want to go either. So, he simply didn't bring me in on his process." I grimace.

We roll to a stop at the red light. I hope it's not symbolic for where my acquaintance with Calvin is headed after that confession. Sigh. Might as well do it thoroughly, then. "I hate to think of myself as a dream killer. A dream underminer. Maybe if I'd realized how important this was to him, I could have rallied. Could have supported him. I'm not sure that's true, though. I suppose in the end it doesn't matter, because apparently, he doesn't really need me in the equation."

"Mistake on his part if you'll pardon my saying so."

"You're pardoned and thank you for that." I smile over at him. "I don't want to make Jimmy sound like a terrible selfish person." I add. "He's not. However, he never let on he was planning to go, and I may be many things, a mind reader is not one of them."

The light turns green, and we roll on. Calvin nods. "So, he turns your world upside down and waltzes off to Peru for who knows how long?"

"Exactly. At least for a year, though the college has a three-year grant, so he could very well stay there the whole time. He says he doesn't want a divorce; I'm wondering what I want, you know?"

"I see what you mean by complicated. I understand, though. Sometimes we begin to feel invisible around the ones we love, as if they're proceeding with their lives and letting us fit in if we can. If we can't, they don't seem to notice our absence, which only confirms our fears."

"Exactly," I repeat, and we ride along in silence for a bit. "So, he's gone, and after I wallowed a while and raged a while longer, I dusted off my old bucket list. That's why I'm house hunting, you see. I decided to navigate my way through my list without considering Jimmy in the equation anymore."

"I admire you for rallying like that. You're bouncing back a lot faster than I did, to tell you the truth." He clicks his tongue and shakes his head. "It took me a good year or more to move forward, and even now, sometimes I'm not sure if I want to engage in life again or simply finish my course as a single fellow trying to do good in the earth. At this point, I'm leaning toward the latter."

I nod. "I get that. I really do. Part of me wishes Jimmy would come home and we could pick up where we left off, even if it wasn't romantic. The rest of me is like heck no. I am not going back to that. If Jimmy wants to be part of my life, he'll have to win me back on a level playing field."

"Good for you," Calvin says, holding up his hand for a high five. "Don't ever go backward. That's what my mama used to say. Forward is best. Fix what you can or create something new and never settle for something less than what brings your heart alive."

"Sounds like you had a wise mama. Also, a brave one."

"I did indeed."

With that, we roll up to Francesco's and am I ever thankful for my black dress and world class corsage as a valet steps out to receive our keys. Before I can extricate myself from the vehicle, Calvin's there to help me, draping my shawl over my shoulders. Then tucking my hand under his elbow, he leads me through the door as if we're guests of honor at a gala event (minus the flashing light bulbs and confetti).

Another item for my Romance Ingredient list: being treated as if I'm worthy and special. It's as if I've entered an alternate universe where everything including myself and Calvin are rimmed in a shimmer of gold. Entranced by the polite way this lovely man interacts with waiters and hostesses, I note how he orders wine, conferring with me as if I know as much about the subject as he does.

I tell him right up front that I wouldn't know a red from a white unless the color gave it away, which he finds ridiculously funny. (I suspect I gave away how ignorant I am on the subject by that statement, but I don't actually know enough to tell if that's so). We chat about anything and everything, and the way he listens, asks questions, and doesn't stay on the surface opens me up in a way that feels both safe and effortless, as if whatever I am is perfect. He's funny and open and engaged, offering himself and his friendship in such a simple unpretentious way, I'm not sure I could resist even if I wanted to. For the record, I do not. In fact, friendship feels like a true gift to me in this lonely season.

"What are some other items on your bucket list besides a house of your own, Eisel?" he asks as dinner progresses.

No way I'm telling him my top item. However, I do give him a few from further down. "Besides hiking a long trail solo, I need to figure out if I still want to do any of these from my original list: Go snorkeling on a Pacific island reef, visit the cliff dwellings at Mesa Verde, and possibly write a book."

"Inspiring. I'd totally go along with you on those first two adventures if you want company. As for the book, what would you write?" His dark eyes study me as if I'm a fascinating puzzle he just discovered.

"Truthfully, I wrote that idea down when I was seventeen. I'm not sure I have a book in me. Maybe a short story?"

"I bet you have all kinds of books in you. I have a feeling you've got a lot going on under the surface, lady."

"You have no idea. However, I don't think books are down there." I shake my head. "I'm not sure I'm that deep. Merely jumbled."

When I say that, his smile fades. "I don't believe that for a moment, Eisel, and you shouldn't either. Just because you don't understand yourself sometimes doesn't mean you don't have important things to say."

"Thank you for that, Calvin. That's very sweet of you."

"Not sweet. The truth."

"I appreciate that a lot. I'll ponder it. Meanwhile, how about you? Do you have a bucket list?"

"Not as such, though I'm now considering a few items I'd like to pursue. I'm looking at one in particular right now, actually." He winks at me, grinning, and then chuckles when I blush. "Aren't you going to ask me what that item is?"

"I'm—I—"

"No worries." He touches my arm, letting his fingers lay there light as a butterfly and setting me tingling in a way no butterfly never has. Smiling at my obvious confusion over that and his words, he adds, "I'll give you a couple more items while you're processing that one, shall I?"

Gulp. I have no idea how to react to his flirting, though I've got to own that after the initial shock, I'm enjoying it. Very much enjoying it and him.

"I always thought I'd like kayaking down some rapids. Not life-threatening ones, though. Just somewhat risky ones so I can feel as if I accomplished something. I'd also like to be in a musical sometime."

"Do you sing?"

"I do. I'll sing for you sometime, shall I?" His fingers still rest on my wrist, his eyes drawing me in.

"I'd love that a lot, actually," I say, trying not to let on how his touch and his attention has me buzzing in my core. "I adore music, even though the only thing I play is soundtracks."

His rich rumbly laugh sucks me in further. My word. Feeling this way could be addictive. He's certainly giving me some romantic elements to consider. All in all, by the time we're through with dinner, not only am I feeling seen as a woman (yikes. Also, fun), I feel we've become long-time friends; friends, yet with a definite man-woman element that has me all starry-eyed and keyed up, buzzing in my core in a way I'd forgotten.

In fact, Cinderella has nothing on me by the time Calvin (he says, "Call me Cal,") offers his hand to lead me to the dance floor. As the musicians lay down some classic big band sounds, we glide across the floor like silk. I don't even know who this woman is, this me coming alive in the care and wonder of a man who has slipped into my life as if he's someone I've always known and enjoyed.

I'm lost in a sort of romantic haze as we flow to the music. Cal smells like spice and sandalwood with a cool undernote that has me captured as he guides me through dance moves as if we're contestants on *Dancing with the Stars*. He's kind and funny. He's also warm under my hands. Muscular. Clean. Gulp. By the time

"Fly me to the Moon" starts to play, I'm soaring right along with the melody.

As the classic words wind around us, I'm unsure if Cal draws me in closer against his body or if I simply melt into him. Or maybe it's both of us. One thing I do know is that it feels wonderful, thrill after thrill shooting through me at this contact. I'm flushed and smiling, so breathless I I can hardly think straight. So I don't think. I give myself up to that enjoyment.

"You're quite a dancer, Eisel," he whispers in my ear.

Smiling up at him, I float on the music and the nearness of him in a way I wouldn't have envisioned possible only a few of hours before. Yet here we are. Here I am. "Not usually, Cal. I really do think it's you." I know my voice sounds huskier than usual, my gaze locked on his. Yet somehow that's okay in this moment as he twirls me out then pulls me back in against him.

The electrical surge that sweeps me as we touch leaves me weak in the knees and clinging to him for support as well as attraction. It's as if I'm living a scene from a movie, enveloped in the music, encompassed by his presence.

Suffice it to say that by the time we dance through a few more classics, we drive home, and he escorts me from the car to my front door, I completely see how kisses can occur at the end of a first date. I'm in such a sweet, mesmerized state, I'm more than prepared for it to happen. Nervous, but prepared. However, he doesn't make that move. Instead, he takes my hand, bows low over it as before, and this time he brings it up to press his lips to my knuckles while he holds my gaze. It's a timeless moment for me. Already alive in every cell, I'm smiling, softened, completely enchanted by a perfect evening with this wonderful human who still holds my hand.

"Well, well, well. I don't know when I've enjoyed an evening more, and that's the truth," Cal says, his eyes and mouth soft as he smiles back. Kissing my hand one more time, he holds my gaze as he releases it. Then with a wink, he walks off into the night.

CHAPTER 8

When I wake up the next morning, I relive the evening before. Relive Cal. Thinking of him and our time together makes me smile. I blush at how engaged I was. How completely I was in the moment. I'm not sure how it transpired in one evening, but I feel on a solid friendship basis with him already. Recalling the night, as short as our acquaintance is, I can't deny that he seemed to have more on his mind than mere friendship the way he flirted with me.

His touch on my wrist, that list "item" he made clear was me, plus the way we danced together—we covered a whole lot of ground in a very short time. Now I almost feel guilty for having experienced Cal before giving Dan a fighting chance, because I'm still basking in the euphoria of feeling so taken care of. So honored and seen, and yes, even desired. How can Dan hope to compete with that? Should I cancel Sunday's date before we roll any further down the road?

Yet as I remember how I felt with him at dinner on Thursday— his blue eyes and his smile, how easy he is to talk with, how much he seemed to enjoy me—I liked all those and find myself reluctant to cancel on him. Besides, it would be so last minute. I can't think of a way to be truthful without being awkward. What would I say? "I met someone on Friday whom I might end up liking more than I like you," when I haven't actually given Dan a decent chance compared to an evening alone with Cal?

Besides the fact that Dan may not be interested in anything more than friendship anyway, such a scenario would be potentially hurtful. But on the off chance he might be, to make that call without a one-on-one time together doesn't seem quite fair.

It does feel surreal to be going out with two attractive men, though. Craziness. Tonight, Dan and I will be alone together without Kate and Eric, and that dynamic should help me gauge whether he's interested in me in a romantic way and whether I want to know him better or not.

I wasn't kidding when I told Cal I'm a jumble inside. I'm in that state most of the time, and this "experiencing a great romance" directive has me more kerflummoxed than usual. So much complexity to sort through. In this case, I tease out two aspects: I can only be romantically involved with one man at a time (studiously not thinking of Jimmy as husband, only as a romantic contender for my heart at this point). Secondly, I can't choose which one at this point.

I can, however, be friends, even good friends with more than one at a time. Jimmy and I are of course friends by virtue of all we've shared together—though right now I don't know if I'm one of his favorites, that's for sure. After last night, I feel a warmth of friendship with Cal in which I can rest easy. In fact, I want to call him and bask in his caramel-colored voice, hear him laugh again, to connect more, and face it—to feel as wonderful and clever as I did last night.

I don't call, though, because when it comes right down to it, what do I really know about how romance feels anyway? Maybe I misinterpreted things last night. Still, as I'm replaying what he said; the way he made intentional longer eye contact multiple times, unlocking me deeper with each pass; how he held me while we danced—respectful, yet close—I didn't make that up. The way kissed my hand and winked at me when he said goodbye—I don't think he'd have done those things if he wasn't at least a bit attracted to me. This conclusion sends a jolt through me toe to cheek.

When I think that less than a week ago, I was still walking around wounded, resentful, and without an anchor, I'm not even sure what's happening to me. Is this an awakening or a rebirth? I guess it doesn't matter in the end. What matters is I'm moving forward, as per Cal's mom's advice, and in doing so am feeling so much more alive than I thought possible. All that from simply beginning on two bucket list items—who knew?

Comparing elements with Dan this evening as he suggested and seeing if we have any overlaps seems like the perfect way to get to know him as a person and perhaps as a friend, wherever else it might or might not go.

I text him. *Looking forward to tonight. How are you with coconut and pecans? I'm thinking German chocolate cake.*

I'm looking forward to it as well, and to seeing you again. Thanks for accepting my invite. German Chocolate cake is one of my favorites. Bring it on.

Excellent.

Then I see that I have a text waiting for me from Jimmy. Part of me doesn't want to open it—doesn't want to think about him after thinking about Cal and Dan. That part also doesn't want to read what Jim has to say about my not experiencing romance with him now that he's had some time to process.

I know I'll have to open his message sooner or later, though, and curiosity overtakes me. Surprise! It is not a protest or a defense. It's a video of a lovely little river dancing its way over rocks, sunlight sparkling off its surface like diamonds, and an early morning mist threading through ferns and foliage along the banks. Jimmy also sent me a poem.

The river ripples past me,
Singing as it goes,

Quicksilver on the surface,
Midnight depths below.
I think, 'It's just like Eisel,'
Alive and wild and free
And I wonder at the wonder
Of the gift she is to me."

I read it through again, then again, and with every reading, my heart slows and softens. Jimmy wrote this for me.

Jimmy wrote this about me.

I have no grid for a version of him who's clearly thinking of me and thankful for me. He hasn't written poetry for me since our dating days. I'm pondering that as I grind my morning coffee. The rich aroma reminds of how he always brought the fresh grinds over for me to smell when he made our morning coffee, and how we'd tell each other which flavor notes we picked up.

Picturing how he'd smile at me while he waited for me to hand the coffee back to him, I wonder why this daily interaction never sent the same thrills through my middle as Cal's smiles did last night. As I mentioned to Maggie, what if I am so accustomed to such small acts of inclusiveness from Jimmy that I don't see them anymore? Has romance been at my fingertips all along, and I had no eyes to see it?

I want to think that can't be true. However, a proverb comes to me that hits too close to home, reminding me of what Maggie said yesterday morning. "To a hungry man every bitter thing is sweet, but a full man tramples on the honeycomb."

Remove the gender references, and it feels applicable, which I find puzzling because I don't feel full. I feel starved for romance. I'm not sure how being both starved and full can co-exist in the same realm. Did I wander around trampling on the very romantic elements I so long for, simply because they were coming from someone I grew too used to having around?

I do not like that thought at all, so I push it to the background, sure it'll come back around to haunt me later. Meanwhile, I need to figure out how to respond to Jimmy's offering of this window into his soul. It takes me a whole cup of coffee plus a toasted croissant with blackberry jam to craft my reply, which is not a literary masterpiece by any stretch of the imagination even then.

I tag a heart on the poem, then message, *Thank you. [heart eyes, thank you hands, heart emojis]*, and hit send. I want to give him more, but I can't. I can't pretend that one poem remedies years of emotional non-supply or his recent abandonment and also can't because I'm now more confused than before about whether or I've experienced a great romance or not.

Maybe the key word here is "experienced." Not "had available" or "was offered." Experienced could mean I have more agency in the equation than I assumed. Whatever. I move on, yielding to an impulse to distract myself from all these thoughts by texting Cal.

Thank you for last night. It was lovely. I hover over the send button. Yet my words seem too generic for the level of connection to him I feel after last night. I delete and try again. *Thank you for last night. I truly enjoyed it and you.*

Too leading? Recalling all the moments up until he said goodbye, I decide to risk it and hit send.

Not five minutes later, my phone pings. It's from Cal.

My exact words, he texts. Then, *I believe I can safely tell Miss Millsbaugh that I like you. :-)*

I smile all over my face as I figure out a reply. I do want the house. Separate from that, I want to know Cal as a person, not as a realtor. I don't want our friendship to be about business.

Adding a heart eyes emoji and thank you hands to his message, I wonder if that is too suggestive, like a woman on the make or reading into his text more than he meant. Talking to him would be better. Texts are so one dimensional, and emojis, despite the fact I use them a fair amount, are stereotyped, hence my hesitation.

I tag his text with *Haha* instead and ask, *Do you mind if I call you to coordinate a visit to said Miss Millsbaugh?*

I'm waiting for his answer when my phone rings instead. "Hello, Eisel? It's me, Cal."

Endeavoring not to gush as his warm voice washes over me, drawing me back into the bubble of friendship we built between us last night, I smile. "I realized after I sent that text that it's Sunday, and you shouldn't have to work on the weekends. Maybe we should figure this out tomorrow?"

"Now, now. Talking to you is not work, lady."

I laugh to cover the zip of electricity that flicks through me at that. "You do know how to say precisely the right thing, Cal. Are you sure you don't mind?"

"I'm sure."

I hear the soft smile in his voice and smile, too. "I really appreciate it, because I do love that old house."

"Still want it, do you?"

"I do."

An unsettling thought intrudes—what if he thinks I went out with him last night and am having a conversation with him now solely because I want to get on his good side so I can buy that house? "Cal, I hope you know that wanting the house has nothing to do with my saying I enjoyed last night and you. I would never try to use someone to obtain what I want."

In the beat of silence following my statement, I die a slow, apologetic death, reviving only as I comprehend his response. "I could say a lot of things right now, Eisel Jane McCord, but I think I'll go with this one: I'm a pretty good judge of character, if I say so myself, and if I may be so bold as to offer an opinion of you, I would say that you are one of the most authentic and forthright people I have ever had a privilege to meet." He chuckles, that deep, rumbly sound almost like purring, but better. "In fact, I'll go so far as to bet that if you were contemplating trying to manipulate me about this house deal, you'd probably tell me your intentions right out of the gate in case I got the wrong impression."

I give a weak haha. "True."

"I'll go a little further out on the limb here, Eisel, trusting you'll tell me to back off if it's not to your liking, because I want you to understand something. Last night with you? For me, it was like being in a forest in the quiet where I could simply be myself and not worry about what I should or shouldn't be doing or saying. It was so—so easy. Not one woman in all my dates since my divorce has opened that space for me."

My turn for silence.

"Too much?"

"No. Not too much," I manage to say, and then before I chicken out, "Actually, I think that was exactly what I hoped you were feeling, because last night—" I gulp and plunge ahead. "Last night was magical for me. I feel like we became real friends, and—" I pause, looking for words that don't assume too much while doing justice to our time together. "I don't mean to read more into your kindnesses and your words than you might have meant, but I loved it all. All of it." I hope he's remembering the dancing and how our bodies felt together, the easy conversation, the enchanted ending, because I sure am. "This morning, though, I've been wondering if you say those things to all the ladies you go out with."

I'm more comfortable with his silence this time, his quiet breathing so close in my ear. When he answers, his voice is as soft as velvet. "Eisel Jane. I don't know who you think I am, like some ladies' man or something, being divorced and such. However, I'm not that way. Not at all. I've gone out with a few ladies over the years, but it's the God-honest truth that I've never—" He clears his throat. "I don't know what you were feeling last night. I only know I had all sorts of feels going on I hadn't expected." He breaks off, and I hold my breath. "That being the case, I'd like to see you again. Soon. I want to spend more time with you like we did last night and see where it goes."

He would? My word. "I'd like that too," I say, almost whispering to keep the trembling out of my voice.

"All right then." He chuckles. "We'll do that little thing. Let me look at my appointments and circle back on that."

"Perfect." I bite my lip to prove I'm not dreaming. One dinner in and he wants to see where it goes? Maybe things just move faster when you're in your sixties. I wouldn't know, but I appreciate the clarity his words bring to the picture. Also, the accompanying tingles.

"As for meeting Miss Millsbaugh, I'll stop by her assisted living residence tomorrow on my way to the office and let her know I like you fine." He pauses. "I won't let on how much I'm enjoying you, of course, because she's very particular about such things."

I laugh, figuring that response is safe. "You're hilarious." Blushing now, once again caught in the euphoria of attraction to this very nice man, I venture further. "However, when we're there, maybe don't wink at me like you did last night. You might distract me so much she'll throw me out. I am not and never have been a good actor."

"Actually, except for real estate deals like we're about to finagle, I'm quite happy about that fact, Eisel Jane. You just be you. I'm thinking that's working quite well for me."

★ ★ ★

I rehash this conversation in my mind for an hour or so, reliving Cal's strategic chuckles and the way his voice softened and drew me in. He's making it very clear he likes me and may even be open to liking me a lot. It's all so new and I'm so inexperienced, when it comes right down to it, I don't know what to think. I call Kate and fill her in.

"Kate, Cal is gorgeous. He's also fun and witty and I know we've just met, but last night at dinner and just now on the phone, he made it clear he likes me and wants to get to know me better."

"Wow, babe. I think this bucket list of yours is turning out to be a whole lot more rewarding than you thought it would. Also moving quicker than you expected. When do I meet this model of masculine perfection?"

I snort. "Not for a bit. I need to get my feet under me, and besides, I have a date with Dan tonight, and if can you believe it, of all things, this morning Jimmy sent me a poem he wrote about me. It's really quite lovely. I have no idea how to process that or really, this whole experiencing romance thing." I sigh. "It's quite complicated going from flat lining in the romantic realm to having two standup guys finding me worth their attention in the space of a week, and Jimmy's poem to boot."

Her turn to snort. "Because you are worthy of it, and always have been, girl. You simply haven't been very tuned into the fact."

True. I need more practice viewing myself from that perspective. "Thank you, Kate. You're such a great friend to me, and that black dress? It was perfect for the occasion. Thank you for insisting I lay out the moola for it. I felt like Cinderella at the ball."

"Sounds to me like you might have danced your way into his heart, or at least into his arms. I had no idea you were such a fast mover, E."

I laugh at the sheer ridiculousness of that description applied to me. But I don't really mind because being with Cal is so fun. I have apparently completely cut loose from my usual moorings, a hot air balloon sailing along in a sapphire sky. "I'm thoroughly confused about all of this. I will say, though, I loved how I felt when I was with him last night."

"I'm so stinkin' stoked for you to have this happening when hardly a week ago you were so downhearted."

"I was, wasn't I? I'm not even sure who this version of me is. I can tell you this, though—it's a blast. Also, emotionally exhausting. Speaking of which, would you help me choose what I should wear to Dan's tonight? He's grilling steaks, I'm bringing dessert, and we're going to see if any items on our respective bucket lists sync up."

"Dang, girl. When you decide to do something, you get 'er done."

"Stop teasing me and help, you rascal."

We settle on informal with a touch of upscale whimsy. Navy leggings. Ariat deck shoes. White linen button-down blouse paired with feather earrings. Then I hop to, making the cake and frosting it (I always make a batch and a half of the coconut pecan frosting so I can "sample" it multiple times without needing to skim bits off my already frosted cake), then shower and putter through a few house chores.

Thankfully, my new haircut is as cute today as yesterday, I'm thrilled to see, and I send Kate a selfie of my ensemble.

Irresistible, she texts back with a star eyes emoji.

For better or for worse, I'm ready for this next foray into the realm of friendship and possible romance. Before setting out, I run through what I know about Dan and what might be the best way to let this time with him be free of any comparison with last night's date with Cal.

1. *Dan is Dan, I don't yet know who that is, and I want to find out (all I know from our double date last week is that he's kind, has a great smile, blue eyes, and is very easy to talk with).*
2. *Dan is not going to be Cal (or Jimmy), and none of them deserve to be weighed against the others. (I will stay in*

the moment and out of my introspective alter ego, so I don't second and third guess myself out of authenticity or sell Dan short).

3. *I'd really like to chat with him about his marriage with Rosalie and ask him what he knows about romance. (Did they have it together? What does romance look like from the man's perspective, etc.).*

3. *If he offers to hold my hand, I'll meet him halfway. Maybe I'd be willing to go a bit further, if it feels appropriate. (Not letting myself speculate what further would look like lest I arrive all frozen and awkward from overthinking).*

4. *Still planning on winging it after that. (The thought of crossing the lip barrier is surprisingly daunting, yet last night on the doorstep after an evening with Cal, I could have done it in a heartbeat, so I now know I can reach that juncture under the right circumstances).*

CHAPTER 9

Dan's place is on the outskirts of town, a rambling Colorado-type house with a sweeping green lawn rolling up to the walk. Like a mountain meadow, it's dotted with pines, maples, and other trees in strategic places as if you just stepped into a mountain meadow. The smell of smoke and steak hangs in the air like a tantalizing perfume. I toss my jacket over my shoulder, extract the cake from the car, and rotate full circle simply taking it all in. As I turn back to face the door, Dan comes down the steps, a bouquet of flowers in his hands and a big smile on his face.

"What a beautiful place you have here, Dan."

"Thank you. Rosalie and I always wanted a house like this, so about ten years ago, we built it." He takes the cake from me and holds out the sheaf of candy pink carnations, sky-blue larkspur, and filmy baby's breath. "I saw these when I picked up the steaks from the market and took a chance that maybe you like flowers."

"I do. I love them," I say, smiling up at him as I bury my nose in the bouquet. "Sorry Jimmy," I murmur there, a pang hitting my heart. Clearly, I have a serious perception error where he and romance are concerned, because as with Cal's corsage last night, this offer of flowers lifts my heart. "This is so kind of you. Carnations are one of my favorites, too—spicy like cloves. These are so pretty with the greenery, larkspur blue, and baby's breath."

He grins. "Good. I wondered if it was cliché to offer a woman flowers these days. I'm out of touch with that kind of thing."

"Flowers are never cliché," I state as he holds out his other arm to escort me toward the house in an almost unconscious gesture. I'll bet it's what he used to do for Rosalie. That makes me smile as he leads the way up the steps, through the house, and out to the back deck, which is truly a mountain wonder, complete with soundtrack as John Denver's greatest hits play in the background.

From that moment forward, everything seems so easy with Dan. So normal, if I can say it that way. He finds a vase; I arrange the flowers. He pulls out a chair for me; I settle into it. Easing into the evening, I'm already feeling so comfortable. We must have covered a lot more ground on Friday night than it seemed at the time, because picking up from there, we're chatting like old friends before the first fifteen minutes go by.

Dan Baker really is a lovely person, straightforward, sincere, kind. He also seems to know what he wants in life, which is rather disconcerting for someone who has no idea what exactly that might be, though it's pretty clear he's interested in me. Something about the way he watches my face, the way he listens, and how intentional and thoughtful he is in his conversation. I'm relaxing into the moment, feeling quite enchanted with him and the night and the music.

Interesting. It's completely different from my night with Cal, which was frankly perfect. Yet this feels just as perfect in its own way. I thought I'd be awkward and uncomfortable on this date after being with Cal. Considering I haven't dated since before I married Jimmy, I really have no clue about dating protocol, and two in a row as if I'm a serial dater? I have no grid for that.

I'm amazed at how effortless it is to simply be with Dan. Maybe it's not the high-level Cinderella feeling of last night with Cal where I felt brilliant and funny and as if I could do nothing that didn't fit into those two categories. This is more of a slip off your shoes, lean back in your chair and enjoy the evening type of easy.

Rather than clarify anything, this date with Dan adds to my inner jumble. However, I can't find it in myself to worry very much about that right now. I'm too busy enjoying the experience.

"Would you like something to drink, Eisel?" Dan asks, giving me one of his killer smiles. "I have pretty much anything you can ask for and can also mix drinks with a certain amount of skill, or so Rosalie used to say."

"What are you having?"

"I generally like a craft beer of some sort along about dinner time."

"I'm not much of a beer lover as a rule, unless it's ginger beer."

"I have that, too. One icy cold ginger beer coming up."

When he comes back, he hands me a goblet with some ice, then cups his hand around mine as he pours the glass full. Looking up, I see he's watching me, head slightly tilted as if gauging my reaction to that contact. I hope he can't tell I've gone all fluttery in my chest.

He gives a one-sided smile. "There you go, Eisel." Not sure what he means by that as of all things, he slides his hand off mine in such a slow movement it takes me by surprise, as does the hitch in my breathing. "I've got more where that came from." His smile deepens, presumably at the way my eyes go wide.

OMG. Not completely sure how to respond to this intentional flirting of his, I can think of absolutely nothing to say in response that won't embarrass the daylights out of me, so I scramble for a completely different subject instead. "T—thanks for inviting me over, Dan. I like your idea of seeing if anything on our bucket lists sync up. I'll warn you, though. I already told you the most exciting item on mine, and as I explained, it was basically bogus."

Laughing, eyes holding mine until I look away, he says, "We might be on solid ground then, because honestly, when I sat down and looked at mine, not only is it very tame, most of the things I listed I've either already done or am no longer interested in doing."

I touch my glass of ginger beer to his bottle of Raymeyer's Pale Ale. "I feel better. What's item number one for you?"

"Climbing El Capitan."

"Seriously? What happened to nothing spectacular on your list? Climbing El Capitan? That's epic. Do you climb in your off time?"

He grins. "Actually, no. I wrote that down while in college, and never got around to it once I met Rosalie and settled down. However, I've been thinking about it since digging out my list, and it still sounds like something I want to do before I'm too old and decrepit."

"Not to flirt with you or anything (though I guess I am, just nothing near the level he already engaged in), but when I look at you, the words old and decrepit do not come to mind."

"Why thank you. I'll take that compliment." His eyes twinkle as he takes a drink. "Seriously though, the tallest thing I've climbed to date is the wall down at Six Flags. It's going to take a lot of leveling up to tackle El Cap."

"Still impressive," I say with a grin. This conversing with attractive men thing is probably one of the more dangerous and enjoyable things I've done for a very long time. "So how do you prepare for that—climb smaller cliff faces?"

"Basically, yes. Does that remotely relate to anything on your bucket list?" He tops off my glass and adds a couple more ice cubes, varying his previous tactic by bridging my fingers with his as he does so while once again keeping his eyes on mine.

He's flirting with me. He totally is, and I'm not sure how to process that info since I'm not the best at thinking things through as they're happening. I'm more of a retrospective learner. For lack of a better idea, I simply carry on talking, blushing as I answer, then blushing more as he grins in response. "Solo hiking on a long trail is the nearest thing on my list to your item. I'll prep by taking short hikes. Though I doubt hiking will do much toward training you for mountain climbing, I'd love to walk some shorter trails with you sometime if you're interested."

Dang. Is this me, throwing out invitations like I'm passing out grocery store flyers? Of course, he paved the way for me with those touches and gazes, so it doesn't seem as if I'm stepping out on a limb, or at least not too far out, though I'm far from my usual, that's for sure.

"I'm very interested." He lifts one eyebrow and one corner of his mouth quirks up. My word. I blush again, grinning in response, and at this auspicious moment, an alarm beeps. "The steaks are done. Let's discuss hiking together further, shall we? First, though, I need to pull these off the grill and put our plates together."

"Let me help," I say, trailing behind him close enough to detect his sage and pine-scented aftershave. Yum. If men only knew how their cologne affects the typical woman—I pause. As Kate would say, "Duh. That's undoubtedly why they wear it, silly." That being the case, maybe I should consider applying a tiny dab of my favorite perfume next time I go on a date. I don't even remember the last time I did so—Jimmy was so sensitive to odors; he didn't wear aftershave and said my perfume burned his nostrils. But I love aftershave. Love when men smell good.

I love my perfume too.

Pondering this, I'm following too closely when Dan turns around, and not only are we suddenly in each other's space bubbles, he almost catches me sniffing the air like old Trencher on the trail of some "niblet" of food.

I'm snagged in his blue gaze as he smiles down at me, one eyebrow raised. Instead of pulling out while I have a chance, though, all I can do is blink up at him, mesmerized. His smile deepens, and suddenly I'm way too aware of how attractive he is with his broad shoulders, obvious biceps, five o'clock shadow and more.

What in the world? Does Jimmy also exude masculinity like this, and I've gotten too used to a good thing to recognize it? Furthermore, how do I answer that question now that he's too far away to test it out?

Dan tilts his head. "What's up, Eisel? Where'd you go just now?"

He saw that? Part of me wants to crawl under the nearest chair and hide (or concoct a convenient lie, the conversational equivalent). I do neither, because the other part of me knows I must opt for authenticity from the get-go or let this be the last date I have with Mr. Dan Baker; I cannot flip off a surface answer to his question and then build on the resulting layer of insincerity. I'm not wired that way (though I will say, it would definitely be convenient in such instances).

"I'll tell you at the table."

Once we've eaten our way through the excellent rib eyes, baked potatoes, and salad (and just as I begin to hope he forgot his question), he fixes those blue eyes on me and circles back. "So, what happened to you earlier?"

I grimace. "Can we just let it pass?"

"I suppose we could. I'm curious, though—one second you were there, and I was pretty sure we were about to have a moment, and then you weren't. I'm curious as to why."

My vitals clench at his "…we were about to have a moment…" statement because as I suspected, it means he knew exactly what he was doing by staying so close and looking down at me with that what-you-gonna-do-about-it" smile. I blush. Again.

Hold it together, girl, I tell myself, taking a deep breath. "Okay, Dan. This is going to sound weird, I'm afraid, and also a bit embarrassing," Actually a lot embarrassing. "I'll throw it out there and hope you can understand where I'm coming from, though I won't fault you if you don't."

"That's quite an intro there, Eisel. Pray tell what is this possibly weird, embarrassing thought you had that I may not understand?" He leans forward and wiggles his eyebrows at me.

I laugh. "I do have a tendency to over explain. Here's the plain unembellished truth, and I hope you don't think I'm coming on to you or anything—" Before I expire of embarrassment, I blurt out, "You smell good."

Grin deepening, his eyes definitely twinkle now. "Glad to hear that."

I power on. "I was thinking about that when you turned around, and there we were—as you say, about to have a moment—and then it struck me—" Gulp. "This is the weird part, because smelling nice is, well, nice and not weird—" I'm officially dying now. "Anyway, my absentee husband, Jimmy, sent me a poem this morning which is not what he has ever done before. That has me suddenly wondering if he is also as—" I try again. "Dan, I'm talking myself into a deep hole here. I'll finish, though, because I also want to ask you a question about your marriage."

His crooked half smile and a nod invites me deeper.

"The truth is, I suddenly wondered if Jimmy also exudes masculine energy like you do, and whether I was too used to him to recognize it." I want it to come out funny, but I choke up as I say that last bit and find I'm blinking back sudden tears. "I'm sorry," I add, waving my hand in front of my face to head them off. "I didn't accept an invitation from you to come think or talk about Jimmy. He's doing his own thing without me anyway, in spite of the poem."

I brace myself to be swallowed the rest of the way by embarrassment, and since I'm already almost there so I go for it. "You know how we're talking about bucket lists? One item I wrote on mine when I was seventeen or eighteen is that I wanted to experience a great romance."

Dan doesn't grin at me or let on that what I've shared is anything but understandable. In fact, his eyes grow soft as an early morning sky, encouraging me to finish out my fiasco of a speech.

"I know it sounds strange considering I've been married forty-three years, but I have yet to experience a great romance. Or even a small one, for that matter, at least that I'm aware of. That's what I thought when I read through my list after Jimmy left. However, meeting you and hearing about Rosalie—it's clear you loved her so much—and thinking about different ingredients in a romantic relationship, now I'm wondering if maybe a romance with Jimmy was there for the taking, even though I didn't experience it. Like maybe my not experiencing it is at least partially my fault.

With all that as background, I was hoping you could tell me what you know about romantic relationships. Ingredients, I guess you'd say, and how to recognize them, so I can figure out if my lack of experiencing romance is more about me not recognizing it for what it is. Or was, I guess you'd say, now."

The candles have burned to a low golden glow, stars winking on one by one as my words hang in the air between us. I don't know if that's a good thing or a bad thing as "Annie's Song" begins playing low, wrapping the deck in melody, filling my senses.

Night wraps us in its cool dark softness as Dan reaches out his hand, palm up, exactly as I envisioned. I place mine into it, which feels every bit as exciting as I pictured it would. Is this really happening to me, Eisel Jane McCord? What a crazy turn my life has taken. As the music plays, the candlelight flickers in Dan's eyes.

"Eisel," he says, slowly running his thumb back and forth across my knuckles as if it helps him think, sending continuous thrills through me. "You're a mighty brave lady, to be so honest with your thoughts and feelings. I really respect that. I'd be honored to tell you anything I know about romance."

We sit there like this for a long moment, him studying my face. Then he scoots his chair over next to mine, holding my eyes with his, and like a love scene in a movie, he reaches out and cups my face in his hand, smoothing my cheekbone with his thumb. "Honored to tell you," he whispers. "But I'd rather show you instead." Then slowly, infinitesimally, he leans in as the sweet song enwraps us. Closer. Closer. Breath catching, my heart beats in double time as he touches his lips to mine, a mere brush at first as if testing the waters, and I hold as still as daybreak.

His next kiss is long and soft and sweet, and I give myself to it, tilting my head, leaning in. It's not pushy or hungry. It's unhurried. On purpose. Off and on, deeper, then backing off until honestly, I'm floating with the music, my senses so full I can't tell you who I am or who he is, only that there's a kind of magic I forgot existed or else I never knew, and I'm caught in its wonder.

Drawing back, he runs his finger gently, slowly down my cheek, then tips my head up so I'm looking into his sea blue eyes once more. "I'd rather show you, Eisel, because romance is an experience. You got that right," and he leans in for another long, soft kiss before folding me into his arms that are strong and warm and wonderfully safe.

Undone by his kisses, I melt into this first hug I've had in four months, and of course being me, tears happen. I don't want to cry. It's too beautiful a moment to cry. Or perhaps that's why I do. It feels so sweet and healing and perfect and sad all entwined together it takes me a long minute to reel myself in.

"I'm sorry, Dan." I say, sitting up and dabbing at my eyes with my dinner napkin.

He simply smiles and pats his shoulder, inviting me to lay my head down if I want.

I do.

There we stay for a lovely, long time listening to music and the night around us until I draw a long breath. "Wow. I did not expect to lose it like that."

He chuckles. "We never do, do we? You're going through something huge right now with Jimmy leaving you like he did. That's something you didn't have time to prepare for, and if I don't miss my guess, it is going to take more time to process. I've had four years now without Rosalie, and it still hits me sometimes." He touches my hand and looks into my eyes again. "Are you okay with what—with my showing you instead of telling?"

I smile. "Firstly, let me say that show and tell was never this fun before. Secondly, I'm not sure what I learned from those kisses beyond the fact that I'm apparently toast around a good smelling, kind, authentic man such as yourself, should he decide kissing is on the agenda."

We laugh together at that (me a bit hysterically, if the truth be told, because I mean exactly what I said), and though I'm still reeling from the wash of hormones, wonder, and sadness I just experienced, I cut us a couple of pieces of cake, and we move to the lighted fire pit. There we sit and chit and chat, and meanwhile, ten and then eleven o'clock comes and goes, and I don't really care.

When a breeze comes up, Dan throws a blanket over our shoulders and puts his arm around me, all of which feels so comfortable that once again, I don't recognize this version of me. Don't recognize it, yet very much enjoy it as I snuggle into his side a bit more closely (though hopefully not so much he thinks I want to start the kissing up again, because that was too perfect to cap at this moment).

On the other hand, now that I say that—who says another round couldn't be as nice?

CHAPTER 10

When I wake the next morning, I lie there reliving last night's long sweet kisses and afterwards, how we stared into the fire while we talked about so many things from our histories. The way Dan's arm encircled me felt so safe, and the last lingering kiss that happened so naturally as he pulled me against him there by my car door certainly elicited all the feels. I'm surprised I could even remember how to start the engine after that, and I smiled all the way home

My.

Goodness.

Gracious.

I suppose at this point people may question what in the world I am up to—still married (though arguably abandoned and by my own declaration right from the get-go, not at all sure I want to stay married due to said abandonment) while exploring relationship with not one but two other guys, both of which have taken a decided romantic turn, (though I will add, as per my original intent, I was not the initiator of those romantic advances in either case). Still, I responded. Yes, I did, and doing so was a blast.

I think Jimmy and I have not had much of that kind of fun as the years passed. We went on trips and such, of course. However, I'm sure I would remember if I was having this level of engagement and anticipation about his attention to me on those expeditions, to say nothing of our daily life. He wasn't paying any attention to me that I can remember, and I'm sure I would recall if I felt that same level of attraction for him and attention to him of Saturday with Cal and last night with Dan.

It's a sad commentary on fickle human nature how we strive to create a life we in which want to live, and once we arrive there, often become complacent, lacking awareness and thankfulness for what we have—for the fact that we're connected to other people, the most precious commodity on the planet. My point is, I would never have thought that I, Eisel Jane McCord, would be in this position of having three—*three*—valuable, desirable humans of the male persuasion wanting to be connected to me and vice versa.

You might ask *does* Jimmy want to be connected to me? Before he sent that poem yesterday morning, I would have said apparently not, as clearly indicated by the way he went about his Peru plans, because you hold onto what is most dear to you, don't you, and I guess that isn't me now for him.

Yet I can't blame him in one way—the ruts of our ruts have ruts, and when you've lived with someone for forty-three years, and you know you're mutually committed to finish out the rest of your earthly existence with that same person, I suppose it could begin to feel less like a gift and more like a given if you aren't careful. You forget you aren't promised tomorrow, and you can let the magic drain out of the everyday and leave life together feeling less than exciting or purposeful. I'm thinking Jimmy and I weren't careful. Or weren't careful enough.

To return to my original subject however, I have no doubt there will be people who are scandalized by the sudden surplus of men in my life, especially since I'm not even legally separated. I might argue that the real separation happens in hearts, not on legal documents, though of course, society doesn't equate those two. More than that, Maggie is going to struggle with all this, and she's the one I'm really concerned about. I'm not sure how to tell her about Dan and Cal, though I'll need to do so if things develop further. I can put it off for now, I think. What feels much more imminent is that soon, very soon, I need to tell Cal and Dan about each other and tell Jimmy about both of them. That should be all sorts of fun.

Do I feel guilty or morally deficient because I'm now being romanced by two very cool, very honorable, interesting men while my husband is off in the wilds of Peru? Actually, no. I do not. I've been very upfront with Jimmy that I may not want to stay married to him, nor has he once offered to return or asked me if I would please come be with him.

I've also been completely transparent with Cal and Dan about my marital status and where I'm at in the process; I did not initiate romance in either case, so no hidden motives there. Besides, I didn't even think about the physical aspect of a relationship when I picked that item off my bucket list, though duh. Of course, that is an integral factor to desiring and feeling desired.

One might argue that I allowed their advances and I responded, flirted back, and allowed kisses to hands and lips, thus I am culpable, and that would be accurate. However, I'll do it again in the right circumstances. I'll even go so far as to say I hope it happens again soon. If I ever knew, I forgot how fun it is to have someone appreciate me for who I am, not what I do. With Cal I feel fascinating and perfect just the way I am. With Dan I also feel seen and valued. With both, I feel desirable.

What do I feel with Jimmy?

I hate to say it—before his poem arrived, with Jimmy I'd say I mostly feel unnoticed. The poem does give me a tiny glimmer that maybe something else is present as well. I think what I feel worst about in this situation with Jimmy is that somehow I have become someone he doesn't share his heart with. Not that I caused his course of action—all of that is completely his desire and his choices.

Dan and Cal: they're both fresh and see me with fresh eyes, though we don't yet have much history together. Jimmy sees me, if he sees me at all, through some pretty solid relational cataracts, I think. We've shared so much over the years. If I could have the freshness, the "being seenness" of these new relationships paired with the rich depths of the years Jimmy and I invested, that would be my best of both worlds in one fell swoop. I feel shaky in my core and that tight line of pressure in my chest to be so unsure whether Jimmy cares to revamp his vision of me or not. To be fair, my relational cataracts toward him are at least on par with his, so definite attention needed there as well.

How I feel with Cal each time we've interacted or how amazing it was with Dan last night—I'm sorry. I'm not willing to back away from experiencing how alive, appreciated, and pursued I feel with them merely to satisfy onlooking people who do not understand the dynamics of the situation and are uncomfortable with packages not tied up all legal and pretty with bows. My morals are really none of their business anyway. Whoever "they" are.

Still, and confusingly, I do love Jimmy even in the absence of romance and despite our ruts, and I won't remove him from the running if he wants to be in it. It's also quite apparent to me that since I don't have fresh eyes with him, I may be blind to whether he actually wants to throw his hat in the ring, so to speak. Here in the quiet of the morning, I can admit to myself that I'm not as curious with him or about him as I am with Dan or Cal.

This lack of curiosity toward Jimmy is not something I'm proud of, either. It's as if the very thing I feel he's done with me I've done with him as well—assumed we already know everything that can be known about each other, which when you think about it is pretty sad, because no matter how well we think we know someone, can we ever know them completely? I like to think I'm a whole undiscovered universe waiting to be explored. I wonder how or if I can find the door into the universe of Jimmy.

However, this time, I won't initiate as I did back in our youth group days. I really, *really* need to know he's doing something with me because he wants to, not because he thinks *I* want him to. He'll need to intentionally communicate that he wants to be with me more than any other thing, including end-of-life dream-chasing through the archeological sites of Peru. I don't think that's asking too much, especially if he's asking me to put my life on hold meanwhile.

If we're going to have a shared future, my efforts alone cannot be the basis of it. However, if he does reach out, if he does want to be with me, I can and will expend the effort to open my own eyes, to see him without the lenses of familiarity I've taken on. I can at least begin to commence to start to try, anyway.

Opening my phone to his poem, I picture him sitting by that river as if he's a man I don't know well—a man who met me, a woman of sixty-four who needs to know if he's interested in her at all. If she matters to him. I sit there until I can see him in my mind, the sunlight haloing his hair as it did not all that long ago in this very kitchen. His intent, brown-eyed focus, his Harrison Ford scruffiness in a plaid shirt and jeans. He trails a hand in the water. Gazes up at the sky. Then he opens a notebook and writes:

The river ripples past me,
Singing as it goes,
Quicksilver on the surface,
Midnight depths below.
I think, 'It's just like Eisel,'
Alive and wild and free
And I wonder at the wonder
Of the gift she is to me.

If Cal or Dan sent me that poem, I'd smile, knowing they see me as a person who ripples and sparkles, and also has depth, recognizing my need not to be pinned down, fenced in, defined. Those last two lines? Those would set my heart beating faster.

Now Jimmy—brown-eyed, thoughtful, creative Jimmy—is saying he can't believe he gets to be in my life? That's hard for me to take in. Also hard to deny. He thought it, wrote it, down there in Peru where everything is new and fresh for him, and I'm guessing fulfilling at least a truckload of his long-treasured dreams. All that is happening for him, yet in the midst of it, he's thinking about me? More than thinking—he sent me a message on purpose, and the timing of it can't be ignored either—he sent it after I told him I hadn't experienced a great romance with him. Is he letting me know that in his eyes, I'm as lovely, as mysterious, as alive as a river, and he can't believe he has the privilege to be with me? That's very romantic, no doubt about it.

In my mind's eye, he looks up and smiles, as if he's enjoying crafting this poem to send to his lady love, one Eisel Jane. Then he sighs and trails his hand in the water again, maybe hoping this message makes it past all the hurt and the years, leaps over the ruts of the everyday functionality of our relationship, and lodges like Cupid's arrow in my heart so maybe he can slip in after it.

I imagine Jimmy typing the poem out on his phone and then standing up, rotating until he connects with a signal, and hits send. What I don't expect is that he then sits back down on his rock and alternately watches his phone and gazes off over the river until a text comes back to him.

My text. *Thank you. [Heart eyes, thank you hands, heart emojis.]*

It may have been all I felt I could do at the time, but I see now it wasn't what he was hoping for as he sighs, trailing his hand in the river again. Clearing his throat, he takes a deep breath, blowing it out long and slow before standing and trudging back up a stony bank, and fading into the jungle.

With this scenario in mind, I compose a new text, striving not to fixate on the fact that no new message from him awaits me, *I'm picturing you down by the river as you wrote that poem, maybe wearing a plaid shirt and trailing your hand in the water. It means a lot to me that you would think it, that you would write it, that you would send it. I'm sorry if my response yesterday was less than it could have been. I'm wondering if we've gotten too used to the way we see each other and have lost touch with who each of us really is.*

Never has Peru seemed so far away and Jimmy so unreachable. Sighing, I write a follow up. *Your poem makes me feel more seen by you. Thank you for that. I want to see you, as well—see you for the amazing human you are apart from the life we built together over the years. All I ask is please don't let me be the strongest person in the equation. I need to know that you're making the decisions you want to make, not the ones you think I want you to make, if that makes sense.*

I hit send, and as I brew my morning cup of coffee, I check my phone off and on, holding the picture of Jimmy in my mind, wondering what he'll think of my text. At the same time, I know he's probably dug in at some archeological task (no pun intended), so I can't realistically expect a lightning reply, especially since my own answers take a cup of coffee plus consumption of a toasted croissant to compose. At the very least. I do find I'm hoping he will answer me and am more than a little hoping when he does, it will carry the sweet scent of romance, be it ever so small, and that I will be able to identify and experience it as such.

Hanging in this space, I picture Jimmy as he labors, how he'll wipe his forehead with the back of his arm and the sweat will shine like dew on the fine hairs there, graying now in his later years. He'll straighten up with his fists in his lower back, bend to touch the ground, then throw his arms open to the sky as if to invite its freedom in. He always does that. I've never appreciated it as I do in this moment. I picture him, the endearing way his cowlick tends to stick up and how he always unconsciously smooths it down after his sky salutation.

"Jimmy," I whisper. "Wouldn't it be so grand if we could experience a great romance together? If this separation needn't end in finding other partners?" I wish I could hear his answer because it sounds as if he feels he experienced romance with me—it may only be me who has not.

★ ★ ★

Dan's text beats Cal's by a half a minute, so, true to my sense of order, I click on it first. *I had a wonderful time with you last night and hope you're still okay with the way I decided to "show" rather than tell you about romance. I tend to be a bit rough and ready, but I never want to do anything that you would not welcome.*

I appreciate this level of consideration. Grinning ear to ear as I wander into the living room, I plop down on the couch to craft my response. *Thank you for that. If you were here in person, we could talk about it in more depth, but I'm quite okay with you "showing instead of telling," though I hardly know what to think about it. Thanks for checking. I do really appreciate that.* Send.

I hardly have time to picture the way his blue eyes twinkle and wonder what he'll respond when his answer pings in. *You have no idea how tempted I am right now to drive over to have that more "in depth" conversation with you. Unfortunately, I must meet a client to go over their remodel. Have no doubt, though—I'll follow up with you ASAP. [Winky face, thumbs up].*

Thankfully, he has no idea how fun that sounds to me or how my stomach does a couple of wheelies while my cheeks tingle. I "heart" his message, and feeling as daring as someone about to skydive, I shoot one more sentence his way. *I'll look forward to that deeper dive ;-).*

[Thumbs up, big grin].

That's what I call a morning pick me up. I sit here wishing I could smell his sage-and-pine cleanness and waiting to see what he comes up with next. Also having a difficult time feeling as if any of this is actually happening to me. However, it's curating a rich, warm glow in my chest to hover in this space.

The reminder for Cal's text pings, and I take a moment to switch gears. I won't be able to maintain this unexpected three-way exploration. Very soon, I need to choose one man to accept attention from and friend zone the others. Yet I've known both Dan and Cal less than a week—how can I choose when I'm not far enough into the process to know for sure what's really coming at me from each of them or from Jimmy?

Dan and Cal are flirting with me, no doubt about that item. However, enjoying their company, regard, and attention is not a guarantee of an eventual romantic relationship. That will require a certain amount of time, transparency, and feeling my way along, building friendship until my choice becomes clear. Right now, the only thing I'm sure about is that this gentle banter I'm experiencing is eye-opening, fascinating, and very enjoyable. I'm grinning as I open Cal's text.

I stopped by Miss Millsbaugh's and convinced her to meet you. She grilled me pretty hard about you and why I like you—I think she suspects I might like you more than the other clients I've introduced to her. [winky face emoji].

I read that sentence again—he likes me more than the other clients? Even his text wink sets my insides fluttering. I wing off a reply I hope will elicit the same response in him *Why Mr. Robinson, whatever might you be talking about? [Wide grin emoji].*

You are a caution, Eisel Jane.

I've never been called "a caution" before, and I like it just fine. I tag the message with a heart.

When would you like to meet her? He texts next. *Today? If you're free, I finish a showing at ten. I could pick you up around ten thirty, and we can go beard the lion(ess) in her den.*

Perfect. Do you think she'll approve of me? I know that could appear to be a leading question, but I'm suddenly very serious.

Somehow, he understands, though, because he texts back, *All joking and other types of truths aside, I think she will, because she is always fiercely herself, like you are. Except I will add that where her fierceness has scared the bejeezus out of me since I was knee-high to her garters, you being yourself is pure joy and revelation.*

Another message pings immediately following. *I mean that.*

My heart does a little leap in my chest. *Thank you for saying that. I'm going to hold onto it when we're with her, because I'm afraid of lions.* I hit send.

Cal's number suddenly lights up as the phone vibrates in my hand. "Hello?"

His voice is soft as silk. "I'll just say this and hang up, because I need to run. I can tell that you really want that old house, and I want you to know I intend to do everything legal to help you own it."

"Thank you. You're a very kind person, Cal." Then even though it feels vulnerable, I add, "Don't be winking at me, though. That is way too distracting."

There's a moment of silence, and I hear the smile in his voice as he answers. "I will refrain from winking, since you've requested that. While we're with Miss Millsbaugh, anyway." He chuckles. "Okay, then, lady. I'll see you right about ten thirty."

"Perfect."

Hanging up, I kick myself for always defaulting to "perfect" as a response, although I literally can't think of a better word for this whole exchange.

CHAPTER 11

Barely twenty-five minutes before Cal drives up to my curb, I finally break out of my romantic haze. No time to shower. Instead. I wash my armpits with soap, rinse, and apply deodorant. Throwing on some corduroy slacks in a warm rust color, I pair them with my gold silk blouse over a black tank top. With the addition of black ankle boots, touched up eyebrows, and a bit of lipstick, I feel ready. On impulse, I dig out my favorite scent—spice, carnation, and a touch of cedar—dabbing a tiny bit on my wrists and rubbing them on my jawline. I hope it's not too obvious, but as the old saying goes, "turnabout is fair play."

In the last minutes before Cal arrives, I locate a little jar of apple butter I made last fall from fruit off our backyard tree, the old-fashioned kind like Mother used to make. I tie on a little sprig of larkspur and baby's breath from Dan's bouquet that lends its fragrant reminder of a lovely evening next to Cal's corsage (also a lovely evening). I'm guessing Miss Millsbaugh doesn't receive many homemade treats. If she doesn't scare me completely to death, maybe I'll try to visit her now and again and bring more such peace offerings, assuming she likes company.

Cal's big black chariot rolls up as I shoulder my bag and step out the front door. Jumping out, he strides toward me. "Now, my friend, please don't deprive me of the pleasure of walking you down the sidewalk," he says, taking my hand as before and this time dispensing with the bow, he raises it straight to his lips, eyes smiling as they look into mine.

My heart lifts at how good it is to see him again. "Hi."

He tucks my hand under his arm like on Saturday night, and the warmth of his ribs on the back of my hand as we walk sets me tingling, deepening my smile. I don't even try to resist the attraction I feel as he opens the car door, assists me up with easy grace, then hands me the seatbelt. "There you go."

"Thank you." I hope I smell as good to him as he does to me. However, I refrain from moving my neck in the vicinity of his nose or sending any of several messages that occur to me. I feel so new at this exploring relationship stage. *Am* new at it, and forty-plus years rusty with a skill I never fully developed. That's what I'm thinking about as I finish buckling in and look back up. My belly does a flip-flop to see Cal still standing there, one arm resting easy on the door frame, hemming me in by his body as he smiles down at me.

"I have so many things I want to talk with you about, Eisel. However, since we need to be business-like for this real estate deal, I'm pushing pause on all that until afterwards. Okay with you?"

Smiling, I nod, very distracted by his proximity, pretty dang sure that what he's referring to about pausing is flirting, which in itself is basically flirting. All of that leaves me completely without words as I snag on his eyes. Breathe in. Breathe out.

"Excellent." He grins and nods, obviously enjoying the effect he has on me. Shutting my door, he hops in his side, and we ride along in silent companionship. I'd say this is definitely a good thing since it gives me a chance to regroup.

Arriving at the facility, Cal opens my door in his usual fashion then guides me through the lobby and down a hallway with the lightest of contact on my elbow, which I find both reassuring and enjoyable. Also anchoring, as I repress an impulse to high tail it back down the hallway. What if Miss Millsbaugh hates me?

"Doing okay there?" Cal asks.

I grimace.

He smiles. "Breathe, lady. I think it will go well." He adds a tiny wink, exactly what I need to distract me as he knocks on door 113.

"Come in."

"Howdy, Miss Millsbaugh. It's me, Calvin Robinson again."

"Well, don't just stand there holdin' my door open, boy. You'll let all the heat out." (For the record, the blast of air that exhales from the room is hot enough to melt butter).

Cal is suddenly a professional real estate agent with a touch of scolded teenager thrown in. That enables me to step into my own everyday persona instead of a starry-eyed first-time house buyer. "Miss Millsbaugh?" I say, stepping forward to shake her hand. "I'm Eisel McCord, and I'm very pleased to meet you."

"You are, are you? I understood you were here to talk about my house, not meet me. Sit down."

I sit. "That's true. Still, it is a pleasure to meet you."

"Hmmph."

I forge on. "I saw your house listed online and drove around to see it on Friday. Mr. Robinson met me out there, and we did a walkthrough. I know it needs a new roof and a bit of intervention on a couple of windows. Regardless, I want to buy it."

"Why?"

I picture the way the house nestles back against the woodland, how quiet and content it seemed as we walked through, as if it had lived a long, full life so far and was ready for its next chapter. "I always wanted to live in the country and also own a house full of history. When I saw yours, I fell in love with it. The way it sits in its own little space, the wraparound porch, and really all of it, is perfect."

"Perfect for what?" She fixes me with sharp if watery eyes.

Quailing inside, I press through. "For me to live in. Also perfect for long walks, growing a little garden, and having a cat." I warm to the subject. "I've never had a place all my own where I can paint it any color I want. I could hang whimsical wallpaper and watch the sunsets from the porch swing or sip my coffee while the snow comes down like feathers."

"Calvin."

"Yessum?"

"You told her my price is firm, didn't you? I'm not payin' to install a new roof or fixin' any windows. I'm sellin' it as is, and there better not be any problems about that nor any of that fallin' out of escrow or what have you."

"Yessum. I did tell Ms. McCord the price is firm, and she agreed to it. If you approve of her, I'll make sure all the paperwork is in order."

"As you should." She glares at him as if she caught him attempting to pull a fast one over on her. Turning her gaze back on me, she asks, "You pre-approved for financin'?"

"Actually, I have some money my grandma left me, and I want to pay cash." I look over at Cal. "May I do that?"

"Absolutely. It will actually make things quicker and easier."

I like this deferential professional side of him, as well. He's at ease, knows what he's doing, yet doesn't posture.

"Did you bring the papers, Calvin?"

"I brought a draft of them, Miss Millsbaugh, ma'am. Shall I run over them with you?"

"Too tedious, boy. If I didn't trust you, I wouldn't a hired you. Just show me where to sign."

I'm sure my eyes are as big as saucers at this sudden turn of events; Cal's remain calm and kind. "I'm mighty sorry ma'am, but to be legal and proper in a court of law, I need to set up to meet a notary public here to witness your signature. I also need to cover a few key points with Ms. McCord regarding the sale."

"Hmmph. Fine. Just don't belabor it, Calvin. I don't have so many more hours of life left that I want to spend them goin' over legal stuff."

"Understood." Cal nods, turning to smile at me, as per his pause decree not flirting, simply reassuring. It's not his fault that his smile sends an electrical charge through me as I meet his eyes. "Now Miss Eisel. How this will happen is that Miss Millsbaugh will sign the papers as the seller, and you'll sign as the buyer and pay the down payment. At that point, we'll have a fully executed contract. I then loop in the Escrow company, and they check to see if there are any liens on the property."

"There aren't any liens," Miss Millsbaugh breaks in. "My pa gave that house to me debt free, and I never borrowed against it."

"Excellent. That will move things right along. With a clear title and a cash offer, we should be able to close within the month."

"So soon! That's amazing. When do I pay the balance?" I'm almost vibrating with all I'm suppressing. That beautiful old house—mine?

"On the date of closing, you'll meet me at the title company to sign the final papers, and then you'll need to wire the money to them. They will then send it to Miss Millsbaugh, who will deposit it in her account."

"Can't you do that for me, boy?"

"If you'd like me to, I'll be glad to oblige."

She nods. "Fine. Do it. What happens if I die before I can sign, Calvin? You know I'm not a spring chicken anymore."

"Excellent question, Miss Millsbaugh, though I think you're looking marvelous, ma'am."

"Don't you try to flatter me, you rascal," she says, though I see the first sign of what could become a smile if she'd allow it to.

"Yessum." Cal purses his lips, keeping a straight face. "Who has your power of attorney, ma'am?"

"That'd be my nephew, Melville Holmes. My sister's son."

"Does he know you're selling your house."

"I told him."

"Would you be willing to give Melville a call right now to declare your intentions to sell your house to one Eisel Jane McCord, should you pass away before the date of closing?"

The man has a gift. He somehow manages to sound professional yet personal as he discusses what to do in case of her demise.

"You dial him, I'll tell him." Believe me, she does, in no uncertain terms. "Melville, it's Aunt Rose. We got you on speaker phone here, so don't you give me none of your sass."

"No ma'am."

"I've got my realtor here—you remember him. Little Calvin Robinson from down the road?" (Cal grimaces and rolls his eyes. I grin).

"Howdy, Cal."

"Howdy, Mel. How's it going?"

"You boys quit wastin' my time with your pleasantries. Now Melville, you know I told you I'm sellin' my house? Well, Calvin found a buyer—Ms. Eisel McCord—and here's what I want: if I die before the closin' date, you sign on my behalf. You got that?"

"Yes, I got it, Aunt Rose. Sell your house to Ms. McCord if you die before closing. I'll do it."

"You better, or I'll haunt you from my grave, you young whippersnapper!"

"Auntie, I'm sixty-five years old. That's an old whippersnapper." He chuckles.

"Don't you get mouthy with me, Melville. Just do what I tell you, and all will be fine."

"Will do, ma'am. Scout's honor."

"Good. Then give Calvin your phone number so we can hang up."

He does. "Bye, then Auntie Rose, and talk to you later, Cal."

"Bye." She glares at Calvin as if he trapped her into the call. "Now, if you're quite finished."

"Yessum, I am, thank you. I think Miss Eisel had some questions she wanted to ask about the history of your house though, if you've got the time."

Miss Millsbaugh glowers at me. "I'm sellin' you my house. What else do you want? They're servin' lunch soon, and I want to get out there before someone eats all the rolls."

Gulp. "We don't have to chat now, though when you have time, I'd love to hear whatever you'd care to share about your house's history. What you love about it, what flowers you have planted and such." I reach into my bag. "Also, I brought you some apple butter I made last fall."

She snatches it from me, her eyes brighter than they've been throughout our conversation. "Lord have mercy. I'm goin' to have that on my roll." She tilts her head as if reassessing me. "I'll tell you what, Eisel McCord. I'll give you three things about that house, and then I'm goin' to lunch. If you want to hear more, you can come back."

"Wonderful. Thanks so much."

"Hmmph. My pa bought the house for me as a wedding present. Then my fiancé up and died of the influenza. Pa gave the property to me anyway; guess he didn't want me mopin' around his house the rest of my life since I made it very clear that if I couldn't marry the man I loved, I'd never marry, and I didn't." She nods. "There. I think I gave you a bonus item."

"Thanks so much." I stand up, wondering if she's a hugger (I very seriously doubt it), a hand shaker, or merely a head nodder. I go with the nod, plus clasping my hands to my heart. "I will be so happy there, I think."

"Well, don't get all effusive. I approve of you, but you don't want to push your luck." She gives me what could possibly be the start of a smile, then she reaches over and pokes Cal in the arm. "Listen up, you young rapscallion. Don't think I can't see right through you. I better not hear of you taking any sort of advantage of this young woman, or I'll haunt you after I check in on Melville."

Calvin's eyes grow wide and innocent. "Why Miss Millsbaugh. What in the world are you talking about?"

"Don't you give me any of your subterfuge, Calvin Felix Robinson. It's as plain as the nose on this old face that you like her more than you should, given I believe you said she's married right now. You better go easy, young man. You're chock full of charm and smooth words and always have been. Don't you be leadin' her down any garden paths." She reaches over and pinches his mocha-colored cheek. "You hear me?"

Grinning, he stares down at the floor. "Shucks, Miss Millsbaugh. Can't I ever be a grown up with you?"

"Maybe when you are a hundred, we'll see about that. Now you two get along so I can snag me a roll to eat with my apple butter."

Cal nods, gives her his brightest grin and a quick and gentle side hug. "Miss Millsbaugh, you're a caution, you know that?"

Remembering his text calling me that, I smile as she calls after us. "Now you come back and see me. Alone or together makes no never mind to me, only don't be showin' up at mealtimes."

I give a feeble wave, and sag against the wall when Cal shuts the door behind us. Seeing that, he holds out his arm for me to anchor myself on. "Well done. Eisel Jane. Lion bearding accomplished. Looks like you have yourself a house."

"I can't believe it," I whisper, squeezing his arm. "She liked me. She's going to sell me her house!" I'm almost floating as we make our way to the car. "My word. She's certainly a force to be reckoned with."

"She is that. But she's also a very sharp judge of character. You have to be pretty special to pass muster with Miss Millsbaugh."

He smiles over at me. "I had no doubts whatsoever that she'd like you just fine."

Warmed by his words, light-headed at my success, I can only grin. When we reach the car, Cal once again stands with his arm on the doorframe. This time he leans in a bit closer than before—so close I'm sure he can't help smelling my perfume just as I'm smelling his aftershave.

He has that flirty half smile of his going now, eyes dancing as he raises his eyebrows. "I don't know about you, but I'm ready to push the play button again now that we survived."

Gazing up into his dark chocolate eyes, they're so deep and focused on mine I hang there, captured by unspoken communication I scramble to decipher. What is he thinking? What should I say? Clueless, all I can manage to do is raise one eyebrow and smile.

He shakes his head and grins. "My, my, my, Eisel Jane. You do know how to distract a man. I'd love to take you to lunch now if you're amenable. Someplace where people are present to prevent me from coloring outside the lines." He winks.

"I'm—I—yes. Please."

Not the most brilliant of speeches. I blush, but he's grinning. "Good. I hoped you'd say that. As an afternote, I'm guessing you do realize you're taking your own life in your hands, smelling as good as you do."

I have until he circles the car at an easy walk to pull myself together after that exchange and at least attempt to fake that I'm not blown away by this experience of flirting and romantic focus coming at me from such a vital man. I'm not used to feeling desired or desirable; I hope I can bring my thinking brain back online in time to stop short of making a complete idiot of myself in response.

Hopefully oblivious to my state, Cal climbs in, clicks his seatbelt closed, and half turns to me. "Where should we go, lady? What are you hungry for?"

I just shake my head. "I'll be honest. I'm too bedazzled by your charm to think straight, much less know what I want for lunch, and that's the truth, Mr. Calvin *Felix* Robinson." I know I'm smiling at him in a bemused sort of way, and I can't seem to stop.

"That's the kind of honesty I can handle." He smiles and nods, his eyes soft and suddenly earnest. "Remember now—you're safe with me. I mean it when I say I will never take advantage of you, no matter what state you're in." He starts the vehicle then adds, "Just so you know, that's been my intention all along and not because ole Miss M. laid down her royal decree."

I grin at that. "If I'm a caution, she's more like a 'bridge out ahead, flashing lights, danger-Will-Robinson level caution."

"You got that so right."

We laugh, and I'm awash in the wonder that a fellow human being has the power to make me feel so valued while at the same time so honored, safe-guarded, and championed. As we order and eat, we take another long step forward in friendship, laughing together, trading information about our pasts, our school days, and the like. The more we sit there sharing who we are with each other, the more I want to go deeper, to see where this journey will take us. I really like Cal. I also like who I am when I'm with him—somehow braver and funnier and more creative than I tend to be on my own.

He begins telling me about some of his experiences with Miss Millsbaugh as we're driving home. Picturing his long-legged, black-curled "gangliness," yes ma'ams and all, I'm enchanted with that version of him and with the one in front of me as well. Yet, it was only last night that I melted into Dan's "show, don't tell" kisses? Does that make me weird? Immoral? Relationally naive? I have no idea, really. It's very confusing. All I know is that when I'm with Cal in all his dark-skinned, dark-eyed glory, I'm immersed.

How, can it be, then, that last night with Dan and the way the conversation went—he, too, filled the night? I saw no reason not to go deeper into seeing where a friendship with romantic overtones might take us. He's a wonderful, authentic, and highly attractive man as well (without a dog, for the record).

Does it feel sketchy to be receiving focused attention from Dan and Cal at the same time while still married and unsure how or if Jimmy still loves me? It absolutely does, and I'm struggling with that more and more as the hours have rolled by today. Still, what do I really know about romance and how it works anyway? Nothing, apparently, except that I'm attracted to each of these men, and I can't make any type of judgment yet because I literally don't have enough information to guarantee I won't make a wrong choice.

I don't understand exactly what's happening with me or in me. All I know is that I am not an immoral person bent on extracting all the good I can out of others, even if it might look that way to observers. At my worst, I think I am a romance-starved romantic who's experiencing that intoxicating substance for the first time and has no idea how to conduct herself. I would have been happy with one such man. Now there are two. Three? Unbelievable.

Those crossroads I thought about only this morning—that future someday when I would need to tell these men about each other? I planned on doing it once I knew who to friend zone, and I definitely don't know who to do that to yet. How can I discern such a key element in less than a week, even given how comfortable I am with them? I went from one absentee husband to having two men friends flirting with me plus a poem-writing spouse. Now, I'm suddenly toe to toe with a decision I would rather ponder for six months.

The thought of making a huge mistake tightens in my stomach. What if I choose too soon and end up ruling out the one person I really want to be with? A haze of uncertainty sets in—impenetrable, wispy, elusive. I'm not ready. But as Cal's big black car draws near my house, I recognize I can't wait any longer before I tell him and Dan about each other. And of course, I must tell Jimmy about them as well.

The one thing that looms out of the fog is that Dan and Cal are both being very intentional in their focus to explore a romantic relationship with me, and there is Jimmy's poem. Even if I don't know who my heart wants to choose yet, they're all three in their own ways being very upfront and clear that I have their undivided attention and intention (okay, maybe Jimmy not so much, though he has prior claim which counts for something, I suppose).

That's what bears down on me as the world passes by my window. Each of these three men assumes I'm bringing the same level of exclusivity to the picture that they are. Yet through no intent on my part, I am not, and I can't pretend I am—wouldn't pretend even if I could—because of course, relationships can only thrive in an atmosphere of complete truthfulness.

So, as much as I don't want to, I know I can't let Cal drive away today without telling him about Dan and my dilemma over Jimmy's poem. Cal needs to know how things stand so he can choose whether to stay in the picture or leave before he invests further. I mean, look at him, smiling over at me, all soft and open and happy. He's such a beautiful soul. There's no doubt he's risking his heart in letting me in. That's a sacred trust.

People might scoff, pointing out that a week ago, I didn't know the man existed. I would argue that you can live a lot of life by going deep rather than accruing acquaintanceship over time. I have known Cal long enough to understand he's enchanting and kind and intentional, and in a lovely, organic process, he's become my friend in a way that transcends time. With him, I feel protected, seen, and valuable, and I'd love our friendship to develop in a much deeper and wider fashion. He already stated that he's interested in exploring more than friendship with me; his flirting and attention confirm that. Dan has done the same, for that matter.

I'm not sure any man in his right mind would be amenable to the level of uncertainty entailed in waiting for me to figure out who has exclusive claim to my heart. So I don't hold out a lot of hope for either Cal or Dan hanging around. The best thing I can do is make sure that they feel no tangled webs of obligation to do so.

This conversation I must have looms bigger and blacker as we turn on my street and pull up to my house. I'm not ready for this wonderful human to disappear from my life with the same suddenness that Jimmy left me. Yet I don't blame him one bit if that is the case.

CHAPTER 12

"I need to tell you something, Cal," I say as we sit in the car at the curb. "Can you come in for a few minutes?"

He glances over and whatever he reads in my face sobers him between one moment and the next. Yet his smile is as kind and genuine as ever. "Of course I can."

I don't stir from my seat until he opens the door and hands me down (why rush when it might be the last time?), and I focus on his fingers supporting my elbow as we walk up to the door. Meanwhile, I attempt to brave up enough to stab myself in my own heart in an effort to spare his, which is basically what it feels like, though I'm sure Maggie would say, "Mom. You're being rather dramatic about this, aren't you?"

To which I'd answer "Probably." It's hard not to feel dramatic, though, when I'm standing in the middle of Disneyland seeing all the wonder, beauty, and magic at my fingertips and about to be ushered back outside the gates by security.

Fumbling around, I manage to fit the key into the keyhole at last. I'm off kilter, and I know it. In fact, as we reach the living room, Cal looks as if he's not sure whether to rescue me or run. "What is it, Eisel? You look upset."

"I am. However, I still need to do this."

"Okay then. I'm listening."

I plunge in. "I already told you about my husband who left me to go to Peru. Now I need to tell you about an item on my bucket list I didn't mention the other night."

"Great," he says, patting the spot beside him on the couch in invitation. "I'm prepared to be impressed. However, I'm not sure how a bucket list could have you so upset."

I perch on the edge of the couch, muscles tight, mind racing. "I know it sounds funny. It's not, though, so please bear with me." I tell it all to him as he stares at the floor, fingers steepled across his lips. I recount how I set out to do the first three items on my revised, updated list—experience a great romance, own a house of my own, and solo hiking, and how Kate set me up on a blind double date, and I met Dan.

"Then house hunting took me to the Millsbaugh place, and I met you, and I've been enjoying getting to know you." I smile at him. "I mean, very much enjoying it. I feel like we're already good friends."

Looking over at me, he smiles back. "Good to hear, because I've been enjoying the heck out of getting to know you as well."

"That's part of the problem."

He frowns. "Seems pretty simple to me. Boy meets girl. Boy likes girl. Boy lets girl know he likes her. Hopefully, girl starts liking boy." He shrugs, holding hands out palms up.

"In the ideal world, maybe. But not when girl goes from having no romance to meeting two really lovely men who both seem to want to know her at the same time, and said girl is completely confused and actually quite terrified to realize she must make a choice without enough data." I grimace. "Plus, to further complicate matters, yesterday after months of no real indication that he even misses me, Jimmy sent me a lovely poem he wrote. Now I'm wondering if he does still care about me and whether I need to back off from becoming acquainted with anyone else."

"Ah. So, you're saying that maybe you want to hang in there with Jimmy now that he's sent that poem?"

"No, actually. I'm still not convinced he loves me more than archeology, and if he doesn't, I don't think I want to stay married to him. I know that sounds terrible, but it's true. If I'm not at the top of the list of priorities, what's the point? I do not want to compete with ancient artifacts for his affection."

Cal begins pacing, hands clasped behind his back, eyes on the floor. "Let me see if I'm tracking here. I like you, and I want you to like me, which you seem to be doing fine. You don't know if Jimmy loves you or whether you want to go in that direction, and there's something about another man in the mix?"

I nod.

"I'm still a bit at sea here," Cal says, coming to a halt in front of me. "I can't see that anything has substantially changed from the original situation. You told me about that when we went to dinner, all except something about another guy. Is that what you're needing to tell me?"

"Yes. So let me try again, because apparently, I skimmed over the key point you need to know. To be clear, I didn't know that element when you and I had dinner." I hold up one finger: "Last Thursday, I met a man named Dan on a double date." Finger two: "On Friday, Dan invited me for dinner Sunday evening." Finger three: "Then I met you later that same Friday and went to dinner with you Saturday." I hold up my fourth finger. "Because of my bucket list item and having never experienced romance whether it was present or not, I've been taken completely by surprise by both of you." Voice breaking, the tears I'd been holding at bay spill over.

Snagging a tissue from a nearby box (my house has multiple tissue stations, thanks to my propensity for crying), Cal crouches in front of me, tucking it into my hand. "Hang in there, friend. I sense you're about to reach the punch line."

I give a weak chuckle, and straightening up, blot my eyes. "Yes. I'm almost there. I really do mean what I told you: Saturday night with you was amazing. *You* are amazing, Cal. For the first time in my life, I think I experienced what romance feels like and—" I hesitate.

"You make it sound as if it's only you experiencing that kind of wonder. I told you the God-honest truth that I don't know when I've enjoyed being with someone so much. That has continued. Today has likewise been enlightening."

He's smiling his soft smile. I want to answer it, but I hold up my hand like a stop sign. "Please don't sidetrack me, Cal. I need to say this. The thing is, I went last night to Dan's house for steaks—I'd already accepted that invitation before I met you. His wife died four years ago, and it sounds like they loved each other so much. I told him how I'm wondering if maybe romance was there with Jimmy—like he was giving it, and I—that maybe not experiencing it is my fault. I hoped Dan could tell me what he knows about ingredient for romantic relationships. because of how much he loved his wife." I swallow. "But the conversation went in an unexpected direction."

Cal starts pacing again, back and forth, back and forth, then sits in an adjacent chair. My heart drops to see that instead of his usual open expression, his face is hard to read. Measuring. Definitely not the soft depths of earlier. "He kissed you, didn't he."

"He did. I didn't realize that would happen. I didn't ask to be kissed. However, that's not the real problem. It's that I—I enjoyed it." I grimace, spreading out my hands. Cal is up and pacing again as I continue. "I don't really know what kind of a person that makes me when even though I felt like Cinderella at the ball when I was with you on Saturday night, I still enjoyed his kisses. I'm not a player, Cal. Really, I'm not, and I never intended to act like one."

Watching him walking back and forth in front of me, brow furrowed, bottom lip caught between his teeth, my heart shrinks in on itself. "Honestly, I thought I'd have a bit more time to figure things out. It got complicated so fast."

He's stands very still now. Facing away.

"I hope you believe me that I didn't start out to create such a mess. Also, I don't know how to fix any of it."

"I believe you." He still isn't looking at me.

"If it were only you, Cal, the solution could be simple." His shoulders relax a bit at that. "It's not that clearcut, though, which is why it's so messed up. I feel this way about you, and today with you has been so lovely. That is why you deserve to know I let Dan kiss me. In my defense, I thought I was simply having dinner with a new friend until the conversation went off road. He has no idea about you because I never got that far." Cal feels so far away I wilt inside. Nevertheless, I must finish this fiasco. "I hope you don't hate me now, Cal."

He turns around, arms crossed, face still unreadable. "No, Eisel. I don't hate you now."

"I'd understand it if you did," I say, blinking back a fresh onslaught of tears. "Now that I've told you, I need to tell Dan about you and tell Jimmy about both of you because he doesn't have a clue about any of this. It's happened so fast. After that, since I have no idea who I want to be with yet or if any of you will be around once I finish telling you about each other, I think I might just crawl in a hole somewhere and disappear."

There. It's all out.

A great silence hangs between us, and I stare at the floor trying my best not to cry. However, when Cal sits down beside me and sets an arm around my shoulders, I lose that battle. Crying on his chest, my tears leaking onto his shirt, I have no idea how I, who have been (as I assumed), completely without romance for all of my sixty-four years, am experiencing romance in three variations when barely more than a week ago, it was merely an item on my forgotten bucket list.

Maybe the issue is the timeline—too fast, too deep, too soon. Maybe if this had all taken place over months, I could sort it out. I guess I'll never know, though, because I'm pretty sure that after today, Cal will contact me only to close on the house. That's what I expect, and really, why would he stick around? Same with Dan. Jimmy? Though he's left me behind like everything we ever built together is worth nothing, I'd bet my new house against his archeological dig that he's not going to take it well when I tell him about Dan and Cal.

Predictably, once I tamp down my tears, I begin apologizing for everything multiple times until Cal stands and offers me a hand up. "Hey, it's okay. I can tell you didn't try to create this situation, Eisel. It happened; a timing thing, I suppose, and I accept your apologies, so no need to keep giving them. We're good, my friend." He smiles, and though I feel a distance between us that wasn't there before, he does squeeze my hand.

"Thank you for listening." It feels so lame, yet I'm out of words.

"Of course. Now I think you might need a drink of water to replenish your tear supply. May I bring you some?"

No comments on what he thinks about my disclosures I notice. Both relieved and devastated by this, I take a deep breath. "Yes, please. Glasses are to the right of the sink and water's in the door of the fridge."

Ahhh. The icy water feels very good going down. Looking at Cal over the rim, I'm melted by the fact that this beautiful human is being so kind and good to me after I informed him, I've inadvertently turned out to be a three-timing relationship train wreck. "Thank you, Cal." I whisper. I hope he knows I mean thank you for more than the water.

Smiling—though it doesn't reach all the way to his eyes—he takes the empty glass from me. "So, here's what we're going to do, Eisel, if you're amenable. We'll drive out to your new house and do a second walk through now that you've been heartily approved by both required parties. Gold star from me on that, actually. The drive will give me time to process my thoughts enough to share them with you. How does that sound?"

"Perfect." As far as I'm concerned, any delay of the inevitable is welcome.

"Can't get better than that."

I miss the caramel-colored chuckle he usually gives after such a statement. What else did I expect? I summon up the best smile I can, though tears are right behind it.

"Hey, now, we barely replenished those water works. Let's give them a moment, shall we?" Then he winks, which seems even more sweet of him than usual considering the circumstances.

I know I've still got two more men to tell this situation to. However, thanks to Cal, at least I've been held in a place of emotional safety thus far. That is more than I hoped for. I expected anger, disgust, or indifference, really, and the lack of those emotions coming at me leaves me disoriented.

Though I don't know what he'll ultimately decide to do, at least I've now faced the worst-case scenario in my own mind. The only thing left is for me to pick up any pieces after he goes and somehow move forward. All things considered, it's probably a good thing I'm buying that old house. I can immerse myself in remodeling and redecorating, and though it will never substitute for the wonder I've had this last week, it may just save my life.

I'm ready to see the property that will soon be completely and only mine. Also, I'm touched that in the face of my announcement of non-exclusivity in relationship, Cal thought of a walkthrough. Maybe he wants to give a bit of distance between my explanation and his goodbye. If so, I'm thankful for this little window of time to spend with him before it closes. Or maybe he somehow knows how much seeing the house will delight my heart, and he wants to give me that, too, regardless of what he decides to do about my three-way split of attention. Intention. Whatever.

I think that's when I truly begin to understand why I always longed to experience a great romance—romantic attention focused on me with the intention of creating a lasting relationship. It is marvelous. Painful. Wondrous. I only wish I could have had it longer.

Cal escorts me out to the car as if I haven't just spilled my guts and a month's supply of tears, and I try not to think of how blotchy my face must be. As he leans toward me as he hands me the seatbelt, I reach up to touch the big damp spot that runs the length of his collarbone, attempting (unsuccessfully) to ignore the way his warm brown skin shows through. "Thankfully, tears don't stain," I joke.

"Wish they did, actually," he says, smiling. "Badge of honor, ma'am."

"That's very kind of you." I smile up at him.

He smiles back, this time his eyes play into the game a bit. I breathe in, savoring the moment and the way my heart lifts as he does so. Then he steps back and shuts my door with as much care as if I'm the queen of England. We're a quiet pair as we roll down my street and head west. I want to give him time to think through things like he said he was going to do on the drive, so I ride along endeavoring to stay as much in the moment as I can.

"Doing okay?"

"Yes, thank you." It's basically a lie, but for his sake, not mine, so I let it stand. Besides, I should be asking him that, I think, if I were brave enough. I am not, though. I settle for "Thank you for this walkthrough, Cal. Also, I'm not sure I said a sufficient thank you for helping me purchase this house. I'm still amazed that it's actually happening."

"You did thank me, and it's my pleasure. As your realtor, I should tell you that you ought to have it inspected so you know what you're dealing with structurally. As I said during your original walkthrough, overall, I believe it's sound. I'm also confident you know what you're taking on, and that you understand roofs and such are not cheap." After a long pause, he adds, "I don't think I mentioned how much I like the thought of you sitting on the porch swing out there, watching the sunset. Maybe with a cup of tea and a good book, or a journal. You strike me as the journaling type."

I sigh. "I am. Also, a list girl."

"That I definitely believe." He chuckles, glancing over and wiggling his eyebrows at me. "Once you close on the house, what is the first thing you plan on doing to it, Eisel?"

"I've been trying not to think about it until I knew if Miss Millsbaugh approved of me, so things are a bit fuzzy as yet. I suppose I should prioritize the roof and the outdoor painting before the fall rains start up."

"Sound reasoning. Do you know a good contractor?"

Gulp. "Dan Baker, the Dan I told you about? He's a contractor in the area."

There's a beat of silence, and the glance I steal shows Cal staring straight ahead, a bit of a frown pulling the corner of his mouth down.

"Ah. Now I understand better how that kiss might have happened. He's a force of nature, Dan is. Tends to know what he wants and goes for it." Cal clicks his tongue and shakes his head. "I'm more than a little jealous he got the drop on me in your bucket list fulfillment duty."

I have no idea what to say to that, and I suspect my one-syllable bark of a laugh is on the hysterical side.

"Leaving that subject for now, what do you plan on doing with your very own house, Eisel Jane?"

My mind in a whirl, I'm perfectly willing to leave that subject alone for now. I lean back, allowing myself to dream about the house, all it's nooks and crannies, fanciful rooflines, original shiplap siding. "I think I'll want to paint it inside. Freshen it up. Maybe hang some special wallpaper on strategic walls. Make some curtains. I should also probably have the floors refinished before I move in any furniture."

"Nice."

"Now that I'm thinking about it, I want to only bring furniture from Jimmy's and my house that is mine or that I specifically love. Maybe I'll start haunting estate sales to see if I can find pieces that resonate with an 1880's Victorian farmhouse."

"A brilliant plan. A house of your very own filled with things you've specifically chosen sounds almost as lovely and whimsical as you are."

I look over at Cal who meets my eyes with an innocent smile. "I think I'm beginning to understand what Miss M. meant by saying you're chock full of charm and smooth words."

Cal chuckles. "Well, I wouldn't know about that. However, to be on the safe side, you might want to watch out for those garden paths she warned me against leading you down, my friend."

Wait. What? I dropped my relationship-killing bomb, and I'm pretty sure I detonated it good and proper, and he's flirting again? Still, he said he's not a ladies' man, and I believe him.

"Duly noted, sir," I say, a relieved grin competing with the confused running commentary in my head.

"Good. We're turning the corner, and your new home will be showing up in three, two, one, now."

CHAPTER 13

It's exactly as I remembered, and I love it all over again. "Wow," I breathe. "It is perfect."

After he parks and turns off the engine, Cal holds out his hand in an unspoken invitation; I don't hesitate to nestle mine into it. I mean, he's a grown man. He shouldn't hold it out there if he doesn't want me to take it, especially given what I just told him about Dan. We sit there in the quiet looking out at the house of my daydreams. I won't pretend it's not a bit dingy, and the yard is unkempt. However, I love it all. "Perfect," I repeat.

Searching my face, apparently whatever he sees satisfies him. "Excellent."

"Thank you again for everything, Cal," I say as he opens my door. "For approving of me and helping me win Miss Millsbaugh's sign off, for listening to my confusing situation, and being kind while you did so." I smile up at him as he tucks my hand under his arm. That contact twists a knife in my heart while at the same time sending an electrical surge through my middle.

As easy as sunshine, he smiles back. Maybe it's wishful thinking that the earlier shadow in his eyes seems to have disappeared. "Those first two items you did all on your own merit, lady. As for the listening, you're welcome." He leads the way up the walk to the porch, me toddling alongside weak in the knees, still very attracted to him while simultaneously gutted to be in this stupid situation I made possible by my desire for romance. Not that I don't still want that. I do. I just wish it could happen without all the pain and confusion.

We end our tour standing on the porch as the sun starts its last drop behind the hills, dragging a blanket of orange and red and gold along with it. "Now, if you don't mind, Eisel," Cal says, leading me over to the porch swing. "You sit right here. I brought something special to help celebrate this occasion."

He jogs to the car with the ease of an athlete, opens the back door, and emerges with a bottle of champagne and two crystal champagne flutes. "I had a good feeling about how our meeting with Miss Millsbaugh would go, so I took the chance and stuck this bottle in my cooler."

"Do you celebrate this way with all your clients?" I ask as I stand and take the glasses from him.

"No." Popping the cork, he pours out, then taking his glass from me, clinks it against mine. "No, I definitely do not. This is special treatment for a special lady." His eyes and his smile grow soft. "To you, Eisel Jane McCord, pursuer of truth and romance. May all your days in this house be ones of joy and connection, and may I have the very great privilege of visiting early, late, and often, once you're settled in. Cheers."

We sip, and as his eyes meet mine, he smiles.

My returning smile falters though. "Cal, I would love that more than anything, but is it really fair to you? What if I feel I owe it to Jimmy to try to find romance with him after all or if in the end, something about Dan Baker wins a part of my heart I didn't know I had? I don't want to hurt you. I know I haven't known you very long, but you said you do want to explore more than being friends, but now all this. How can—I mean—help me understand."

He takes another contemplative sip and tilts his head as if it helps him see me better. "All the way out here, I thought about those very questions, asking myself if it wouldn't be better to cut my losses now before my heart is hooked good and proper, if it isn't already."

I blink back tears again. Here it is. This exciting, enjoyable, smart, sweet-smelling man is about to exit stage left, leaving a black hole where delight has been since our first meeting. After Jimmy's leaving, I don't feel strong enough to face this. Yet I must. "I'm so sorry, Cal. I didn't mean for this to happen."

"Whoa there, lady. I'm not finished." He wiggles his eyebrows and gently lifts my glass to my lips for another sip, then takes one of his own. "Hear me out. Like I said, I asked myself those questions, and here's what my heart answered: Hell no. I am not moving aside for your Jimmy who has not been careful to curate your heart and has left you to your own devices. Nor am I making room for Mr. Dan "come-into-my-parlor" Baker or any other fellow who happens to take a fancy to you. I will keep showing up and romancing and respecting and enjoying you as much as you'll let me." Still holding my gaze, he adds, "At sixty-five years old, I don't want to play it safe anymore, now that I've met you. If in the end, you choose someone else, I'll know I gave it my best. Also, I want you to know that I'll be your friend either way so I can still enjoy the heck out of you and your authentic way of going through life."

Reaching out, he takes my free hand. "You let me worry about my own heart, okay? All I ask is that you please do not think that the best way to proceed is to withhold yourself from me for my own good. That would be cruel. I'm a grown-up man, contrary to what Miss M. seems to think. The only way I can feel good about this whole thing at the end of the day is if I try my darnedest to win you, so at the very least, you end up experiencing the romance you deserve. Along the way, we'll continue to build our friendship such that should I not be the one you choose, we can still grow old sharing moments here on your porch like true if not romantic friends."

For a moment, my soul leaves my body, I'm so taken aback by those words. "You—you're sure about that, Calvin Felix? You sure you want to keep investing your heart knowing a solid chance exists that I won't—I don't—I—"

He touches his finger to his lips. "Hush now, Lady Jane. Please continue being yourself with me. That's all I'm asking and what I'm finding so very attractive. You being you. I'm learning I can trust that. I'm not sure you realize how rare such a thing is in this old world. I'm surrounded by people who need something from me. Business deals. Insider tips on the brokerage side. Ulterior motives up the wazoo and playing strategy games when all I want is to be real. Folks are always saying things they don't mean in hopes of gaining leverage over me or from me. You though?" He smiles and touches his glass to mine again. "You're different."

"I'm different all right," I say, gulping back the flood of relief that has me once again and unsurprisingly, on the brink of tears.

His laughter washes over me, and I sway toward him. "Whoa, lady. You should have warned me you're a lightweight in the drinks department."

"It's not the champagne, Cal. It's you. How can you be so kind and gallant when all this is my fault? My stupid bucket list and sorting rule of considering only myself in the equation has put you in this position, and all you're thinking of is wanting me to be happy?"

He gives a lopsided grin and snorts. "I hope you don't think this is altruism on my part. It's not. I'll be taking measures, as much as it lies with me and without obligating you in the least, to make sure I have squatter's rights to this porch swing right here beside you. If it all comes out right, that's going to include enough romantic overtones and undertones to cross that little item off your bucket list."

I raise my glass to that and drain it dry.

★ ★ ★

The sunset is fading to dusk as Cal and I drive away from my soon-to-be-home. "I know this has been a very intense day for you," he says. "Do you want some dinner, or would you like me to take you home, my friend?"

"Home, I think. Thanks for understanding."

"Of course."

Finding my hand in the dark, he holds all the way back to my house. "Cal. What a day. I know I keep saying this but thank you again. Thank you for who you are and your kindness, loaning me your shoulder to cry on, and for your friendship regardless of how things turn out. That's such a gift to me. I feel very cared for and seen."

His smile is sweet beyond words. "Definitely my pleasure. It's been a day for the record books, that's for sure." On the porch now, he faces me, holding my hands in both of his. "How are you doing?"

"Surprisingly well, thanks to you. However, we should not be standing here in full view of the neighborhood watch. Don't you have a reputation to uphold?"

He chuckles. "Have you forgotten I'm divorced? I ruined my moral credibility twenty years ago."

"Be that as it may, if news spreads that you're standing on Jimmy McCord's front steps with Jimmy McCord's wife in the dark—I don't want your association with me—" I correct myself. "Our association with each other to reflect negatively on you. You've been nothing but thoughtful and courteous, and gossip is so unkind."

He's shaking his head the whole time, and when I reach this part, he interrupts. "Hey, hey, lady. Whoa now. My reputation, my choices. Truth is, your neighbors and this whole town can go to

H E double toothpicks for all I care. They have no idea that for the first time since before my marriage dissolved, I feel hopeful and alive and very interested in finding a way to remain so." He touches my cheek, holding my gaze. "That's because I met you."

I swallow, blinking at the sweetness of that statement and his touch. "I'm so mixed up, Cal. This is all happening so fast. From meeting you to liking you to thinking this day would end without you, and I'll be honest—facing that felt like the bottom was about to drop out of my world again, this time of my own doing. Part of it still may, because at the very least, I have to tell Jimmy about you and Dan."

Lips tightening, he nods. "How do you think he'll respond?"

"I don't think he'll respond. I'm pretty sure he'll react." I grimace. "I mean, what would you say if your wife told you she was seeing another man? Men?"

His eyes flick up to mine, and the intensity of them takes me aback. "I would be furious. At her. At the man. Men. So hurt and betrayed." He takes a deep breath and blows it out. "Sorry. I'll tell you my story another time. As much as I hate to say it, I think you'd better batten down your hatches for a hurricane. I know you didn't mean for this to happen and that also you served him notice you weren't sure you'd still be around if or when he got ready to be married again. However, I can tell you from experience, your news will hit him completely out of the blue. It'll slam him in the solar plexus with a truckload of anger, pain, and betrayal. I really wish you were on the other side of it already, my friend."

I sigh. "That's exactly what I'm afraid of. You may not have noticed this about me yet, Cal, but I tend to be conflict avoidant, and the thought of telling Jimmy has me shaking inside. I think what's hardest about it to me in this particular case is that none of this would have happened if he'd not gone to Peru, yet it will look like I'm the one who's scuttling our marital boat." I sigh. "You can see that I need to tell him, though, right?"

"I wish I could say no, you don't. However, I do think you should. You wouldn't be you if you left him in the dark to discover it on his own, which, if you remember, is one of the many aspects I'm enjoying so very much about you." Capturing my hand again, he looks down at me for a long minute, and I'm very aware all of a sudden of how close we're standing to each other. I can't help it—I lean toward him, and he seems to do the same, then takes a deep breath. "May we go in for a tad, lady? I want to see your face more clearly than I can right now. I promise I won't stay long."

Part of me wants to say "Stay as long as you want. Stay forever, you fabulous human, you," while the more rational part of me appreciates the wisdom of his intent. "Of course. Let me make us some tea."

"If you're sure. I commandeered the bulk of your day, one way or the other, and I can see you're about worn out."

"I am. I'm sure. I'm also worn out," I say as I usher him into the entryway and through to the kitchen. "However, your leaving is not going to fix that, Cal. I'm afraid I won't feel any better until I let Jimmy and Dan know about this unintentional quadrangulation I have going on." I smile over at him. "Though it could be argued I was simply calling a realtor to look at a house, like thousands of people do every day. How was I to know it would be you, and that you being you is such heady stuff?" Don't ask me why, and I kid you not, I then bat my eyelashes at him as if this whole afternoon didn't happen. What the heck? I am way out of my depth right now.

"Mercy, Lady Jane." His eyes twinkle. "You know I'm having a hard time keeping it slow, and you're not helping."

He's "keeping it slow?" Still shocked at my own audacity and grinning with his response, I turn to put on the kettle while

I scrabble back off that slippery slope. Until I tell Jimmy and Dan what I need to, I can't let my heart go any further down the road with Cal, even if all my physical and emotional gauges are reading "full speed ahead." I find some cups and change the subject. "I didn't take my phone with me today. In case Jimmy texted me."

He nods, elbows on the island, chin on his fists as I ready our cups and pour the water. "What are you afraid of besides his anger?"

"I think when it comes right down to it, I'm afraid of losing emotional connection with him, what little I have left from the huge hit it took when he launched his Peru adventure, anyway." I chew on my lip. "I try so hard, yet it seems as if I always do something that cuts that connection, and then I must labor even harder to repair it."

"In my humble and very solid opinion, it sounds as if you're taking responsibility for someone else's repair job. In fact, I'll go out on a limb and say you might've grown up in a household where love was conditional upon your behavior, and it appears that your marriage has not dispelled that fallacy."

"You're not wrong." I slide his cup across the countertop to him. Actually, he's scarily spot on for both counts. "Do you want sugar? Honey? Milk?"

"No, thank you. Got all the sweetness here I can handle right now." He gives a slow wink at me over his cup.

I almost choke on my sip of tea.

"You okay there, sugar?"

"You're incorrigible."

"I'm inclined to agree, seeing that incorrigible means not able to change or alter the behavior."

I roll my eyes, sitting on the stool beside him sideways so I can see his face. He did ask me not to curate his heart for him and to simply be myself. That seems ridiculously easy considering how complicated everything else in my life is.

He laughs, and we sip our tea for a bit before he clears his throat. "Back to what I was saying. Taking a risk here, so tell me to hush up if it's too much, but I think I'm understanding maybe a little better how you could be married forty-three years and still feel as if you never experienced a great romance."

"That makes one of us who understands, then."

"Sounds to me like instead of knowing you're loved for who you are, you think you need to perform in order to receive connection. You know that's not really how love works, don't you? Real love isn't dependent on what you put into it. Unfortunately, those of us who have the challenge of growing up with conditional acceptance don't always see our own value or the other person's part in the equation."

As amazing as it is to be this understood, it's not comfortable to have my dysfunction spread out on the table in plain sight, so I search for a witty reply. Cal doesn't give me time to deflect, though.

"The point I really want to make here, lady, is that I don't understand how your Jimmy could live with such a lovely, interesting, fresh, funny person such as yourself for so long and not treat you as if he's the luckiest man alive. You're the greatest treasure he'll ever hope to have. Maybe once he gets over being angry, the thought of losing you will be a wakeup call for him. It should be, anyway, and I suppose it wouldn't be ethical to pray otherwise. However, if he doesn't rise to the occasion on his own, then maybe his trip to Peru is not the disaster it appears to be." Cal reaches out his hand, palm up, and I slip mine into it, thrilling at the warmth. "Eisel Jane, please promise me one thing."

"Which is?"

"Don't try to make a quick decision about who to be with just yet. If you can stand the not knowing, the not being sure, would you please give it some time? A month. Two. However long you need until you know which way you're leaning. Any man worth his shoe leather is not going to toss away his chances to be with you simply because you're not sure how you're inclined just yet. We need some time to jockey for your heart anyway."

He gives me a soft-eyed smile. "You're worth the risk, whether you realize it or not, and I want you to hold that thought close when you talk to Jimmy and Dan so you don't give your heart away for peanuts. I know that at some point, you'll choose, and I'm sure your need to make everyone happy feels like pressure to make that happen soon, if only to minimize damage. Please don't rush into a decision, though. Give yourself the respect you deserve and allow each of us men the honor and courtesy of trying to win you by our own merits, okay?"

Some of the tension in my chest unwinds. He distilled the essence of my dilemma into exactly what I need—time to make a good decision. Time to know my heart in order to choose well.

Setting his cup down, Cal leans close enough to reach over and tips my chin up so I meet his eyes. "Will you promise me that Eisel? That you'll give this situation time? Give us all time?"

"I promise," I whisper, wondering how in the world any of this is happening to me.

His eyes keep drifting down to my lips. I know he wants to kiss me and honestly, I'd be quite okay with that. It feels as if we've lived months together since I met him. A kiss would be amazing. It would help me feel anchored. Connected. Comforted.

He doesn't, though, which is simultaneously disappointing and wonderful. Every time he hovers on the edge of deeper intimacy and makes a decision not to press the edge builds my respect, trust, and appreciation of him, especially in this moment with my emotions so raw. It reassures my heart that Cal's not a taker. He's a giver, and he's careful with me in a way I'm not sure I ever experienced before.

Walking him to the door, I watch him climb into his SUV, then flip the porch light off and on as he pulls away. He flicks his headlights off-on-off-on in answer. Heart fractured, I don't know what hits me hardest—that he received and responded to my message so easily or that it's been years and years since that terrible argument with Jimmy robbed us of this same sweet exchange.

When Cal's taillights turn the corner down by the stop sign, I lock up, take a deep breath, and collapse on the couch to relive the day. As Cal said, it's been one for the record books, and somehow, in a miraculous way I don't quite understand, I am not lost somewhere in the darkness of despair and disappointment as I expected to be.

Not yet, anyway.

CHAPTER 14

I almost hate to go to bed. It's like saying this day is over, and I don't want to do that, remembering all it's held: approval for buying my own little house, the lovely lunch with Cal, surviving the ordeal of telling him about Dan. Then on the porch swing, his declaration to always be there with me and for me, in one capacity or another. Remembering how he picked that gentle flirting back up where he left off before my update and maybe a bit deeper, and he way his eyes roamed, I smile. Garden path indeed.

I know I'm about to repeat the update ordeal with Dan and Jimmy, yet I feel rescued. Sometimes life is just too kind and beautiful to bear, and the way this day has ended is one of those times. I don't know how it will all turn out—who my heart will want the most or how I will ever decide, which sounds both pitiful and powerless. Then the promise Cal asked of me floods me with gratitude; I don't need to choose right now. In fact, I promised *not* to choose yet.

Turning out the light, I find my love songs playlist to fall to sleep by. James Taylor singing "You've Got a Friend" seems to be capture what fills my heart right now—how when I expected to be left alone, I ended up with a friend—a friend who promised to be with me through whatever comes and whether I choose him or not. I don't know what to do with that level of wonderful. That I can call Cal and he'll answer, showing up for me no matter how big a mess I am or have made? Yes, it's very good to know that.

★ ★ ★

I wake up in a bit of a bleary-eyed dream world, feeling in my being how near I was to drowning yesterday, and how very rescued I was as well. It seems especially mundane and maybe even a little cruel to know I must rally to face whatever this day brings instead of basking in Cal's assurance of friendship and intent to do his best to win my heart. I want to ponder what that could look like. Instead, today I must tell Jimmy about Cal and Dan, and tell Dan about Cal. I'm dreading those two tasks in every pore. Knowing that's not going to change until I've done what I need to do, I pick up my phone to see if the world is still spinning and if I've missed any texts.

I have.

Maggie: *Mom, you didn't answer any texts yesterday. Should I call the fire department or something?*

Me: *Sorry hon. I've had a lot going on. Left my phone behind yesterday :-P. Maybe we can meet at the park soon so we can catch up while Portia plays.*

At this time of morning, I won't have to field any replies from Mags, as I know little Miss Sweetness will be in the middle of breakfast.

I open the next blue dot, Kate.

How's it going, girlfriend? We need to catch up. Coffee this week?

Absolutely, I reply. *Can you do tomorrow morning at ten, our favorite table at The Other Mermaid?*

Kate will respond yea or nay when she has a chance. Heaven knows I have a lot to catch her up on.

Dan. Yesterday was so full of Cal and house business and crisis and joy and grief I haven't thought much about the tall, thoughtful contractor man except to remember his kisses, the warmth of his embrace, and to confess his existence to Cal. Oh, and to dread telling him about my crazy situation. Now I smile as I open the text. What did Cal call him—Mr. Dan Come-into-my-parlor Baker? Haha. I guess that does rather fit him. He certainly doesn't drag his feet, that's for sure.

Yesterday at twelve pm: *Hope you've had a good day so far. Finished all my client meetings and am wondering if you want to go hiking this afternoon.*

Yesterday at three pm: *Hi, Dan again. Guess we missed our hiking window today. What about tomorrow, Soapstone Ridge Trail at one o'clock?*

I text, *So sorry. I was gone all day yesterday, left my phone at home, and didn't check texts before I crashed last night. I'd love to go hiking with you today. See you there."*

I leave Jimmy's text until last, and before I open it, take a few deep breaths, remembering what Cal said about me being the greatest treasure Jimmy could ever have. I'm not at all sure Jim feels I am. For that matter, I'm not sure I really embody the description as much as Cal seems to think I do. Be that as it may, I'm so thankful for my promise not to rush into a decision. In truth, I couldn't make a decision to save my life right now. Three perfectly wonderful humans, three entirely different life trajectories I suddenly have an opportunity to choose from. I don't have enough data to make a call I will live with the rest of my life.

Breaking with my usual first texts first routine, I don't open Jimmy's yet. I can't face what he might say, good or bad. Not before coffee, anyway. Not with the day I had yesterday. Not with Cal's sweet presence still lingering in my kitchen like his own alluring aroma.

Instead, I text Cal. *Good morning, my friend. I now suspect you of knowing exactly how stabilizing I would find that promise you extracted :-) On the strength of that agreement, I'm endeavoring to let go of needing to reach a decision until I see the whites of its eyes. Thanks again for your kindness and your insights, and for everything yesterday. You're my hero, for sure.*

I'm brushing my teeth when his texts pings in. *Good morning, lovely lady. Thank you for your promise and for sharing yourself with this confirmed old bachelor who is suddenly not quite so content to remain so.*

That's certainly a whopper of a way to start the morning, and I smile ear to ear as I text back. *Incorrigible. That's all I'm going to say right now until I've done what I need to do and the dust settles down. I see Jim has sent me a text, so wish me luck, because I'm going to try to call him and tell him the situation.*

I'm taking my first sip of coffee when Cal returns my text. *Sending all my good wishes your way for a communication that is everything you need it to be with none of the fear and pain that makes life so hard sometimes.*

I don't open Jimmy's text until I finish my cup of coffee. No doubt about it, I'm procrastinating. However, prepping for a hurricane is difficult in the extreme, and I must gear up. Way up. Pouring myself a second cup of liquid courage, I stand for a moment picturing how I will soon have the option to take my morning cup of joe out to the porch swing in the early morning air when the birds are waking up and everything is fresh and new. Here in town, I could take it to the deck. However, that would mean dressing in something besides my robe, because the fence between our house and the Dixons gives them prime row seats to my coffee time.

No thank you.

Instead, I settle on the couch and open Jimmy's text. Four messages wait for me, plus he tagged a heart on my mine, which reassures me. He probably likes that I did a better job the second time around seeing the poem for the olive branch and gift he undoubtedly meant it to be. Maybe with the poem he's telling me he's internalizing my statement about not experiencing a great romance, and it constitutes an effort to do something about that.

That's sweet.

Jimmy is sweet. He always has been, and that's one thing that has allowed our marriage to last all these years. I'm not so sweet. Or maybe I'm sweet in a different way. More of a subtle acquired taste that (hopefully) grows on you. He's the kind of guy who is genuinely interested in people, their stories, and their struggles. A loyal friend, he still has buddies from his high school days, and everything he sets his hand to seems to turn out well because he brings a level of focus and care that is a joy to watch. To be honest, sometimes I've wondered why it hasn't occurred to him to apply that same intentionality to his interactions with me. I guess that's hardly fair, though, because when I think about it now with more equitable eyes, I see that he often does.

Or did.

Yet I don't feel special or especially approved of or enjoyed by him, which as Calvin pointed out, may have more to do with my family of origin than with Jimmy. Very true, and yet what Jimmy gives seems more like maintenance care than focus. Again, I suspect I'm at least half of the issue. Relationship myopia strikes again: not seeing the other person clearly and not being seen clearly myself. Not on the level of seen I feel with Cal and Dan, anyway. Not even close.

What a crazy set of circumstances to land in. It's confusing and more than that, feels as if I'm defrauding each of these men in a different way by even entertaining the possibility of the other two. Remembering Cal's words of last night, though, I relax a bit. "Give yourself the respect you deserve and allow each of us men the honor and courtesy of trying to win you by our own merits," he said, as if I'm a prize they're competing for. That feels unexpectedly sweet. I promised, and if you think about it, that promise allows for me to focus on only one at a time, though any onlooker would be scandalized that I could dangle the three of them along in uncertainty.

I can do so if I want to, though. Applying a modified split focus if you will—concentrating on each one completely when I interact with him. Them. Wow. Even the grammar is messy. I won't be able to maintain a trio of romantic interests forever, nor would I want that. For now, I promised not to rush a decision, and I find that fact strangely centering. "Thank you, Calvin Felix," I whisper.

I read Jimmy's text. *Thanks for sharing that picture of me down by the river. I'm always amazed at how intuitive you can be, because that's exactly how it was. I think of you a lot down here in Peru, as if my heartstrings are tuned to yours over the miles. [Heart eyes emoji].*

If he'd been saying these things to me all along, maybe I would have crossed that romance entry off my bucket list upon reading it and moved on without a backward glance. Yet then I wouldn't have met Cal and Dan, and that feels sad.

I suppose if I had romance already, I would be feeling as valued and seen and desirable as I do when I'm interacting with those two, so maybe the sadness would only be that I wouldn't have the privilege of being friends with such great humans of the masculine variety. I don't know. My thoughts are as tangled as a pile of baling twine.

Jimmy goes on to say, *You make a valid point about being too used to the way we see each other. These days, I'm pondering things I didn't take the time to think much about before—including how blind I tended to be to the fact I'm married to an incredible woman. That is something I regret. I know we irritate each other sometimes, but I don't want you to feel un-romanced by me. I love you Eisel, and I always will.*

> *You're the cream in my coffee*
> *The sun in my sky*
> *You're funny, intelligent, hardworking, kind*
> *You go through your days*
> *With a wise sort of grace*
> *And make the world glad by the sight of your face.*

Awww. He's done it again, and that throws me off balance. Again. It was so much clearer cut when I was mad at him. When he didn't want or need me in his life. Is this poem because he misses me or because he's trying to counter my "no romance" info with a healthy deposit in that account? Either way, it does seem as if Peru is truly being good for him.

Moving on to Jimmy's fourth text, though, my smile fades. *I am puzzled about your final statement. What did you mean?*

I reread my previous text, especially the last sentence, feeling tightness rising in my chest, like preparation to run or hide. *All I ask is please don't let me be the strongest person in the equation. I really need to know that you're making the decisions you want to make, not the ones you think I want you to make.* I don't think clarity is the problem here. Rather, I suppose he didn't like my statement because it does make certain assumptions about how he lives life with me.

Honestly, I knew when I wrote it that he wouldn't appreciate my implication that he sees me as the person who has the power in our relationship. Whatever. I have something much more momentous to discuss, and I'm not in the mood to piddle around explaining myself on lesser matters in order for him to continue to disagree.

Instead, I text, *Jimmy, I need to talk to you about something important. Is there a chance you can call me? I'm available now if you are, or I could chat this evening as well.*

Send.

I shower and am dressing when my phone buzzes. It's Jimmy, and I take a deep breath, hoping our connection will hold on long enough for me to say what I need to say. "Hi Jimmy John. How's it going?" (Striving for casual, here).

"How great to hear your voice. Let me see if I can FaceTime you."

Wonder of wonders, we connect. "It's great to *see* you," I say, because it is. Such a dear familiar face and voice. I love him, and I still can't believe that after all our years of marriage, he'd simply up and leave me. It's as if he's been a good provider, husband, father, and so on for all that time, and thinks that somehow earns him the right to shed those roles and be the heroic world-changing figure he always admired and dreamed of being. I guess I wouldn't know about that because meanwhile back in my universe, I wasn't role playing, and I didn't understand that he, apparently, was.

"You said you need to talk to me about something important? Did Trencher have to go to the vet, or do we need to call the roto rooter man out to look at our drains as I was afraid of?"

"No, it's nothing like that."

"Good. So what's up?"

"Remember the bucket list item I told you about—experiencing a great romance?"

"I do. That's why I wrote those poems, actually." He smiles up at me from the phone screen, the jungle green around him. "I started thinking—we love each other, and for me, that's the definition of romance. Meeting, marrying, raising a family, living together—that's romantic in my book. It was pretty counterintuitive for me to hear that you must have a different definition of romance than I do."

I nod.

"I was upset and texted Maggie, and as I thought about her explanation, realized maybe I've not been the best about letting you know how much I appreciate you."

I nod again. Normally, I'd be all over this conversation. However, knowing what I'm about to spring on him, I struggle not to blurt it out over the top of his confession just to get this over with. Then again, he's given me a lead in, so I take it. "Jim, I really appreciate what you're sharing and the thought you've given it, and the poems are very sweet. I think you're right about our definitions of romance differing. I need to tell you something that's transpired in the last week that has to do with mine."

I pause to gather my wits and my words. "It all happened very unintentionally on my part, and it's confusing. What I wanted to tell you is that there are two very nice men here in town who currently think I'm wonderful and want to spend time exploring whether we could have a relationship beyond being just friends. Frankly, that is both unexpected and enjoyable, and I find myself in a dilemma."

He frowns. "Wait. What do you mean, dilemma? Where's the dilemma? Tell them to back off. You're taken. We're married, Eisel. End of story."

I know that tone of voice—the clipped words. The tight mouth and hard eyes, and I very badly want to bail out right now before the engines catch fire. I also know I need to do this, do it completely, and I need to be as clear about it as I can. "I know you said you don't want a divorce. If you remember, I said I wasn't sure what I want. You left me to pursue a dream that was—that *is* more important to you than I am, and I decided if you can up and do that without considering its effect on me, then I am just as free to make decisions and live my life without considering you."

"Whoa now. In what universe does that mean letting guys come on to you while you're still married?"

"Would you please hear me out, Jimmy? I want to explain what occurred and where I'm currently at with their attentions. I'm not trying to hurt you. I'm being honest with you, and I do still love you." I steady myself and drop the payload. "However, the long and short of it is, you no longer have exclusivity."

CHAPTER 15

"What the hell are you talking about?" Jimmy demands, and I brace for the full force of the hurricane. "You mean to tell me that while I'm down here working and sweating and thinking about you—writing you poems—you're up there flirting with other men? I can't believe what I'm hearing right now. Forty-three years of fidelity, and suddenly you're involved with not one but two other men as soon as your husband is out of town? I don't even know what to say. That's—that's immoral. That's shallow and ridiculous and petty."

"Jimmy—"

"I'm done with this conversation."

"Would you please listen to me? It's not what you're making it out to be."

"So, you're not flirting and carrying on?" He glares at me through the screen and dang it, I blush.

"It's not like you're making it sound." Because I am flirting, though in a very chaste and thoughtful way. Dan and Cal are being very gentlemanly about it all as well. Of course, that is not helpful information for Jimmy right now.

"Who are these men, anyway? They're going to hear from me. No way they can simply waltz into my house and make a move on my wife. My *wife. My* wife."

That irks me right there. *His* wife? Like I'm property that belongs to him to do with what he will? I snort, dropping the buffering layer I usually maintain to minimize damage. "On paper, yes. However, the way I see it, you abdicated your position. It's called spousal abandonment. If you want a relationship with me now or when or *if* you return from Peru, I consider that you're starting with a handicap. Also, if you don't act soon, you may miss your chance with me."

"What's that supposed to mean?" He's reached the snarling stage, at which landmark I tend to shrink to a dried-out mushroom inside. Dare I hang up? We're already at the point where he's about to start lobbing short range missiles.

Then remembering Cal's quiet voice and dark eyes last night as he asked me to give myself the respect and the men the honor and courtesy of winning my heart, I take a breath. Wow, Jim, I think. Of all the responses you could make here that would advocate on your behalf, this is not it.

I brave up, say what I need to say while staying as much in my prefrontal cortex as I can, though I feel it shutting down with every moment that passes under his barrage. "It means that you need to know that two other men want to be with me. Care about me. They enjoy me and think I'm wonderful. I want that kind of wonder in my life. I want to feel that special—not like a can of green beans at the back of the pantry shelf waiting for you to decide whether you want them for dinner at some point in the next fifteen years. At this time, I don't yet know which one if any of you three I will decide to be with."

"That is the stupidest thing I've ever heard in my life." He grows louder and lower pitched with every word. "Can you even hear yourself? You're with *me*. I'm going to call the police and have them serve a restraining order on those—those—I cannot believe this! You're throwing away everything we built together because some guys you didn't even know a short minute ago are paying you compliments and trying to steal you from me? Well,

I'm not having it. You're mine. I can't believe you'd betray me like this."

Me throwing everything away? I laugh. That's completely ludicrous after his leaving precipitated this entire state of affairs. I should save my breath, though. Nothing I come up with will penetrate his anger. Looking away from my phone screen for a moment, I do my best to put myself in his position. In a way, I don't really blame him for being upset. I imagine he thinks because he's not becoming all friendly with some other woman down in Peru, he's being faithful to me. In reality, I'm not the one who threw away forty-three years as if our life together was a sock with a hole in it. Tears leak out, streaking down my face.

"Oh, yeah, why don't you just cry about it, Eisel, like you're the one who's hurt," Jimmy spits out. "You have no idea."

I think I do, Jimmy, I say inside my head. I also realize that no one can fully comprehend what another person is feeling, and no matter how much my heart aches over all this, I don't want to minimize his pain. It's the very reason I hated to tell him. That and the inevitable anger I was pretty sure would be directed at me. I wasn't wrong on that count, either, whatever else I am.

I suppose from his perspective, anger makes complete sense, though it's only one of multiple possible responses, of course. However, it doesn't necessarily follow that I must stand in front of the firing squad and be riddled with bullets. "That's under-standable," I manage to croak. "I feel really bad for you. I do."

I so desperately want him to receive the empathy I telegraph through the phone connection, yet he rants on until I try to break in. "Jimmy? Jim?"

"What, for God's sake? Did you just remember yet another wife-stealer you forgot to mention?"

"Jimmy. That's mean, and I don't appreciate being yelled at. I understand this has blindsided you, just as your Peru announcement blindsided me, but—"

"No. Don't you do that, Eisel. You can't say that my going to Peru to join an archeological dig is on the same level of betrayal as you running around on me while I'm gone. I can't—"

I touch the green button, and his voice cuts off mid-sentence. I refuse to make a decision about who to be with for the rest of my life based on anger. Mine or his. Pacing the room, I shake my hands and attempt to bring my breathing under control. I'm a spring wound so tight one more ratchet will cause everything to explode. Or implode, which is more probable with me, anyway.

My phone rings. It's Jimmy. I let it go to voicemail.

He dials again. I hit the red "decline" button. I know better than to answer when he's raging. Usually, I don't have the leisure of silencing him, and for this small blessing I'm thankful.

My phone continues to blow up. "Jimmy, enough already," I say out loud, safe in the knowledge that he can't hear me. "Can you please just take a minute to cool off? I know you're triggered out of your gourd, and I'm sorry. It probably feels as if I'm leaving you alone when you need me to be able to field your big emotions and help you find your way out of them."

For the fifth time, my phone vibrates like a trapped wasp. That seems an especially accurate simile, as if his anger could break free and sting me to death. Shuddering, I leave my phone behind and go stand out under the sky in our backyard, despite the chance of being observed by the Dixons. I hug a tree. Practice deep breathing. Anything to center myself, but as soon as I stop, everything rushes back like the incoming tide.

Finally, in between Jim calling and sending texts, I message Cal. *I told Jimmy. As you predicted, he's beyond furious.*

My phone rings the next second, and my heart leaps up out of my belly where it's been riding and back into my chest when I see Cal's name, not Jimmy's displaying. "Hello."

"Hi, brave lady. Are you okay?"

"No." I groan. "Working on it, though."

"Would you like me to come over to be with you for a while?"

I picture the complete and utter comfort it would be to not be alone while I process my shell shock and gather myself back together. I can't do that, though. The relationship, the kind of great romance I want, must include two strong people. Not him strong and me drawing on that whenever I have a meltdown.

"Eisel?"

I sniff. "That's incredibly sweet and kind of you and part of me wants very much for you to do exactly that. Probably why I texted you, to be honest, though I didn't stop to think about it before this."

"There's nothing wrong with that," he says. "That's what friends are for—to be with each other in times of need. I won't try to make it go away—couldn't do so if I tried. I also don't want to make light of the situation or help you stuff it down or ignore it. I only want to lend you my strength as you go through this hard thing."

I take a deep breath. "Cal, I don't want a relationship with you where you always give, and I always take. I'm having a hard time right now, yes. However, I can't be running to you every time that happens."

"Why not?"

"For our friendship or anything beyond it to exist, I need to be as strong for you as you are for me. Equals. Yet I'm already so deep in red ink on my side of the ledger, I'm not sure I'll ever catch up."

"Eisel, if I show up on your doorstep in fifteen minutes with a vanilla cappuccino in hand, will you let me in?"

I choke on a sob. "You're impossible."

"I'll take that as a yes. I'll be there momentarily."

Not two seconds after he hangs up, my phone rings again, and it's Jimmy. Swallowing tears, I watch until it goes to voicemail. Poor, dear, angry man. I hate it that he's all alone in his pain. No friend (at least that I know of) to do for him what I usually do—listen and sympathize and absorb his reactions as he verbally processes, moving through the various stages of emotions until he reaches equilibrium and waltzes off to resume life, leaving me to put myself back together in the aftermath.

Jimmy calls again. His anger makes sense, and it guts me. Heart aching, throat tight, sick to my stomach, I hate that we've come to this point. Hate that there is nothing that can be said or done to soften the blow. Forty-three years, and we end up here? Can we come back from this?

As Cal comes up the steps, a coffee cup in either hand, I meet him. "A thank you seems pretty lame for what I'm feeling right now."

"I do aim to please," he says, wiggling his eyebrows at me and handing me one of the cups. "I have you pegged as a coffee lover, noticing your coffee setup, and I think the vanilla cappuccinos at Sierra are mighty nice."

"You're not wrong. Yum. Do you want to come in and sit down?"

"Not yet. First, I want to give you one of those side hugs so I won't spill my coffee on you. Then I'd like to sit down, if you're fine with that." He lifts his arm, inviting me into an embrace.

I come in underneath it, wrapping my free arm around his back as he folds me against him, my face on his chest, my nose mighty near his armpit. This turns out to be a marvelous choice. I feel guilty that my phone has just stopped ringing for the millionth time—Jimmy's face lighting up the caller ID so there's no doubt it's him—while all I want to think about is how nice it is to be snuggled up to Cal's warmth, enjoying the smell of mingled aftershave and deodorant, soap and clean laundry. I melt against him, absorbing his calmness, letting his heartbeat help regulate mine, and he snugs me closer, releasing me only when I draw back slightly.

"I'm open for sitting now, if you're amenable."

"I am."

Without any hint of commandeering or insistence, he leads me over to the couch with that feather touch to my elbow, sits down, and like yesterday, pats the spot beside him. Then with his arm around my shoulders, I lean my head back against him, and there we sit, sipping coffee, saying nothing. No need for words. It is enough—no, so much more than enough—simply to be supported right now. I don't need solutions. What could anyone say that could fix this situation anyway? I don't need platitudes or adages or anything along that line, including problem solving, or blaming Jimmy. Cal does none of the above. He's simply here with me, and I underestimated how companionship in the midst of a difficult spot really does lend a solid strength.

Jimmy's picture lights up on my phone again, and again I let it go to voicemail.

"Want to tell me about it?" Cal's voice is low and calm.

I sigh. "It was as horrible as I was afraid it would be. Jimmy accused me of running around on him, hinting if not downright stating that I have suddenly taken up an old and very disreputable profession since he left. To compound that, he acted as if I'm his property and you and Dan are trespassing."

"Taking it pretty hard, then."

"Yeah." I fill him in on the conversation, and the more I review it, the tighter my throat grows until I'm one sniff away from bawling again. That is exactly what I don't want to do to Cal. I refuse to install him in the position of rescuer.

"You okay, my friend? That sounds pretty rough."

"I'll survive," I croak, leaning into him, and he hugs me closer in response. "Jimmy said he's going to call the police and take out a restraining order against you and Dan. Can he do that?"

"No. That's not how they work. We should be okay as long as he doesn't hire a hit man or something."

My laugh sounds a bit hysterical even to myself. I can't picture Jimmy doing any such thing. "Silly." I shake my head, grinning weakly. "When he's not triggered, Jimmy is one of the nicest, most compassionate people you'd ever hope to meet. I doubt the term "hit man" is even in his vocabulary."

"We can't rule out these possibilities," Cal says with a twinkle. "I don't think you understand how men's minds and hearts work in this type of situation, my dear. I'm also not sure you realize how devastating it would be to face not having you in his life, especially after all the years you've spent together. That said, in my personal opinion based on the way he left you behind, I'd say he tends to take you for granted. We men can be that way, becoming complacent and forgetting that fragile and precious things like wives and children can wither under that kind of neglect. May I tell you how I know that?"

"Of course."

"I know because I did that to my wife, Kalisha. I was living my dream. I had a pretty wife who loved me. Two sweet, funny little kids. A nice house, nice cars, nice life. Yet the more I had, the more I wanted, I guess, and the more I grew blind to the cost of that. I began spending more and more time at the office, giving after hours property showings plus some financial consulting and brokerage on the side.

Kalisha would talk to me about my workaholism, and I'd reform for a week or two, but there always seemed to be a compelling reason to take this appointment or that commitment. The kiddos were often in bed by the time I returned home, and I'd leave before they woke up."

He pauses and I wait, trying to "lend strength" as he put it.

"Then one night I came home, and those little nippers were bundled up in their jammies as I came in the door. After they jumped on me and climbed my legs up into my arms, and I'd kissed them all over their sweet faces, Kalisha sent them to the kitchen for a cup of warm cocoa. It felt in that moment as if I had the best life ever until she led me to the living room and told me she was done. Done with me being married to my profession and my income and my prestige-based aspirations. Done with me never being there for her or the kids."

I take Cal's hand, not knowing what to say, pretty sure that he doesn't need me to say anything anyway. He's simply letting me into his world, giving me a chance to be with him in that painful memory, and it feels like a privilege to be trusted like this.

"She wanted out. It turns out that while I was busy conquering worlds, she'd been running the kids to sports and music and school events, and without meaning to, met someone who thought she was amazing and who wanted to spend time with her, the time I didn't seem to value. She was starved for my love, and I didn't see it." Cal breathes a shaky sigh.

"I wonder to this day if I'd really seen that and asked her to give me one last chance, she might have. Sadly, I responded exactly like your Jimmy has. I blasted her as if she was to blame for the whole situation, and I was ready to find that teacher and be the hit man myself, not merely hire one. Instead of seeing it as my final chance to salvage our life together, I ranted and raved as she bundled the kids into the car, and that was the end."

He drops his head into his hands and just sits there, my arm around his shoulders now. After a bit, he straightens and shakes his head. "Later, when it was all too late, I realized I'd lost the only things in life that actually mattered to me. Kalisha was a gem. I think I neglected her too badly for her to want to try anymore. Forgot to keep romancing her once we were married and had the kids. She eventually married the teacher, and I'm glad for her sake and the kids' that he had his priorities in the right order.

"Oh, Cal," I breathe. "That's so hard. I'm really sorry."

"Thank you. Yeah, it was my own fault, same as your Jimmy has created quite a situation for himself. I eventually saw that, so something good has come from it, I think I can say. I reorganized my life so I could be there for my children as they finished growing up, even if I couldn't be with their mother."

"Somehow it's hard for me to picture you being neglectful, detached, or complacent."

"I was. Believe me. I was a classic workaholic and absentee husband and father. They needed and wanted me, and I gave them stuff. Nice house, clothes, etc. Afterwards, though, alone in that house night after night after night, I vowed I would never take people for granted again. Never assume they belonged to me. I've been through all sorts of counseling and anger management classes since then, and I've vowed to walk lightly all my days, so I never inflict that kind of pain on anyone ever again."

"Thank you for sharing that with me," I say after he's been silent a long time. "I guess that's why you had such an accurate idea of how Jimmy would respond."

"Exactly," he says, giving me a lopsided smile. "At least, I thought he might. That is also why I'll be keeping an eye peeled for suspicious characters following me around. Jimmy isn't close enough to run Dan and I off from you personally, so he's got to hire it out."

I laugh. "You're a caution, Calvin Robinson." I'm amazed that I feel less traumatized over Jimmy's anger than I would expect at this point in the aftermath. Also, I appreciate that Cal doesn't try to solve this romantic fiasco I find myself in just because he's had one of his own. Instead, he takes my hand and holds it against his cheek.

Centering in the warmth of his skin against mine, I breathe, focusing on gratefulness. Then my phone rings again, jerking me back to earth. It's Maggie. "I'm sorry, Cal. It's my daughter. I should answer."

"Of course."

CHAPTER 16

Jimmy called Maggie, of course. I probably would have put two and two together if I hadn't been so transported out of the moment with Cal coming to the rescue. Now she's practically yelling into the phone, and I hold it away from my ear so Cal hears everything.

"Mother. I just got off the phone with Dad. He said you're dating two other men, and you don't want to be married to him now. I'm calling you to confirm or deny."

"I both confirm and deny."

"What is that supposed to mean?"

"I have met two very nice men. I don't understand how or why, but they both seem to like me quite a bit, and you know what I told you about my bucket list item regarding experiencing a great romance? I think that's what's happening." I shrug, though of course she can't see that. "I called your dad to tell him about it and to explain that if he wants to have a romantic relationship with me, he needs to know that as far as I'm concerned, he's on a slightly less than level playing field with these two gentlemen, thanks to him chucking all our years together like they're moldy leftovers."

"Mother, stop joking."

"I'm not joking, honey."

"You really are running around on Dad with not one but two different men at the same time, while he follows his dream?

Do you have any idea how disgusting that is and how angry and betrayed he feels right now?"

"He already treated me to that anger, thank you."

Cal is as still as a meadow at daybreak, his hands steepled under his chin, his expression sad and kind. It calms me, and I take a big breath. "Maggie. You know I love you to pieces and would throw myself in front of a train for you day or night. I appreciate that this is rough news for you and also that your dad is so hurt and angry right now he unloaded all that on you. He shouldn't have done that. However, he's given you only his perspective. I'd love to give you mine sometime."

"What other spin can you put on it, Mom? Either you're carrying on with those other guys, or you're with Dad. Which is it? I can't believe my own mother—"

I break in. "Maggie, dear. I'm sorry. I know this is unexpected for us all and more than difficult, and at the same time, I will not sit here and have you shred this fragile, beautiful thing I'm experiencing for the first time in my life. I'm hanging up now, and you let me know when you're ready to chat about it. I'll answer your questions and tell you my thoughts. Then. Not now. Not this way."

"Mother. Don't you hang up on me like you did Dad. What has gotten into you? I don't even recognize you."

"I love you, Mags. Talk to you soon. Bye." I touch the green button, set my phone down on the coffee table with excessive care, then sit there stunned. I don't have tears. I don't have thoughts. I am frozen.

What was I thinking to have gone on dates with strange men and let them pay attention to me as I have? Seeing it from Maggie's viewpoint all of a sudden, I'm floundering in whitewater, heading for a stretch of rapids I'm pretty sure I won't survive. What am I to do? Should I have kept settling for the life I had, void of romance and left alone? Should I not have dug out my bucket list or picked up the pieces of my life and tried to fit them together knowing that the whole center of the puzzle is missing? I don't know. All I know is that Maggie is disgusted by me, and I'm lost in that reality.

Standing, Cal pulls me gently up and into his arms. Inside, I'm all empty space without any stars, an iceberg cast adrift in uncharted waters. Jimmy's anger I'm used to, if you ever really become used to such things. Maggie's words, though, reverberate in my head—"I don't even recognize you"—and whatever equilibrium I was holding onto drains away.

Then into that maelstrom, Cal begins to sing, and his voice is every bit as warm and mellow and sweet as Josh Groban's as he sways slowly back and forth to the tune of "I'll Stand by You," all about being sad, not being ashamed to cry, and not being alone in all of that.

The words, the music, and Cal's kindness erase any control I had over my tears. I'm crying huge, gulping sobs, so swallowed by sadness I can't catch my breath. It's bad enough that Jimmy John is furious with me. Blames me. Shames me. Now my little girl, my darling and my joy, looks at me with disgust, and somehow that feels like the end of life as I know it.

Jimmy, that's one thing. We've had a lot of ups and downs. I learned I can survive those, can forgive, can regain ground bit by tiny bit within myself until we're okay again. But this? Maggie and I, we're more than mother and daughter. We're friends, and she's never talked that way to me, even in her teens. Disappointing her? It feels like I've lost everything we had in one short conversation.

Cal cradles my head against his shoulder, apparently unfazed by tears, his free hand on my back, patting me as gently as you'd pat a newborn baby, still singing about not letting anyone hurt me. I wish. I'm aching inside right now from multiple woundings. Yet as I listen to the rumble of his voice against my ear and let the words begin to wash over me, my breathing and heartbeat begin to sync with his. Tears slowing.

I'm not sure how long I'm wrapped in his lovely voice, so rich, resonant, enveloping. In a sort of timelessness, I eventually realize that now we're slow dancing to music of his making, swaying with the melody, little steps and the movement with the music helping me center. Helping me regulate inside.

Dancing with him before was enchanted. This is on a whole different level. This being held by friendship—seen, given all the time and the freedom in the world to feel the height and depths of grief and anger, loss and confusion, and not going through it alone is a special healing magic. Moving in time to the vibration of his song thrumming through me, the words take on nuance and meaning they never had before. I don't have words for this level of wonderful.

Bit by bit, I relax into the rhythm and the rise and fall of his voice, standing a little straighter. The whole situation still feels big and sad and unsolvable, yet it's as if I've somehow reached a quiet eddy in the rushing river and am starting to crawl to safety. Placing my hand in Cal's so he can guide me in a gentle circle, soon I'm tuning to his leading, my mind letting go of this thing with Maggie. He still holds me close, my cheek resting on his shoulder as I let his music, his movements, and his calmness reset me.

Into this sacred space, my phone intrudes. It's Maggie again I see at a glance, but Cal swings me away from the living room, breaking into a new verse a bit louder to mask the buzzing. Then he starts into the jazzier chorus, picks up the tempo a bit, never missing a beat as he sends me out to the end of his arm, eyes on mine as he tugs me back against him, whirling me as if I actually know how to dance like this on my own.

Our eyes meet again, and he smiles, dropping into a hum and swinging me into a tight circle that slows to a halt with our faces only inches apart. It's heady stuff, I'm past my limit, and I know it. For a moment, I hang there feeling his soft breath on my cheek, anchored in his eyes. His smile deepens. Stepping back, I close my eyes, re-centering. I am so far out from my normal, I have no memory of this place.

"Cal, I don't know how to thank you for coming over and simply being with me," I say, cradling his hand in both of mine, holding it up under my chin. "I thought you shouldn't, and that I should handle it on my own and not burden you with any of it. I'm so very grateful you came anyway."

"You're very welcome, Lady Jane. Once again, the pleasure is all mine."

"That's a good thing, because as a bonus, I see I've left tear stains on your shirt again. A lot of them."

"Thank you for that honor, ma'am."

"You're incorrigible. You know that?"

"So I understand." He grins.

I smile, amazed to be so calmed in the face of what just happened. Then his alarm rings.

"Shoot," he says with a grimace. "I have a closing at the title office in ten minutes. Like we're going to be doing for you in the near future," he adds.

I shake my head in wonder. "It doesn't seem real. Any of this. I don't know how you managed to reel me back from the brink like you did. Especially after Maggie. You really helped me. I promise I won't make a habit of this."

"Now Eisel, please. You think that's good news?"

I laugh. "Okay. Whatever. You'd better take off before you're late, and I hope you have a jacket to cover that spot on your shirt. Again, thank you for everything. You helped me move through all this. I'll be okay now."

"Good." He runs his fingers down my cheek, stalling at my lips for a breath, then enfolds me in a last hug. That touch fizzes through me like a gift in this moment, a little proof that my world has not lurched completely out of orbit. Or if it has, it's found a sweet new alternative.

Only as I'm walking with him out to his car do I remember what my afternoon still holds. "Cal? With all the mess this morning with Jimmy and then Maggie, I forgot to tell you I'm going to tell Dan today as well. About you. Please send up a little prayer for me that I do it well. That he takes it well."

He stares at the SUV for a beat, then smiles and nods. "Lots I could say right now, except I don't believe in crippling the opposition. Let him bring his best because I'll bring mine. You deserve that. He better not hurt you, though, or I'll come looking for him." Then he touches me on the chin, a bare whisper of contact, and off he drives, leaving me to shuffle back up the walk and collapse on the couch. I feel as if I've run a marathon, and it's only nine thirty in the morning.

* * *

Thankful for familiar chores as my system slowly resets, I text Kate as I eat a quick lunch and pull on my hiking boots. *Send all good vibes my way. I'm going hiking with Dan this afternoon, and I've got a ton of stuff to tell you.*

Spill it, girl.

Tomorrow :-)

What a day so far. Telling Jimmy about Cal and Dan. Having Maggie side against me. Cal singing me back from the brink of an emotional Niagara Falls (and I do not think that's describing it too strongly). I'm not sure I feel sufficient to finish this self-appointed, self-inflicted task, yet no use delaying. Every day that Dan doesn't know about Cal is one day more he may be hoping, thinking that

I'm as completely unencumbered as he is himself. I don't think I'm assuming to much in thinking that. His "I'd-rather-show-you" kiss and what we shared on the deck and out by the car and in his texts—I'm sure that he doesn't go around doing that with every woman he meets. I may not understand his why or how, yet I think I'd be more naive than I already am to think he's not interested in a romantic relationship with me, and so I know I have to do this today.

As if my thinking about him is the cause, my phone pings with a text from Dan. *Unless you'd prefer, I see no reason for both of us to drive. I'd be glad to swing by and pick you up.*

That's kind of you. I hate for you go out of your way, though.

No worries. I'll be in town picking up some roofing supplies for my crew. Twelve thirty sound okay?"

Perfect :-).

Roofing supplies. That reminds me. Cal said I should have an inspection done on the house. Maybe I can talk with Dan about his availability to do that. I text Cal. *You have lovely voice.*

Thank you, Lady Jane. How are you doing?

So far, so good. Dreading telling Dan Baker about you. Also, I remembered I was going to ask him about inspecting the old house. Do you think I'd be tacky to do both today?

Lady, you'll never be tacky. You're in the middle of a very complex situation and simply trying your best. You're a class act, however you look at it.

I read that through several more times, simply for the lift it gives my heart. *Thank you for that, Cal. You're so kind. I hope it's true. Is it okay if I use the lockbox code to take Dan through the house?*

Of course. Aside from my resentment of him as a person also interested in you, he's arguably the best contractor in the area. He's honest, turns out a quality product, and won't take advantage of you.

Thank you. For everything. [Star eyes emoji].

One more text comes in from Cal: *I'm pretty much in awe of your communication skills, your bravery, and a whole lot of other things as well. I'll be thinking about you.*

Honestly. Complications aside, being treated this way is lighting up some spaces inside that have dimmed down over the years.

★ ★ ★

"Great to see you again, Eisel," Dan says, my momentarily awkwardness erased as he gives me a quick hug, his blue eyes even brighter than I remembered. "Gorgeous day for hiking. I'm looking forward to spending time with you."

"Same here," I say and find it's true. Two minutes in, I remember why his kiss on Sunday evening did not seem like too big of a stretch—Dan emanates masculinity like a sonar device. It's pinging off of me; caught in his tractor beam, he's drawing me in already. That feels crazy and does set me wondering how I can respond to him like that after yesterday and this morning with Cal? That was completely immersive.

Is there something wrong with me, like Jimmy and Maggie are convinced is the case, that I can enjoy more than one man concurrently and engage with their attention? Have I lost the "taken" sign I've worn for more than forty-three years so I'm fair game these days? I don't know. I can't invest a lot of energy in those questions right now. I need to figure out how to tell Dan about Cal and the mess I've unintentionally created due to dusting off my bucket list. Yet, thanks to the promise Cal extracted, I'm free to focus on the man in front of me, giving myself and him that honor and respect.

I swim through all these thoughts as we roll up to the trailhead, park, and don our gear. "I should probably tell you I haven't hiked much in the last few years," Dan says as we adjust our Camelbacks and check out the map.

"This is merely a training mission, shall we say. I have no doubt that you can hike circles around me right now, even though I do go walking most weeks."

He laughs. "You just keep that good opinion of me. Maybe it will inspire me to do more than think about prepping to climb."

It really is a lovely afternoon. The sky is that impossible deep summer blue with a few high clouds for contrast, and with every step, I feel more like myself. Or maybe more at home in myself. More at peace. We pass in and out of shadows, sun patterning the trail in tiger stripes. "I love being outside," I say when we pause at a viewpoint bench. "It helps settle me."

"I know what you mean." Dan takes a big breath and lets it out slowly. "It's as if the world spins at the right pace out in nature where the hands of man have not messed with the inner workings of it all."

"Exactly." Maybe I should just tell him now, before this easy connection starts down the slippery slope of physical attraction and makes everything that much more complicated.

As I open my mouth to begin, though, Dan takes my hand in his as naturally and easily as sunshine, and that throws me off. Especially when he gives me a little half grin as if he knows it.

"Ready?"

Ready for what, Mr. Dan? I think, not about to throw that out there for explanation. "Ready."

"Excellent." He pulls me to my feet. "How's house hunting coming along? You know, item number two on your list?"

"Good. Great actually. I found one and put an offer on it."

"Well done. Tell me about it."

He still holds my hand, a fact that sets my stomach fluttering as does the warmth and strength of his fingers and how they wrap mine so gently. Part of me wonders why I'm allowing him to do so, and the other part is holding on for dear life to these last man-woman moments before I tell him what I'm pretty sure will alter our easy give-and-take dynamic forever. I fill him in about the house, touching on Miss Millsbaugh, who it turns out he knows, though only by reputation.

"She's sharp as a whip, Miss Millsbaugh. However, I don't know how well she maintained her house, these last few years especially."

"Funny you should mention that," I quip. "I was going to ask you if you'd be willing to look it over and see what I'll need to fix first off. I mean, I want to buy it, regardless. I just need to know what I'm dealing with cost-wise. The realtor says it probably needs a new roof and a couple of the exterior windowsills need some attention. He thought most other things are more cosmetic and advised me to have it gone through by someone who knows. Of course, I'll pay you for your time and services."

"Pshaw. You absolutely cannot pay me for the pleasure of spending some extra time with you, Eisel," he says with a grin. "As it happens, I'm free the rest of the afternoon. What say we drive over there after we finish this hike, and I'll go over it for you with a fine-toothed comb."

"Amazing. I'd love that. If you'd be so kind, I'd also like to have you add my name to your wait list for projects. I'm sure you're booked solid as I have it on good authority that you're the best contractor in the area."

Dan laughs. "You do know how to wrap a man around your little finger. You bet I'll add your name to my list. Depending on the size of the job, I might have an opening next month. It would be good to wrap up any outside projects before the weather turns."

We chat about renovation ideas I have for the house, some of which may need carpentry skills, while others can be accomplished by paintbrush and wallpaper tools. I can't wait to start, and designing and decorating fills my mind as I hike, distracting me from my primary objective of bringing everything out in the open. I'm also struck again by what a very nice human Mr. Dan Baker is. Easy to talk with, easy to be with.

"How did you get started in general contracting?" I ask as we arrive back at his truck, and I buckle in.

"I worked for my dad while I was in high school. He was a carpenter craftsman in the area, and I discovered I liked building quite a lot. So I learned from the ground up, you might say. I took a break for college, then when Rosalie and I married, we decided to settle down here, and I stepped back in as head carpenter on one of Dad's crews. As he aged, he handed more and more of the business over to me until here I am. These days I'm often so busy on the contracting side, I don't have the opportunity to pick up a hammer myself, and I miss that. Also, I do love restoring historic houses like the old Millsbaugh place."

"You're completely welcome to do that anytime. I don't want you to feel in any way obligated though."

Smiling, he shakes his head. "You might not know this about me yet, Eisel, but I've reached the point in my life where I do nothing I do not choose to do, so if I show up with my tools, I hope you'll read that to mean that I want to be there."

"Fair enough." Then before I miss the opportunity, I add, "Once we finish the walkthrough, I have something I need to tell you, if that's okay.

"Sure thing. Here we are. Let's see what your own little house has going on, then have that conversation. By the way, I took the liberty of stowing a couple of ginger beers in my cooler, in case we needed some refreshment after hiking." He fishes a couple of cans out from the back seat of his pickup, opens one, and hands it to me, his fingers contacting mine in a way I'm sure is intentional. I blink at the jolt it sends through me, masking as best I can with a sip of ginger beer. "This tastes heavenly. Thank you for your thoughtfulness."

"My pleasure." Looking right into my eyes, he smiles that killer smile of his that wipes my brain clear of any truly objective thoughts and makes me want to go swimming in that blue, blue gaze. "By the way, "He adds. "I'm hoping we can have an installment soon on that deeper dive you referred to in your text."

CHAPTER 17

Be still my little heart, as Grover of Sesame Street fame is fond of saying. I hope we can finish the walkthrough without skating too close to the edge of that drop-off, so our upcoming conversation won't be quite as difficult. Dan Baker is a beautiful, vital man, and I like him a lot. Besides being straightforward, respectful, and decisive, I enjoy his company. I think we could have fun doing a lot of things together, maybe even some bucket list entries I don't want to do solo.

When I'm with him, he fills the space. Inhabits it, I guess you'd say, so comfortable with himself and who he is, no posturing or need to impress. Being with him is like stepping into a whole landscape that reminds me of the oak woodlands of northern California, all sweeping grasslands and hills and ancient spreading trees under an endless sky. As Cal said, Dan is a force to be reckoned with. However, he's not like a hurricane. He's more like the midsummer sun that envelopes and warms and cannot be ignored.

I really, *really* wish I didn't need to tell him about not being the only man in my equation. What's he supposed to do with that? Jimmy demonstrated one option. Cal another. How will Dan interpret me after he knows? Will the sun go away? I have no idea. At this point, all I know is that things are shifting, and where two weeks ago, I would have said I knew what love is, now I don't know what to think.

John Denver's song, "Perhaps Love," runs like a soundtrack in my mind as we walk through the old beauty of a house. Love as a resting place, a shelter, comforting and warm in times of trouble—that reminds me of Cal. What about the next verse? It's like Cal as well, yet in it, I also see Dan as he kissed me Sunday night and gathered me in his arms to show me what romance feels like instead of merely telling me. It's a window or an open door, inviting me further in.

Jimmy. What about Jimmy John McCord? What would he say love is, this man I know so well yet not at all, it seems? Between us, love is like a churning ocean right now. Other times, it's been the warmth of fire when it's cold, thunder in the rain. Will all his memories of love be of me? Will mine be of him? I don't know.

I seem to be summed up in the bridge between verses and chorus: Nebulous as clouds, as enduring as steel, yet where love has been a way of living for me all these years, suddenly it's more a way to feel, and I have no compass to point me to the true north. I thought love was holding on, and I held on so long and so desperately. What am I to think now, though?

Jimmy with his new (old) love, Peruvian archeology, and so maybe for me in this season, love is letting go. Letting go of him so he can have this new life he's chosen to pursue without being encumbered with me, despite claims that I'm his. Letting go of what I thought my last years on earth would look like: the companionship and security of nearly a half century of shared memories, experiences, difficulties, joys. Should I give up such wealth and start over?

Perhaps love is not so easily defined as all that. Maybe it's all of those aspects and more in a great cycle of life, spiraling, intertwining, weaving an endless tapestry from which we'll never be far enough away to see the whole picture. I don't know, and I don't know what to do. Should I hold on to whatever I may still have with Jimmy, waiting for him to return and pick up whatever pieces are left between us after this morning? I'm not sure he wants to. I'm not sure I want to either. What if he does and I don't? What if I let go and then wish I had not?

I have no idea how you decide these things. I know people think rules give the parameters, and all we have to do is color within those lines. Rules like "you're married." As Jimmy said this morning, "What's the dilemma?" That's what I always thought as well. I promised to love and cherish him, and that was the bottom line. He promised as well, and maybe he thinks he's keeping his end of the contract, but I can't see how that's true when here I am, and all I have left is not so much the memories of love as the knowledge that I'm left behind, left out of his world. He's living his own life. I have no place in it now.

I don't think memories of love are going to be enough to take me through the years to come. I need the now. I need a presently unfolding kind of love, the kind that lights his eyes when he sees me, has him spending his time thinking of how to be with me, how to let me know he values me more than anything else. Yet right now, I don't know that, and I don't think Jimmy feels that way, because wouldn't he be here in Ranger Falls and not in Peru if his heart was still with me?

I know love is so much more than this aspect, yet it looms like Everest in my sight. Jimmy himself is the only one who can move that mountain from in between us. It terrifies me to realize that if he waits too long, he won't find me on the other side.

These are the things I'm thinking inside while my body follows Dan around as he taps on the water heater and checks the level of sediment in it (needs to be replaced, as Cal suspected). The attic could stand some insulation. Chimneys should be cleaned (Dan knows a guy). The bathroom needs an upgrade (Dan says he can schedule that in once I close on the house), and we talk about installing a little half bath in the roomy space on the landing between the two upstairs bedrooms, each of which have quaint built-ins, angles, nooks and crannies, and fireplaces.

I'm envisioning a clawfoot tub with a window above it so I can soak while gazing out over the rolling hills behind the property. In the midst of the complexity of my life, this sweet old home fills my heart with a bubbling joy for the future I will build here.

We eventually make a full circle; I'm no closer to understanding love. All I know is that I need to tell Dan about my lack of exclusivity before he moves in for a deeper connection. Before my romance-starved heart takes over again, and I let this lovely intentional man closer than I should until he knows what he's dealing with. He doesn't deserve to be hurt. He deserves honor, consideration, and friendship, and no matter what's in store for us in the romantic realm, I'm hoping we can end up still being friends. Because real friends are as rare as diamonds in the sand or the sound of wild geese flying.

I guess we'll find out.

"How are you doing on your drink, there, Eisel?" Dan asks as we step back to the porch. "Can I interest you in another?"

"Why not?" Maybe the kick of the ginger will help me stay mentally alert and able to navigate what I'm hating to do just as much the third time as the first and second renditions. These last few days have played out like a soap opera, a genre I never watch because I can't handle the continual drama and how everyone always ends up in some love triangle or another. Yet dang, if I haven't landed myself in a doozy. In fact, it's a straight up quadrangle.

"I'll shoot these bids over to you for each project—time and materials, so you can decide which you want to tackle first," he says as he opens another can for me. "Meanwhile, you said you had something to tell me?"

"I do. Shall we sit?" I sink onto the porch swing, shaky with anxiety, wanting to do this well, uncertain of the outcome. He settles beside me, and we turn to half face each other. "Dan. I'm not going to give you one of my long introductions. You already know about my bucket list and my desire to experience a great romance."

He leans back with his arm laying across the back of the swing within touching distance of my shoulder and grins. "Are you thinking you need another installment on experiencing that?"

Whoops. We're already headed off the rails, so I give one a weak "haha" and leap before he goes any further. "You know that old adage about 'when it rains, it pours?' I guess you'd say it's been raining in the romantic realm since I dusted off that item. In fact, it appears I've gone from famine to feast, in a way of speaking."

He tilts his head, brow furrowed. "Are my attentions too much? Because if that's the case, I can move slower, and I apologize—"

"No, no," I protest, touching his arm for a second. "You've been perfect, and I'm enjoying you (blush). What I'm trying to say without sounding like a—a flirt or a profligate, is that I've gone from effectively having no romance in my life to there being three men who're volunteering for the job."

He frowns. "Three? How is there now three of us?"

"It's a huge mess, Dan. That's what I need to tell you about. I feel terrible. I had no idea of any of it when I accepted your dinner invitation. However, yes, all of a sudden, there are three—or two and a half, anyway—because there's you—" I pause, struck by a fear that I've made a massive false assumption about his intentions. "That is unless I misread you on Sunday and in your texts."

"No worries there." He laughs. "I'd say you've got me pinned pretty accurately. I am definitely interested in continuing in the same vein. I always did prefer showing over telling. So, I'll admit it's a bit unnerving to learn that I'm not the only one interested in the same."

My heart drops. "That's what I was afraid of. I would never in a million years want to hurt or unnerve you, Dan. What happened is that I began on item number two on my list. Owning a house, you know. I went on some drive-bys and then met the realtor who's handling the sale of this place." I take a deep breath to steady myself and power on. "He's a very nice man as well, and he seems to like me in an—an intentional way as well, which is very unexpected, and to be completely clear, I hadn't met him when I accepted your dinner invite, and besides, I had no idea that you would—" Gulp.

"Kiss you?" His face is less open than a moment before, but he's hanging in there with me.

"Exactly. Or that I'd like it, and that you'd also be so comfortable to be with and—and all." I'm stuttering, though at this point, I'm less concerned about my delivery than I am about being able to finish. "Then there's Jimmy. I thought he wasn't in the running, if I can say it that way, then out of the blue, he's written another poem for me that clearly fits in the romantic realm. I've suddenly gone from having no admirers, as far as I knew, to having three-ish. It's so mixed up."

Dan sits up a bit straighter, removing his arm from the back of the swing and facing front. "Okay. So there's me. There's this realtor person who I'm going to risk doing the math and checking it against the realty sign over there on the fence post, and assume you met Calvin Robinson, who is arguably one of the nicest, most intelligent, and honorable men I have the privilege of being acquainted with. Am I right?"

"Yes."

He gives a low whistle. "I'll admit it does surprise me that he's engaging in the romantic realm, because the last time we talked about our love lives, he declared himself a lifelong retiree from such activity."

"Apparently he's making an exception?" I shrug and grimace.

"I hope not." Dan says with another frown. "That's some stiff competition. So, I'm up against Cal Robinson and your Jimmy? Or is there someone else I should be aware of who has discovered you're a gem?"

I snort. "No, thankfully, that's the lot of you. What a crazy situation. I told Cal about you yesterday, and I told Jimmy about both of you this morning."

"I really appreciate that your attempt to get ahead of this train and flag it down before it runs too far from the station, if it hasn't already." He manages a smile that doesn't quite reach his eyes and squeezes my heart further. "What did Cal say?"

"That he'll take his chances."

"Ah. How'd Jimmy take it?"

"He's currently furious with me."

"I'm not surprised he's angry. I'd say it also indicates that apparently in his own mind, he thinks he still has first rights to your heart."

"I think that's the gist of it, though it feels more like proprietorship than romance to me. I know that probably sounds terrible since you were so happy with Rosalie, and now that I've experienced with you a tiny bit of what it feels like to be understood and seen and valued, and meeting Cal who is also very intentionally ticking off some boxes on my Romance Ingredients list as well, I'm not sure that a claim staked four decades ago and not exactly inhabited is enough to trump those things. I'm also not willing to remain starved, waiting for Jimmy to get over being mad, live his dream, and eventually maybe return, only to pick up where we left off."

"Dang, girl. I must say, you don't do things in half measures, do you?"

"Apparently not." I sigh. "To make it complete, my daughter is disgusted with me for even considering being involved with someone not her dad, so that's going to be hard to repair, and I know what I'm doing looks questionable."

"You certainly have yourself a whopper of a situation, Eisel." Dan stares off across the fields for a long moment, shaking his head. Now he's squinting up at the sky.

I have no idea what he's thinking. His eyes have turned a deep gray-blue and he doesn't meet my gaze. Maybe he'll say, "It's been fun while it lasted," and drive me home. I sigh again. "Yes, it's quite a dilemma. The only thing I know to do about any of it is tell each of you the truth about the others so it's out in the open, and I've done that. Now I guess I simply let the situation play out. Assuming any of you two and a half/three wonderful men decide to stay in the picture, I know there'll come a time when I'll have to make a choice. However, I can't choose right now."

"Nor should we expect you to at this stage."

At that response, the tears I've been suppressing spring up (I certainly do cry quite a bit, I realize). "Really?"

"Really."

I blink them back. "Please. Tell me why you say that."

"My thought is that if we weren't all in our sixties with all the givens we've acquired—say, if we were all eighteen again—how reasonable would you say it is for three dudes to decide they're interested in one desirable gal, and then force her to choose between them with a week's worth of measurable data?"

"Interesting." Sitting up a bit straighter, I fish around in my pocket for a tissue.

"I've been chatting to Rosalie in my mind, here, because she's much less hot-headed than I am and also wiser. I think she'd advocate on your behalf, and that makes me want to do the same. I'll say to you what I would have said if I'd ever had a daughter who had several guys interested in her at the same time, or even if there was only one interested party. I'd tell her, 'Honey, you don't have to pick up the telephone simply because it's ringing.'

In the same way, just because someone likes you doesn't obligate you to like them back or decide in their favor if you don't like them enough to commit in that way. In this situation, if we remove a few details—age, marital status, and such—you're simply the high school dream girl every sane guy wants to date. It's not your fault that you're attractive, funny, honest, and kind."

It's crazy. I just gave him some tough info, yet here he is breaking the situation down into digestible chunks when to me it's a mammoth obstacle. "That's very kind of you, Dan. I guess one thing that complicates the situation even more is I'm struggling with how much I'm enjoying the attention from both you and Cal. I can't seem to find the bravery to put the kibosh on that when I'm barely starting to catch a glimmer of how lovely it is. Yet not doing so feels selfish. Disingenuous. Maybe even narcissistic, as if I'm more interested in how you make me feel than caring about how it might play out for you."

He nods. "I appreciate that, Eisel. I do. If you didn't feel that way, you wouldn't be you, from what I've seen so far. I understand, though. In a way, whether it's because you didn't see it or didn't receive it or both, you don't know what it feels like to be romanced by a man. So going back to my analogy, maybe you're like a teenager in that way as well. First romances are heady, absorbing things. We learn as we go, and it can be confusing. However, I'd say you have a couple of advantages over a teenager even so."

I manage a grin. "Like?"

"Like we three men are, theoretically, more intellectually and emotionally mature and less hormone-driven than our teenage counterparts, so you have a better chance of seeing our true colors without being pressured. You have the same maturity to know to be careful with our hearts and how far you let us go toward engaging yours. That said, each member of this foursome we're discussing is in charge of their own emotions. For good or for ill, we each have the choice of whether we're going to invest."

I blink, wrapping my mind around all these thoughts. "You're right, of course. I hadn't seen it that way before. So, you don't think I'm a terrible immoral person for being a still-married woman letting two perfectly innocent and unsuspecting men pay attention to me while knowing that I can only give my heart to one of you three?"

He gives a lopsided grin. "While it's true that if I heard about this situation down at the coffee shop, I might think you were playing it a bit fast and loose, no one who has actually met you and spent even a little time with you would believe that interpretation. Remember, you didn't ask to be liked. You've done the honorable thing as soon as you realized what was happening. You told us." He nods. "However, there's no denying that you do have yourself a situation, Eisel."

"Don't I just."

He laughs. "Now it's my turn to be honest with you. I've been letting my heart dream about you these last few days, and I'm really enjoying that. I know you're not exactly a free agent, so to speak, and at some point, if you don't want to be with Jimmy, you'll need to take steps to be released from your marriage contract. I understood that from the get-go."

He nods, then reaches out and takes my hand. "I will own to being a taken aback by your announcement about Cal, but you know what? I guess since that's where things stand, I'm okay with it being the situation for as long as it takes you to figure out where your heart is leading you because I like you and enjoy being with you. The fact that other men also like you ramps up the competition and sets me on my mettle." He squeezes my fingers.

"I say let's you and I learn to know each other the old-fashioned way. Go on dates. Have conversations. Do more data gathering, you know? See where it takes us."

I throw my arms around him in a hug. "Thank you, Dan. That is a huge gift. Everything you just shared. I thought you'd become angry, dump me off at my house, and wish you'd never met me."

He holds me away from him so he can see my eyes. "I would never do that," he says, his lips turning up ever so slightly at the corners and his eyes now matching the summer blue backdrop of the sky. "That's not how I operate. Too much hidden agenda in that. Whatever happens, I'll be honest with you all along the way. If I need to step back, I'll endeavor to do it as well as you've done this today." He chucks me under the chin. "Thank you for your honesty and integrity, Eisel. It means more than you know."

For a moment I just sit there. I'm completely at a loss, really. I guess being with one man all these years, I've never really registered that there are other wonderful men in the world besides Jimmy. Men like Dan and like Cal, and probably like my neighbor down the street, if the truth were known, who are simply endeavoring to live their lives in such a way that the footprints they leave on this earth are lasting and life-giving.

I give Dan another hug, longer this time, and we sit there in that embrace until I get a crick in my back and have to straighten out. "My goodness," I say, standing up and twisting side to side to loosen the kink. "This has been quite a day. I feel—I feel—I don't know how I feel."

"Who says you must define it right now? I say we lock up here, and seeing as it's nearly five o'clock anyway, call it a day. If you're up for it, we can swing by Big Maxx Burgers, grab ours to go, and park at the bluff overlook on Highline Drive to watch the sunset before I take you home. Or I can take you straight home if that sounds better."

I slip my hand into his and let myself be in the moment. What *do* I want? "Burgers and sunset with you sounds perfect, Dan Baker."

CHAPTER 18

The burger is magnificent and watching the sun slowly dip below the distant hills even more so. Dan and I sit there on the bluff in the dimness holding hands, and I'm awash with thankfulness that this day that started so badly is ending with friendship from both Cal and Dan, and an open-ended opportunity to let that grow into more.

I don't want to hurry, to miss sweet, still moments like this by jumping to the end merely to erase the uncertainty of the process. Thanks to my promise to Cal and the way both Cal and Dan have stepped up to the plate, I have time, despite what some people might think of me for not making a decision immediately.

Looking over at Dan, I wonder how he's experiencing this moment in the here and now. He catches my eye. "Penny for your thoughts, ma'am?"

"Funny. I was just wondering about yours."

"You first, since I got the drop on you."

I laugh. "I'm sitting here letting the past stay in the past, allowing the future to keep its secrets, and meanwhile endeavoring to stay as completely as possible in the beautiful here and now. Watching the sunset with you. Not sure how I'd improve on this even if I wanted to. Your turn. What are you thinking right now?"

He grins. "You're pretty brave, asking me an open-ended question like that while I'm sitting here watching you watch the sunset."

"I guess I walked right into that, didn't I?" I laugh as if his "watching you" statement didn't just send a jolt of tingling through my center. "But I do want to know, so—"

"Okay. Besides thinking about how nice it feels to be here with you and how much I appreciate your honesty and also how much I'd prefer being the only one on your horizon though I'm up for the challenge? I'm thinking how I should probably let you know that I'm not a very subtle man, if you haven't already figured that out. More doer than planner. I see something I want, and I go after it. This situation has me reining myself in even though I'd really rather strap on my six-shooter and make sure my competition understands where the lines are drawn."

"Cowboy, huh?" I feel that energy emanating off him and have to admit, it's attractive.

"Yes, ma'am." He tips an imaginary hat. "What I said earlier about you not being obligated to return those feelings is striking a little too close to home right now. However, it still holds true, and I'll be reminding myself of that at every turn."

I'd have to be quite oblivious to not see how he watches for my reaction to all of that; how intentional he is with how far he goes with his teasing, testing the limits, not getting too far out in the weeds, but definitely flirting. It's difficult not to be drawn all the way in. He's all-encompassing in a respectful, intentional, and very masculine way. Also, I think he's right—I'm like a teenager without a track record in this realm of romance.

Hopefully my "winging it" approach is going to suffice, because by the time Dan drops me off at my house, I feel fully in sync with his sense of humor and personality. The more we laugh and chat, the more I admire him, and the less I can decipher my feelings. He's an all-around great guy, worth knowing a lot better. He hops out of the truck when I do, walks me up to the door, then faces me, one arm up on the door jamb, definitely in my space bubble and hemming me in. However, with his smiling down at me and how good he smells, I don't feel in the least intimidated. More like attracted. Again. Still.

"Eisel, I've enjoyed this day with you quite a bit, even given your news. I know you have a lot to sort through, and I understand you'll need to be gathering more data than you currently have. I intend to add to that information on my behalf on the regular."

"I'm okay with that, if that feels fair to you," I say, smiling up at him. Not flirting, merely telling the truth.

Grinning, he raises one eyebrow. "Like I said—you didn't ask to be liked, so you let me worry about me. I'll trust you to inform me when you do figure out how your heart is leaning." Then he very intentionally slips one hand behind my head and bending down, gives me a soft, lingering kiss before lifting just enough that we're not touching. "Good night, Eisel," he whispers. "Thank you for sharing this day with me." Then he kisses me once more, quick and hard, grins as he brushes my cheek with the back of his fingers and strides off like a cowboy into the desert.

* * *

I wander about in a romantic haze for the rest of the evening, not trying to sort anything out. I relive the moments over the past few weeks when I have experienced that precious commodity I'm calling romance for lack of a more specific term. It's a lot to process. Still, confusion and Jimmy's and Maggie's anger aside, I like it quite fine, thank you.

Speaking of Jimmy, when I check my phone, I see I have a text from him (no surprise there), Maggie's (ditto) and Cal's. The only text I open tonight is Cal's.

I hope things went well with Dan and that your heart is at peace, or as much as it can be with three men setting siege to it. [Heart emoji with bow]. For my part, I plan to do my best to know you deeply and thoroughly, trusting that things will come out right for you in the end.

Smiling, I reply. *You have no idea how much I appreciate that and you, Cal. [Heart eyes emoji].* On the heels of that, I add, *Thankfully, Dan took the news like a gentleman and a friend. Like you, he said he's up for the challenge, and a couple of thoughts he shared give me a bit of perspective as well, so I do have more peace now that all is out in the open.* Send.

As a parting text, I add, *Cal, again, thank you for this morn-ing, for the coffee and the way you sang me out of my emotional nosedive. You're a true friend. Hope you sleep well and that I see you again soon. Very soon.*

After making myself a cup of chamomile tea, I find *Pride and Prejudice* on the TV (the version with Colin Firth and Jennifer Ehrle), to immerse myself in a more graceful era and someone else's drama. I'm more than grateful for the way Dan received my communication today, blown away over his parting kisses and his stating his intentions so clearly. However, I'm worn out after my second emotional marathon of the day and unwilling to think about any of the three contenders or what I should do about them.

★ ★ ★

The next morning, though, I force myself to open Jimmy's text thread. I thought about it last night as I went to sleep; I'll start with his last message, because he would have processed the situation longer at that point than if I took them chronologically. I have no doubt that besides the ten-plus blistering voicemails I'm sure are waiting for me should I decide to listen to them (the answer is no. I will not be doing so), the first six or seven texts will be in a similar triggered vein.

I don't blame him for feeling upset. However, I feel no obliga-tion to shoulder his emotions. As I've already established, they're his. I have a hard enough time dealing with my own. On a good day. So, armed with coffee in my favorite cup, I read his last entry.

Eisel, I'm guessing you're not responding because that's how you deal with my anger. I get it. I am still angry, very much so. However, I know that until I stop aiming it at you, I can't hope you'll engage. I suggest you delete my earlier voicemails. You know how I tend to say things I shouldn't when I'm mad. Maybe texting rather than phone calls is the best way to stay out of the weeds as we talk through this situation, because at the end of the day, we do need to figure it out.

Okay. I'm going to stop texting now and wait for you to answer. Love you. Take care. [Heart emoji].

I breathe out the breath I'd been holding. Actually, that was better than I expected. I'll figure out my response here in a bit. First, I need to touch bases with Kate to confirm we're still on for this morning and apply the same "last text first" strategy with Maggie's messages. Then I'll allow myself to open Dan's and Cal's, as I see a blue dot on both of those, like saving dessert for last or rewarding myself for doing the hard stuff first.

Morning, girlfriend. We still on for ten?

I'll be there. Can't wait to catch up.

I paste a thumbs up on her response and then move to Maggie's thread, hoping she's had some time to process. As it turns out, she has. *Mom, I'm sorry I went ballistic with you,"* she texts. *The truth is, your life is your life, and your love life even more so. I have no right to demand anything of you or judge you. I'd love to meet you at the park on Thursday, this time to listen. I love you. Thank you for loving me even when I throw a fit.*

Sweet Mags, I text back. *Thank you for this text. I look forward to seeing you and Little Miss Preshiness on Thursday. Meanwhile, know that I completely forgive you. I understand this is a lot to process for all of us. See you there, and please send me some Portia pics :-) [heart eyes emoji].*

I sit for a moment letting profound thankfulness envelope me for this olive branch from Maggie. Finishing my coffee, I ponder what the day may hold, and ultimately revisit Dan's statement that in some ways, I'm like a teenager experiencing romance for the first time. I had suspected this, and it's hard not to feel sheepish about how completely inexperienced and naive I am in this realm. He's right when he says it's heady stuff. Saying I'm the high school dream girl every sane guy wants to date—that's completely sweet of him.

When I think about teenage Eisel Wellington, the truth is, I never got to be a teen emotionally or relationally, because my mother was so paranoid I'd do something immoral with a person of the male gender—though how she thought that could happen I have no idea, since she watched me like a Navy Seal team on a reconnaissance mission, complete with spy network, and never allowed me to be anywhere alone with a guy. Thus, I never made it further than the edge of the pond in the flirting department, much less the ocean of romance, because Archer and I were barely beginning to learn the basic elements when we broke up.

When I met Jimmy a couple of years later, he was recuperating from being rejected for coming on a bit too strong with his girlfriend. From what I remember of our meeting at the young single's group at church, I caught his eyes and smiled. He smiled back. I went over and struck up a conversation, and that pattern continued until we were walking down the aisle, because when you have one person desperate to escape their home situation and the other merely hoping not to do anything wrong, you don't have romance. You have two young people who cling together.

There was no need to flirt or discover the wonder of a romantic connection. Then we were deep into the logistics, complications, and joys of marriage and parenthood, and any longings I had for romance were smothered under the sheer workload, then veneered by time and routine.

Bottom line, I never actually ended up getting to be that starry-eyed teenager in the first flush of a romance, experiencing the level of wonder I'm having with Cal and Dan. Teenagers don't have a clue about what they're doing most of the time. They're exploring and learning from their experiences. In this way, I think Dan is correct. I find comfort in knowing I have a precedent for what I'm doing. Even though sixty-four is a bit late for first times, it is a blast. Complicated, yes, full of drama, and a blast.

Dan also nailed it dead center that the teenage version of me would feel obligated to give those guys a quick decision while trying not to hurt any of them. Not so different from the Eisel of today, I think with a grimace. I know I can only have one man in my heart in a romantic way. That's never been the confusion or the question. It's the "who" that has me stymied right now.

I'm still in shock that both Cal and Dan decided they're up for the challenge of vying to become that one person for me, and though I don't know where Jimmy will stack out in the long run, he left no doubt he considers himself in the running as well, whatever questions I may have about that. I'm thankful for the clarity clear intentions bring, because it takes the responsibility off me for the present. They're grown men, and as Dan pointed out yesterday, I'm not forcing them to pay attention to me.

As unlikely as this scenario is, all I need to do now that I've told them about each other is to simply be. Leave the wooing and the winning of my heart in their court and give myself the freedom to respond so I can know whom my heart chooses.

That feels scary. Also nice.

The thought that I could finish out my days with someone who adores me boggles my imagination and sparkles in my heart. On the other hand, I could end up with none of them, I guess. That's a harsh reality I pondered last night during *Pride and Prejudice*. What if my heart leans toward one of them, and he throws in the towel before I reach the point of choosing? Like

Miss Elizabeth Bennett, I'd rather have no one than to be with someone but missing the mutual romantic element that frankly seems like the rarest, most fragile, and elusive commodity on the face of the planet, now that I've had a few opportunities to experience what it is like. If I do end up with that, I will treasure it. I won't take it for granted and become blind to the gift that it is.

I know I've not been amazing in that realm thus far; I can do better. I *will* do better. The thing I need to remember right now is that I've got time. Hearts can't be rushed, mine included. Feeling bolstered by both Cal's and Dan's thoughts along that vein, I repeat the mantra to myself. "I've got time." Time to let my heart relax. Time to gather data. To respond on a deeper level. To be less starved, more open-eyed to what is in front of me, and to figure out where Jimmy ultimately wants to be in the mix.

It may be a dilemma, yet it's also feeling a bit more like an adventure than the mad downhill plummet of yesterday.

I open Dan's text first. *Thanks for yesterday, Eisel. It was a real pleasure, despite developments. I intend to send those bids for your house improvements by end of day. Meanwhile, I want to reiterate that until I notify you to cross my name off your list or you give me notice, I'm considering you fair game [Cowboy hat, pistol, winky face, thumbs up].*

I tag that with a heart as a placeholder. Grinning about his message as I dress, I apply a bit of makeup and give a final tweak to the hemline of the seafoam linen tank I've paired with my jeans and huaraches this morning. Confusion and uncertainty aside, I'm happy to report my new outfits have boosted my overall look. I find comfort in this small brightness.

I text Dan as I locate my keys. *I think yesterday was so nice because you are. Thanks again for understanding my dilemma, for being so clear in your intentions, and for the perspectives you shared. For the record, I have a soft spot for cowboys ;-)* I add a second message. *Regardless of where this crazy quadrangle ends up, I'd love to establish a monthly "burgers by sunset" routine with you, if you're amenable.*

I can't see Jimmy thinking a burger-on-the-bluff with Dan is necessary, should he come and win me back. No worries. I'll cross that bridge if I come to it. We've lived so much life together, Jimmy and me. Every up and every down for four decades and counting. I'm sure we could solve that as well. If. If archeology in Peru or somewhere else in the world isn't more important than me. If it is? That's another conversation.

Jimmy's where he is right now inside as well as geographically. That makes sense. He's a person, and that personhood needs to count for something in the overall equation. The fact he feels dead-ended is not my fault, though I empathize. Who wants to dribble out their last years doing same ole same ole? I don't, and I wouldn't want him to feel he must, either.

At the same time, I struggle to see where I fit into his picture. What's the value of carrying on my end of the bargain while Jimmy's not present with me emotionally, mentally, or physically? Do I sacrifice the rest of my days on the altar of a vacated marriage? I'm not interested in doing that. This much I do know—I'm in a season I didn't ask for, inching my way through, searching for a clear path. Still, for all the upheaval, it's at the same time somehow slightly magical.

Or is that how romance always feels?

Maybe what I need to consider is removing the obligation between Jimmy and I so if we discover that the most important thing in life is each other, it'll be a cognizant choice for both of us, not a default setting we're already locked into. How did Dan express it—remove the contract? That way, romance will have a chance if Jimmy still wants one with me. After all, I would never have gone to this place of separation even in my mind without Jimmy opting to follow his archeological dream before he dies.

To be clear, I don't think anything is wrong with him doing that. Actually, quite the opposite. I see something very right that at this stage in our lives, he's still growing and dreaming and not merely sitting by the fire in an old rocking chair, as has been portrayed as inevitable. In my eyes, it's rather remarkable he's brave enough to do it.

Could he have done so in a better way? Absolutely. Could he have done so in a way that didn't turn my world upside down and leave me behind? Knowing me, I'm not sure. Honestly, I don't think that even if he'd prepped me and included me and walked me through the details for the past however long, I would have accepted his desire to go. Rather, I would have resisted to the bitter end, because I wouldn't want to go to Peru with him, and I wouldn't want to live here in Ranger Falls without him. Unless—and I'm speculating here—unless he also romanced the heck out of me while including me in the plan in some form or another, which is hard for me to visualize.

He didn't, of course, so that's neither here nor there. I'm not wrong for not wanting what Jimmy wants, though I'm not super proud about the fact that I'm ninety-four point-six percent sure I would have focused on keeping my world stable more than on assisting him in dream fulfillment if he *had* tried to keep me in the loop. Without a doubt, it would have been braver and more inclusive. I would have felt wanted. However, I'm not sure it would have affected the ultimate outcome.

Now that he's been the brave one, and I'm seeing him from a bit of a distance (no pun intended), I would rather be (read that as "become") the kind of person who views others for who they are in themselves rather than from how they affect or intersect with my life. I know that's a human tendency, yet now that I'm out of the boat and navigating the rapids of relationship solo, I want to let this experience be an opportunity to grow, not see it as a threat to maintaining life as I know it.

I need to message Jimmy back. Later. After I've had a few hours to process these thoughts. It's a good thing I'm about to have another cup of coffee with Kate. My first one was apparently not enough to lift me out of my usual mental-emotional stewpot, though today feels less intense than I expected it to, so maybe I'm progressing.

Opening Cal's text, I feel myself relaxing. Interesting. Even thinking about him is starting to have that effect on me. Of course, he has rescued me in a remarkable way and then made sure I know he'll be my friend regardless of the direction my heart takes me, so that makes sense on a neurological level as well.

Any chance I could talk you into going to dinner with me tonight?

Those words send a tingle through me along with a whole-body release of tension. *One hundred percent chance. I pay this time.*

His text shoots back so fast I hardly have time to smile. *You might have to fight me for the check. That could be fun. [Winky face emoji]. I'll pick you up at six. Any special spot you'd like to go?*

Six is perfect. When I snatch the bill from you, please don't make a scene. [grinning face with sweat drop]. As far as location, feel free to surprise me as long as you don't choose a seafood exclusive menu and give me a heads up if a dress is required.

You got it, Lady Jane. See you then. [Heart emoji].

I will be looking forward to that, Mr. Calvin Robinson. I will indeed.

CHAPTER 19

"So, Eisel, spill the beans. I haven't had a catch up with you in days. Plus, you'll never believe the latest at the office," Kate says as we settle into our favorite leather chairs at Sierra Roasters.

"You first. Office drama seems fitting over coffee." I grin and clink my cup to hers.

"I think you could sum it up in one word: incompetence. Of course, I could use a few thousand to make sure I'm thorough."

I choke on my drink. "Let me guess—another variation of 'Did you want *me* to do that? I thought you were simply making a suggestion'."

"Basically. Also, someone keyed the CEO's car. I think I know who, and really, except that I'm philosophically opposed to the concept of revenge and vandalism, he deserves it. It wasn't me, though. I swear."

"Kate, you're a caution." I like that word a lot since Cal tagged me with it. It feels daring and funny and out there in a good way.

"Haha." She regales me with anecdotes from her office until I'm laughing so hard, I have to cross my legs to prevent an impromptu dash to the ladies' room.

"How about you and your last few days, E? You're looking pretty twinkly eyed for someone whose husband left her for the wilds of Peru not all that long ago."

"You have no idea. You know about how I told Cal about Dan, and how nice he was about it, so you're caught up to yesterday morning." Then I tell her about Jimmy's anger, how Cal brought coffee and Maggie's tirade, and Kate "oofs" in all the right places. However, I find I want to keep the sweetness of Cal's kindness, his singing and our dancing to myself, so I skip over that. To me, though, it's the one piece that makes sense of everything.

"Then Dan and I went hiking yesterday afternoon and afterwards we went out to inspect the house I'm buying so I'll know what I need to fix first."

"Girl, you pack more drama into a day than everyone in my office combined," she says, toasting my cup. "To Eisel McCord, off-roader extraordinaire."

"Silly." I grin. "I'm merely living my life."

"Yours makes mine look like kindergarten nap time. Without the graham crackers. Come on, spill the rest, girl."

"Okay. So, after Dan did the inspection, I told him about Cal."

"No way. What did he say?"

"You've known him longer than I have, so you can probably guess he was phenomenal. He told me that without a doubt, he does like me, wants to continue getting to know me, and he gave me some very helpful perspectives on how a basically sane woman could think about finding herself the center of so much male attention."

"That's Dan Baker for you. Was I right or was I right? He's so gorgeous, too."

We chat about everything and anything after that, catching up until she runs out of time. "What do you think you're going to do about Jimmy?" she asks as we bus our dishes.

"Excellent question. I'm still figuring that out."

"If anyone can do so, it's you, girlfriend. I'll be waiting for your next update."

I head back home where I plan to spend a long, leisurely day doing odds and ends, catching up on emails, bills and such before Cal picks me up for dinner. Jimmy left me with a crash course on which ones we have on auto debit and which require other payment methods, thankfully.

Jimmy.

I need to answer his text, and it takes me until early afternoon to ready myself for the task. I want to be so careful with his heart and also with mine. For so long, those two have seemed to be one and the same. Sadly, not anymore. I think of all the love songs we used to listen to together. The many long nights we've spent in each other's arms. I'm not sure what happened. When did we stop listening? Dancing? Being so integral to each other?

I know we reached a point where each of us began to go after the ghosts in our pasts, and that is ever a solitary journey. You start out young and defenseless inside, and you must let go of blaming other people for not preparing you, for the way they left you tiny and trembling and needing the nurturing and the comfort they didn't seem to be able to give you when they were your only hope for those essentials.

That window closes for all of us, and we must forge on, giving to our own little inner person the compassion and comfort it needs from us first before it can receive it from others. I think that's really what was going on when Jim and I had some of our largest collisions over the years. I used to want Jimmy to change—how he talked to me, how he was in so many ways in order that I wouldn't trigger and feel those old wounds aching. He did the same. Bit by bit, though, we've been learning to own our own "stuff," gaining in health within ourselves. I think we've turned a corner and are on converging paths.

At least that was how I saw it until he went to Peru. Maybe we have more road to travel, but I did think we were in the final solo stretch. Hoped we were anyway. I hoped that we are grown up enough to walk together again, this time not codependent but walking hand in hand as fellow humans sharing our journeys with each other, interdependent. Entwined on the heart level.

I say a little prayer that Jimmy will hear in my words that I am for him, not against him. That I think he's a hero, not a villain in our story. That there are two heroes' journeys here, and if he wants to try, there may still be a chance we'll find each other at the end of them. I guess the real question here is whether we'll end up as friends or restored lovers. At this point, I'm hardly out of the woods from the wounds he opened up with his leaving.

Though I've tried and tried to make sense of it all, I'm not sure of anything except that I've got to answer him before more time goes by. I know this is going to be long. How do you curate two hearts at once? Texting can't do an adequate job, so I opt for email.

"Dearest Jimmy John," I type.

"Anger is hard, and I appreciate you not aiming yours at me. This is perhaps our biggest mountain peak yet. I don't know the path through. I did have a thought, though. I don't think it will sound like a good one to you on the first reading, but I'm hoping you'll look at it from all angles and see it as a way to move forward without either of us sacrificing our dreams. Maybe they're not the same dreams we used to have. Maybe we've grown and forgotten which things really matter. Or maybe what matters has evolved. Yet we're still here, you and me. Still friends in spite of everything. Maybe what we end up with will not look like it did, and in some ways, maybe that's alright, because what we could find may be better.

The thought I referred to is that I plan to have divorce papers drawn up. Not because we don't love each other, but to clarify exactly where romantic love fits into the rest of our lives. You're in Peru, and I'm proud you're brave enough to pursue your dream of working an archeological dig again. It appears that dream has eclipsed me in your focus and passion. I don't blame you, though, and I think what you said is true—maybe it could be good for both of us, because I would have gone on to the end of life the way we were, not perhaps giving you what you are worthy of and not seeing or dreaming big enough to ask for more for myself.

Now that I've had time to think about it, one thing I'm certain on is that I don't want to take your dream away from you, Jimmy John. That would be selfish of me. Unfair to you. At the same time, neither do I want to wait until you feel you've done all you want to do down there in Peru. What if there's more after that? Another dig you want to explore, another adventure you don't even know about yet that will capture you after your time in Peru. Maybe you'll fall so in love with this season of your life you won't ever come back to Ranger Falls and life with me."

Putting those words out in plain sight—that he may never come back—shreds my heart. What wasn't already in tatters from his leaving. Blotting my eyes, and blowing my nose, I proceed. "I don't want to wait to see if you do, and I don't want to spend my days wondering if you will. Pushing pause on my life for years simply waiting to see if our paths will converge again isn't how I want to end up. I really think that the best thing for us both is to let you go, Jimmy; set you free to be and do anything you want, go anywhere that calls to your heart."

"I want that same freedom. It means you need to know that if you come back—even if it's next week and you're wanting to be together with me, that may not happen. Or it could. I don't know. You may be too early. Or too late. Or perhaps exactly in time."

I try not to think of how he'll take that. I just need to finish this email. "Please don't take that as a threat. I hardly know how to navigate what's happened to me. To us. I believe removing the obligation of marriage will give us both breathing room. It will free you from feeling compelled to return before you've even had a chance to really live this dream of yours to its fullest. It will also free me of competing with that dream of yours. I want to level the playing field and see where things lie once the dust settles down.

"Finally, I want to remind you of this song we used to enjoy, 'Setting Sail.' Some of the lyrics maybe don't fit our situation as well as they once did, but I know you'll remember the things worth remembering, which are many. I think early on, I did feel as if we were invincible together as the lyrics say. I assumed we still were until you made your announcement. Now somehow the second verse that never quite resonated with me before seems most fitting, the one about us building a house out of nowhere and hanging our hearts on the walls, then becoming so familiar with that life we let it crumble around us."

Tears stream unchecked down my face as I write. "We're facing the wind and hail again, aren't we, Jimmy-boy. I don't know about you these days, but me? I'm scared of a lot of things. Of being stuck. Of being alone. Of hurting the people I love. Of being hurt by them. Maybe these particular waves and wind we're navigating solo instead of hand in hand, yet whatever comes, one thing I know—I will always love you and love the years we had together."

"If we have more, living in the same house together, sharing coffee every morning and figuring out what's for dinner—if we can find a way to repair this chasm that has opened up between us, that could be lovely. If we don't, please promise me we'll always—*always*—be friends. Maybe sometime I'll even come and visit you in Peru, simply to see you again and hear your voice telling me what you're doing and loving and dreaming about, even if it is not a world we built together. Because I treasure you and your friendship, Jimmy John, and I always will.

With all my love,

Eisel."

I don't even read the email through again to soften or change or agonize over the wording. It feels like the truest thing I can say, the best way to clear the rubble so Jimmy can decide what his world needs to hold, and so I can do the same. Now that I've sent it, though, I don't know. What if all this questioning and angst and pain is only on my side? What if Jimmy really is fine and wants to come back once Peru is out of his system? Can I wait? Can I pick up where I left off with him, now that I've tasted how amazing it is to be as seen and understood and valued as I've felt this past week?

How hungry my heart has been—has always been—to feel what I'm experiencing with Dan and Cal. I can't really sort out if it was there with Jimmy all along, because he's gone, and they're here actively initiating and wooing me. I'm not willing or brave enough to tell them to exit my life and leave me to carve out a single existence on the off chance that the lack of romance with Jimmy may have been a false perception.

I don't believe that's all on me, though. What I'm seeing about romance is that it's not passive. It seeks. It seeks and gives and looks for. It initiates and also responds. Receives. Enjoys. Maybe ultimately, Jimmy and I have been more focused on hoping the other person would be the seeker, and in so doing, we haven't risked being the one to reach out. Traumatized children do that—life is too uncertain for those of us that have grown up anxious to push out into the relational unknown. At least that's what strikes me at this moment.

I wanted Jimmy to woo me, romance me, not merely because that's fun and easier, but because initiating without certainty is scary. Knowing his history—his childhood was no walk in the park either—he's been largely doing the same. Granted, there are the flowers, the coffee, and I'm sure other occasions I never picked up on, though I do so wish I had. There are also things I did that he didn't seem to notice. Maybe things would be different if we tried again. That's not clear to me, and we may never really know for sure.

Having had to let Jimmy go, having my life turned upside down, and endeavoring to pick up the pieces, I feel so altered these days. I'm still confused, yet clearer about what I want in the relationship realm, much more so than I would have thought a few months could produce. I'm stronger. More capable. I feel more valuable. Not that I would never make this a practice—this having multiple men paying me attention—yet having Cal and Dan, these amazing, thoughtful humans, be so respectful and honoring of my heart, desiring me, championing me, and willing to spend the effort and risk the pain of investing their hearts while waiting until I figure myself out? That has been eye-opening.

I don't know what Jimmy will think about my plan. The D word. I'll wait to send the actual papers until he answers my email, because I don't want him to be blindsided. I can give him that. I guess I also want to hear in his own words where his heart is at with me. That said, my decision to have the documents drawn up and when to send them will not be based on whether he wants it to happen or not. I don't say that in a flippant or combative way, plus I can't see him ever thinking it's a good thing, though I hope he'll eventually be okay with this course of action.

Either way, from the standpoint that we each make our own choices, it makes sense to me, and I'm half this equation. As long as that marriage contract stands, I am held static even though one half of the relationship has left. Left with no declaration or intention, apparently, to return any time soon if ever, and that changes everything for me.

Kate asked me if I was suffering from abandonment trauma, to which I answered, "Duh." I've struggled with that my whole growing up, and up to now, Jimmy was the only important person in my life who hadn't let me down or left me alone.

Until now.

Most of our marriage, I let Jimmy's decisions lead, even if I didn't love them. I was too afraid of abandonment and too conflict-avoidant to scuffle over the bulk of them anyway. I have a new choice in front of me now though: I can continue to let his decisions dictate what I do, or I can make my own.

★ ★ ★

My reaction when I see Calvin on my doorstep that evening is visceral. It seems like forever since I saw him instead of only yesterday morning. I don't say anything. I just step out the door and wrap my arms around him, bury my face in his neck, and breathe him in.

He softens to me as I hold on, enfolding me in his arms, pulling me closer into him "Well now, Eisel Jane. You sure do know how to make a fellow feel welcome."

Something about his words and the husky way he says them strike me funny. "You seem to have a magnetic effect on me, Mr. Robinson, if you haven't noticed." I give him a quick squeeze and step away. "I'm sure my neighbors have given up trying to figure out what's going on over here at the McCord's," I say as I close the door behind me. "Next thing I know, one of them is going to come borrow some sugar or butter to get the real scoop."

He laughs as he hands me into the car, and we follow our usual routine. I'm so raw from composing that email to Jimmy, I'm like a snail that forgot its shell. All my emotions are close to the surface and sensitive beyond the norm (which is saying something, since sensitive is apparently my middle name most times as it is). So when Cal pulls my seatbelt out and hands it to me, I tear up at the simple kindness of his gesture.

"Hey, hey, honey. What's wrong? Are you okay?" He catches an escaped tear with his thumb. "We don't need to go tonight if you're not up to it."

I shake my head. "I'm okay," I whisper, squinting my eyes. "I wrote Jimmy an email, and it brought so many things to the surface. I sent it, and that's that. I don't think he's going to like it, though from what he texted earlier, he'll try not to aim his anger at me."

"Hmph. I should hope not." Cal huffs as he shuts my door.

I'm thankful for the quietness as we drive. For the lack of questioning and solution giving.

"You okay with a steak dinner, Lady Jane?"

"Sounds lovely."

As we settle in at our table in the upscale restaurant, I sigh. "I don't want to talk about my situation right now, Cal. Would you please tell me more about yourself? Tell me about how things you think about in the night, dreams you have, and some of your favorite things."

He smiles at me across the table and shakes his head. "There you go doing that thing you do."

"What would that be?"

"Wanting to know me. Do you know how many people are so intent on being known that they never even think to inquire?"

My turn to shake my head. "Their loss," I say. "Because I find you intriguing. You're like an ever-unfolding book. Every page holds something new and interesting, and I never want to come to the end of the story." I reach out for his hand, and something about the way he lays it in mine seems like a statement of trust. "I really do want to know you better, Cal."

"I'd like that as well. However, I've never been very good at sharing those details. Maybe we'd better play Ten Questions or something to prime the pump."

The evening is full of our laughter and questions and a few tears on my part. Fill in the blanks any way you'd like to, with the understanding that by the time Cal walks me to my door, I'm feeling much more myself and completely taken by him. Again. "Can you come in for a few minutes?" I ask. "I promise I'm not going to drop another dilemma on you or collapse in tears. At least, I'm sure about the first and relatively certain about the second."

"I'm willing to risk whatever you want to dish out in order to spend a bit more time with you."

We sit at the kitchen island sipping tea and picking up from dinner, chat about nothing and everything. He tells me more about his two kids who live in a different state. We trade pictures of grandkids—he's got three to my one. At last, he drains his cup and stands to go.

"Thank you for the lovely evening, Eisel Jane. Apologies for rigging the check situation." He winks, and I laugh.

"You're tricky. I'll hand that to you. Not to worry. I'll get back at you for that."

"Sounds like something to look forward to," he says, his smile soft as we're standing there in the entryway. I want him to take me in his arms, to feel the electric buzzing as we touch, and experience the comfort and care soaking into me in his warm embrace. I worry that is selfish of me, though, so I hold where I am, gazing into his chocolate eyes for a long moment.

Time hangs in the balance, and just when I'm sure he's leaning in to kiss me, he doesn't. Instead, he traces my hairline with a gentle finger, stroking down the side of my face until he reaches my chin, then tips it up so our eyes meet again. "You're mighty hard to say goodbye to, lady. I'm hoping—" As if listening to a voice I can't hear, he pauses, then finishes his sentence. "I'm hoping that someday I won't have to."

CHAPTER 20

Over the next week, I turn the question of divorce inside out, examining it every which way, and then I call my lawyer, Scott. I need to do this now. I can't allow Cal and Dan to risk their hearts while mine is legally not available. I also can't live with the limbo of always wondering if Jimmy is going to rally, hoping, not hoping, hoping again. Nor can I continue acting like I'm not married to him when I still am, at least on paper.

I thought I could wait to file until I knew which, if any of the three my heart would choose. Now I see I need to make this decision about divorce independent of who I may choose. My original thought holds true. I need to level the playing field for all our sakes, including mine. So I sign the papers, citing abandonment as cause, because it's true.

"Jimmy," I think as I flip through the pages of the divorce decree. "Whether by intent or default, you really have abandoned me. Emotionally and physically. The longer you go without answering my email, the deeper that drives into my heart. I think you could still rescue our marriage if you wanted to try, but only if you don't wait any longer."

The finality of signing that document shrinks my heart down to golf ball size, dense, aching, and uncomforted. I don't tell anyone what I've done, thus the whole ordeal is riddled by loneliness. At the same time, a little of the weight on my heart eases as I walk out. Scott will wait to send the papers to Jimmy until I give the word, but I know I've begun the process, and that's what matters.

If Jimmy responds to my email by saying he's heading back to Ranger Falls because he decides he loves me most and wants to spend his last years with me—that he wants to romance me—I'll let Scott know to hold the papers in my folder for now, and I will try with my whole heart to build the kind of romantic connection with Jimmy I so long to have. But—and this is a solid full stop—if Jimmy doesn't do that, I'll call Scott and have him serve the papers.

The days roll by. Two weeks. Three weeks. Four, then five. They're full of Cal—closing on the house, dinners, long conversations, and dancing to music that makes my heart soar. Full of Dan—replacing the roof and overseeing various repairs on my very own historic house, long hikes in the mountains laced with laughter, an occasional burger by sunset.

I visit Miss Millsbaugh with another peace offering, this time homemade blackberry jam. She's less prickly than before (which may be because I made sure not to go close to mealtime) and I learn a bit more history on the house, which I can't wait to move into once Dan and his team finish all the improvements.

However, Jimmy is still missing in action. Why is he delaying? Does he care at all? Should I simply have the papers served and be done with it? However, every time I start to call Scott to initiate delivering the decree, Jimmy texts to say he's writing an email and thanks me for my patience.

I miss him as if he's already gone far beyond Peru emotionally, and I'm increasingly afraid of what his email will convey, afraid of his anger. Afraid of further emotional disconnection. I have a feeling that when he sends it, the life I've built over the months since he left will come crashing down, too fragile, too sweet to withstand the blow. Yet when it does arrive in my inbox, it's not the accusing, resistant version I anticipated. It's the Jimmy John I know and love and desperately miss, and after this email, I lose my bearings a second time.

Dear Eisel, it reads.

I don't want a divorce from you. That seems so final. I don't know how long I'll be here in Peru, and it's hard to think about coming back to Ranger Falls and not being with you there. So if you decide to file papers, that's your call. Please know that's not my choice or preference. I don't want that, and I'm not asking for that. However, if I'm served papers, I'll sign them, I guess, because at that point, it will be clear you have moved on or you want to. If that occurs, I won't blame you. I'll blame myself. I didn't realize it at the time, yet I can see now that if I hadn't left for Peru, none of this would be happening.

This situation is all on me. I admit that, and because it is, I appreciate your validating my dream all the more and how you've made space for me to explore it without incrimination or guilt. I guess I didn't realize the ramifications at the time. I also want to say that I'm really very sorry about how I sprang the whole thing on you. That wasn't brave of me nor kind. I was so afraid of not getting to go, I made you into a big, powerful opponent who wanted to prevent me from doing so. In reality, you were just my sweet wife whose dreams don't include living in the wilds of anywhere and whom I blindsided and then abandoned.

I'm not proud of how I went about it at all, and knowing your family history, I'm deeply sad at the way I did that to you, who has never not supported me once we hashed out the particulars.

I'm also struck as I write this that I still have at least a small chance to turn this whole thing around right now if I was willing to leave what I'm doing here and endeavor to win your heart back. I know you'd let me try, anyway, because you're kind that way, and you always play fair.

I still feel incredibly angry when I think of other men paying attention to you and of you responding to their attention. However, I have to face the fact I could be doing that also. I could be up there with my hat in the ring, like the song you sent (and yes, I remember listening to that with you and the way we smiled at each other, and where that smile took us).

I even reached the point of looking up airplane tickets back to you and Ranger Falls. Yet every time, I didn't click that 'purchase ticket' button. So as much as I flinch to admit it, I've got to call it what it is—I'm not throwing my hat in the ring this time.

I guess I thought prior claim cinched things up tight enough to let me do whatever I felt I needed to do and still be able to keep the life we built together. That was my understanding, and now that I'm seeing it's not yours, I know I need to act if I'm to salvage anything between us. Yet I've let another week go by, which tells me what? That I'm too chicken to risk it? That I'm too desperate to sacrifice this last adventure of a life that has held very few true achievements on the chance I can win your heart back to a better place than where I left it? Or that my love for you is not the most important thing to me? Maybe a bit of all three, and that's hard for me to admit to myself, much less to you.

I know you realize all of the above, and it must feel terrible to you, my dear. The more I think about what I've done to you, the sadder I feel for you. For me. For us. I want to think that if we'd lived our everyday lives differently—if I'd focused more on how special you are to me, and if you'd done the same, maybe our marriage would have seemed like the greatest adventure I could have, eclipsing Peru and archeology and anything else, and we'd be having coffee together this morning.

Yet here we are. I don't hold you responsible for that. I hit the ball into your court, I guess you'd say, and only the fact that you yourself deal in authenticity forces me to concede that you have free choice to do with it what seems best to you and for you. Demanding otherwise is not fair nor kind. I can't ask that what you've been handed by me — a nebulous "maybe someday"—be enough for you.

Dear Eisel. I do love you. I feel we're so enmeshed, sometimes it seems as if we're one and the same. Yet I'm having such an amazing, difficult, wonderful time down here in Peru I don't want to give it up. I know that sounds terrible and selfish, and what can I expect you to do about it? It's not fair to ask you to take second place, to put your life on hold for mine. A location and an experience shouldn't be more important than a person. More than that, archeology itself is not more important than a person, for all its historic value. I know that, and feel like a relational disaster—a selfish, self-oriented man—especially when I picture you there at home without me.

Yet I also know that if I were to leave now, I'd never make it back to Peru or any other dig, and much as I wouldn't want to, I'm afraid I'd end up regretting that choice and resenting you for the rest of whatever bit of life I have left–as if I could blame you, because you're not asking me to come back—you've set me free and even have the grace and maturity to wish me well. I appreciate that more than you know.

I'm so sorry, sweetheart. You don't deserve this. I'm sorry that after all these years and all we've lived together, I haven't kept you at the top of my priority list, and I'm so sorry I can't seem to reorder that list even now. If I thought I could be different—if I could rid myself of this fear of dying and having nothing to show for my life—I'd do it in a heartbeat. I'd show up on your doorstep and give it the old college try anyway.

I've even thought about inviting you down here if you cared to come so we could be together again, but I'm sorry—I think I'd still be on this strange scary solitary journey that has shut you out from my inner heart. I don't know how to stop doing that. You deserve more. It's not fair of me to keep you hoping I can rally. Not fair of me to ask you to take me back only to break your heart again, and as much as I wish it wasn't true, I'm afraid that's how it would go.

Maybe it's like the dragon in the story we used to read to Maggie—I didn't realize I was nurturing something in my heart that would lead me away from you and consume the life we made with each other. Not another woman. A different life altogether. I can't see me ever, ever being with anyone except you. I'm turning seventy, and I feel as if I've ruined everything I ever built. Yet somehow down here, I feel more alive than I have since we walked down the aisle all those years ago.

I don't know what that makes me, but I know what it leaves me—your friend. Definitely that. I promise with all my heart that I will always be your friend. I will try to love who you love just because you are precious to me. I will come to your aid any time, day or night. I'll help you when you need it. I look forward to the day when you step off the plane in Lima, and I throw my arms around you and—

I must stop. I need to close this email, gather the pieces of my heart, and try to make sense of it all. You've done nothing wrong, dear sweet Eisel. I'm sorry for how I reacted when you told me other men are attracted to you. Of course they are. They'd be foolish not to see what a wonderful woman you are.

I wish for you the very best. I wish that if you want it, some-one will love you in the way that I don't seem to be able to these days. I wish for you that you would feel full and free and secure, and that you would know I cherish all the days we had together, even if I can't seem to find it in me to cherish ones to come.

Thank you for loving me like you have and like you do. Thank you for understanding. For not blaming. For being the perfect woman, and for letting me be the imperfect man that I am while still holding out your hand in friendship. I suppose a braver person would call you to say all these things, but I don't know if I could really articulate all this on the phone, and I think if you started to cry, I would begin to as well, and we might never stop.

All that being so, I trust you, dear Eisel Jane. I know that you will never take advantage of me, and in fact, I charge you with being fair to yourself in this situation. Like I said, I will never ask you for those papers. However, if you reach that point, promise me you won't overcompensate. I really don't care about any of our assets. It's merely stuff, and we've got it all in trust anyway. If you're okay doing so, we can leave the trust intact and use the money as we're doing now. You take what you need. I'll do the same. When we're both gone, it goes to Maggie. I'm still great with all that. If you could hold on to my dad's old twenty-two caliber rifle and his Korean war medals for me, I'd take that kindly.

Signing off for now and sending my love and prayers your way to soften this message, if that is possible,

Jimmy John, your lifelong friend, whatever else I am

PS. The song, "Through the Years," says what I feel, and as I listen to the part about staying, I wish I had. I really wish I had. Because all of these words fit except those. We could have had it—had it still, Eisel, except somehow, we let our individual paths become more important than our love, I guess, or at least I did. I allowed my own dream grow past what we had and take me roving when I could have stayed home. Should have, if I'd realized it in time.

Now I can't go back to what my life was when I left—when the most excitement and challenge I could look forward to was rolling the trashcans to the curb before the garbage truck arrived.

The lyrics are all true about you, though, and what you've been in my life. I wish they were truer about me for you. I've let you down in this, and in the end, I don't think I can work it out. For that I am everlastingly sorry.

PPS. Again, I'm also sorry for not realizing what was happening inside me and for not talking it over with you. What I've learned since leaving is that those feelings I was so afraid you'd talk me out of can't be ignored. I shouldn't have blamed you for my fear of not being able to leave. That wasn't on you. It was on me. I'm so very sorry that I shut you out until you believed I didn't want you anymore, and wounded your sweet heart so badly when I could have been kind in the telling and patient with your shock and surprise instead of turning anger on you. Foolish words.

Foolish me.

* * *

I spend the rest of the day on the couch in a fetal position, curled up with a blanket and a box of tissues. This is what has been lurking down underneath everything since Jimmy's announcement in the kitchen months ago. I've glimpsed it but managed to armor up with irritation and be the one to call the shots to keep it at bay. I thought being in control of the narrative that way, it wouldn't be able to leap out of the pit and devour me. Now it has. Now that he's come right out and confirmed it all—that I'm lower on his list of priorities than his Peruvian adventure and that he's not going to try to change that—I don't know what to do.

With this information, my world has fallen out of its decaying orbit. Lost its guiding star. I'm not sure anything will ever, ever be the same as it was. Henceforth, I'm destined to live with knowing that even if Jimmy returns to Ranger Falls, he won't be returning to me. I've articulated this to myself many times over the months, yet I see now that I never quite believed it to be true. Now all that is left me is to allow our relationship to move into the realm of friendship.

That has never felt so inadequate as it does at this moment. I'm losing Jimmy as a lover, a possible romantic partner, a husband. Friendship compared to that is a dry and dusty crust of bread. We're not going to have the storybook ending after all, the one where it turns out he loves me most, and we enter these final years on the crest of a wave of romance that settles all my questions and fills my starved heart to brimming over.

That's not going to happen.

Ever.

Every time I try to wrap my mind around this fact, my heart shatters further. What if I called him—if I begged him? Would he come home? Come home to me? Oh, right. To me and the excitement of outracing the garbage truck. No matter how many times I run the scenario, I end up at this conclusion: I can't be the one who kills Jimmy's dreams and smothers his brave wandering spirit.

I know we made vows to each other. However, if he doesn't want that now as much as he wants something else, who am I to hold him to a lifeless promise? Is it a gift to him to require that of him in his last years? To keep him back because *I* want him? No, it's not, and moreover, it sounds like adding punishment to pain for me if there's no romance between us. If he can no longer be happy here with me, why would I ask him to stay? Even if I want that in my heart of hearts, it looks as if we've gone too far down this river to pull out now.

Really, I don't know anything anymore, except that I ache as I've never ached before. Mourning forty-three years of sharing. I thought I had done that already or at least partially. I hadn't. Not really. I was angry and hurt, for sure. I drew up divorce papers, though only for the clarification it could bring. I never touched on—never let myself really dare think about—what it would be like to actually let Jimmy go. I'm grieving that now as if I'm burying my best friend and lover, because I guess that's really what's happening here. One by one, I'm prying my fingers off this thing we built and shared, and the act of relegating it to the past where it can only be accessed by memory is shredding me inside.

Memories? They are not enough. Not enough to fuel me and sustain me and give me hope. Because that's the thing—I *was* hoping apparently. Even through frustration and anger, in my secret heart, I held out hope of Jimmy bridging the chasm. I guess I thought that in the end, he'd throw me a lifeline to connect our hearts stronger than ever—that he'd give me a chance to romance him and be romanced in return. Absolutely I wanted that, and now? His email has ripped the roots of a giant oak tree out of my heart, and all that is left behind is brokenness.

"Jimmy," I wail. "Please, please come back. I want you so much. We can save our relationship. We can. We can."

But I don't pick up the phone and try. I'm hamstrung by his words and my knowledge that he would probably come home and try to make it work if I asked him to. But I couldn't bear it if he spent the rest of his days wishing he were still in Peru on that dig of his and trying not to resent what I'd asked of him. I also don't think I could bear the weight of trying to compensate for requesting such a thing, not year after year until we die.

If home is where your heart is, then mine must be in Peru right now with Jimmy. That in itself is a disastrous truth, because Jimmy's heart is not here with me in Ranger Falls. It's there on site with him. For a long minute, I even entertain the idea of going down there just to be with him, to be together again like we've always been. Yet what would that accomplish? He already said it wouldn't bump me into first place in his affections, that he's still on a solo journey, and at the end of the day, being second fiddle to any love is not something I can live with, especially now that it's out in the open.

Yet I'm not sure I can live without him, either.

You might ask," What have you been doing these past five months, then?" to which I would reply, "Play acting. Role playing what it feels like to be a single, 64-year-old woman who is no longer needed/wanted in the relationship and is setting out on her own adventure of experiencing a great romance."

Only now—suddenly and too late—I'm seeing that a great romance is not made up of only being seen and enjoyed and respected and desired. It's also forged in the flames of difficulty, the pain of process shared, and the building of history together. Jimmy and I, we already did the hardest parts, and it rips the bottom out of my heart that we've failed when it came to the easiest, most enjoyable ones.

I'm too late to kiss away his fears.

Too late realizing that I love the life we've made.

Yes, he's let me down. But I've let him down as well, and that breaks my heart as much as all the rest of it. All the sweetest times we've experienced? I'm afraid I'll cry every time I remember them, because we don't have them anymore. Not making any new, dear memories together ever? How can I bear this thought?

I can't.

Yet somehow, I must, and that brings a fresh flood of tears.

I keep coming back around to the same brick wall: Jimmy has been honest with where his heart is. To go against that because I hope I can change his mind and heart at this point? I think I should not try. After all, if we don't own our own hearts, then what do we have left? I can't tell him what to love the most. If I love him more than all else in my life, and he doesn't love me that way anymore, my only choice is to live with that hard truth. To mourn it well or poorly, because he's not coming back. That's all that's left to me now, and I am going under.

CHAPTER 21

I think there's no doubt about it: I mourn my loss poorly at first. Though I suppose if being thorough is mourning it well, then I excel. I spend the days in my pjs in bed, getting up only to pee or to brew some coffee that I then let grow cold as I sit there slumped in the empty kitchen. I'm alone here with my pain, and I want it that way. Like a burn victim who can't bear the touch of a cloth on her ravaged skin, I can't talk to anyone.

Can't see anyone.

Can't eat.

Can't sleep.

Can't think.

I can only feel, and it's all on the dark side. I don't seem to be able to find my bootstraps to drag myself up by them, nor, after a few faint attempts at rallying, do I even care to try. Why should I pretend to myself that it's going to be okay? How can it ever be okay without Jimmy in my world—across a cup of coffee? A foot touch away at night. To talk to and at this point, I'd even welcome him to argue with, if only he'd come back.

I don't answer my phone when it rings. I don't reply to messages. The first day, I text Cal and Dan and Kate to let them know about Jimmy's email and ask them to give me some breathing room to sort out my heart. Of course they do, because that's the kind of lovely humans they are.

Back when I wrote my email to Jimmy, I sent a copy to Maggie. It was easier than telling her my thoughts face to face.

So now I send her Jimmy's reply as well. She needs to know, to internalize and understand what he says there, and I don't have the heart or the strength to inform her myself. "Maggie, honey," I text. "I'm sending you your Dad's reply."

She'll know, once she reads it, why I'm going to ground like a wild animal with a mortal wound.

"Please don't call me," I add. "I can't talk about any of it right now. I know it's going to be rough for you, too, and once I surface, we'll talk. Lean on Jared, and for God's sake, appreciate what you've got together."

Dramatic? Of course.

I listen to Jimmy's and my favorite love songs, bawling my eyes out through them all, because now so many of them seem like a mockery or an impossible dream because they're no longer about us. Remembering our conversation that day when life as we knew it changed forever, I feel gutted over the lyrics of "When I'm Sixty-Four" when it comes up on the list. The whole song, despite its upbeat feel, drives me deeper down. No, he doesn't need me. He doesn't need me at all. Not any more.

I'm dreaming of Jimmy whenever I manage to fall asleep, and in those dreams, I'm always trying to save him from one disaster or another, or we're separated by uncrossable obstacles, and he drifts out of sight. No smiling there. What reduces me to one deep ache is that I'm almost certain he's not dreaming of me. Not like that. The promises we used to keep with each other? They're reduced to the promise of friendship, and right now, that is about as life changing as a teaspoon of water to someone in the final stages of dehydration.

Kate texts me on day five. *Girlfriend. I'm dropping a coffee off in your kitchen and checking your fridge to see if you need anything. I'll text you once I'm gone, and of course, if you want anything, please let me know.*

I text a heart emoji back, and after she sends me the all clear, I shuffle to the kitchen for the hot mocha latte sitting there along with a bag of Hershey's kisses. That girl knows me. I grab a handful and take my coffee back to bed.

The next day, I can't stand it any longer. I call Jimmy. It goes straight to voicemail. I don't leave a message, texting instead. *Jimmy, I just want to hear your voice, if you don't mind. I won't try to talk you out of anything.* I hope he'll see it and call me. Instead, the message bounces back seconds later. Not delivered. I try again. Again. Again. Twenty times I try. Twenty times my cry goes unanswered. I need help, and the person I've turned to for over four decades can't be reached. That seems especially symbolic in this moment.

I'm lost, wandering in a labyrinth whose walls are made of razors, where the floor conspires to trip me, and there is no light. I've never been this adrift before, and I have no tools, no strength, and no desire to move forward. As evening draws near on that sixth day in, terror creeps in with it, fear that if I don't do something to escape this dark place now, I may never find my way out.

Hovering there on the rim of a bottomless drop-off, I remember how Cal sang me back from the brink on the day I told Jimmy about him and Dan and was afraid I'd lost Maggie in the process. Cal knows what this feels like. He managed to survive his own version of it. Perhaps he can tell me what I need to do, because maybe I don't matter to anyone else in this world, not really, but Maggie at least, will be devastated if I don't find a way forward out of all this. That's the only thing I have to hold on to—I can't do that to my baby girl. For her sake, I can't give up.

I text Cal. *I'm drowning. Do you think you could come and sing for me again?*

I'll be right there. Leave your door unlocked.

I do, then wrap in my fuzzy blanket and curl up on the couch where he finds me less than fifteen minutes later. "Hi, you," he says, crouching down beside me, stroking my hair back from my blotchy face with a whisper soft touch. "May I hold you?"

That sets me crying again for the 973rd time, but I manage to nod and let him gather me into his arms.

"Poor darling," he murmurs. "It's so hard. I remember. Just let it out. I'll stay with you as long as you need."

Of course, that makes me cry even harder. "Jimmy says—" I try again. "Jimmy says he loves what he's doing in Peru more than he loves me. He's not coming back," I wail.

"I'm so sorry. So very, very sorry." Cal rocks me, holding me warm against him, and the tears soaking through his shirt this time make my former installments look amateur. "I'm sorry. I know it hurts," he murmurs. "Hurts so bad. I've got you, baby. Go ahead and cry all the tears you need to cry."

"I thought—I thought I was okay with him going," I sob. "Okay with moving on, but now that I know it's really true—now that he's said it himself—I realize I still hoped somehow he'd come back. I've lost myself in the sadness of it all now that I know for sure he doesn't love me enough to try. I'm not important enough to him for him to want to win my heart back, and I don't know how to live with that knowledge. How did you survive when you went through this, Cal?"

He's sniffing too, his voice choked with tears when he answers. "I just cried a lot. Like you're doing. I let the grief take me every time it came over me, and eventually the troughs weren't as deep and didn't last as long. There are no guidelines here, my friend, and no deadlines. You should take all the time you need."

He rocks me in a tiny forward and back motion, the kind you do with a little child, and that in itself feels so poignant I cry about it as well. Then he begins to sing, a quiet rumble beneath my ear, and the sound is so sweet and so soft, my sobs lessen so

I can hear. This time he's singing an old folk song, one my father used to sing in the evenings sometimes, "Oh, Shenandoah."

Cal settles me a bit more comfortably, cradled there against his chest, arms wrapped around my shoulders, my cheek resting against his calmly beating heart, and he lays his chin on my hair. Song after song, he holds me and rocks. After a while I realize I'm falling asleep, and I startle awake.

"No, baby. It's okay," he soothes. "Sleep now. I'll stay here with you until you're ready for me to leave."

That brings more tears, though this time there's a bit of ease in them. Nodding, I relax again as he starts on another song, and this time when I come awake, it's dark in the house. Cal is still here. My head on a pillow on his lap, I'm staring up at his chin. With his body turned a bit toward me so that his head rests on the back of the couch, one hand lays on my shoulder as if to reassure me; the other holds my head against him as he breathes long and slowly, sound asleep.

I lie here in the dimness. For the first time since I read Jimmy's email, there's a small space in my brain that is quiet. Not thinking. Not grieving. Not anything. Simply being. I don't know how long it will last, but I'm so grateful for the respite, I almost start to cry again. I'm thankful for this moment where I'm not drowning under the weight of the great sad ocean that crashed down upon me. Grateful for friends who bring me coffee and chocolate, and who come to keep me from being so completely alone in my loneliness.

That's the last thought I remember thinking until the morning sun reaches through the windows and touches me awake. Dragging myself into a sitting position, I smooth my pjs and my hair, tugging the blanket around my shoulders again like a protective skin. Breathing in, the tears come right behind it. This time they don't feel as if they're ripping my insides out though. They're only scalding my cheeks as they run down, and I hug a pillow to my chest. Then I smell coffee and hear Cal's hum approaching.

"Ah, there you are, sweet lady," he says as he sets two steaming cups on the coffee table. "I took a guess that someone who has cream in their fridge probably uses it in her coffee, and you have a bowl of stevia packets in the coffee area, so I brought a some along."

I smile. "Thank you, Sherlock. Two, please."

He nods, soft eyes, soft smile, watching me as he stirs then offers me the cup. "Careful now. It's pretty hot."

However, he doesn't release it. He helps support it as I take a sip, only letting go once I cradle it in my hands and nod. "Thank you," I whisper.

"There now, my friend." Sitting down beside me, turning toward me, he takes a tissue and blots away the streaks from my latest overflow. Then he takes his own cupful, sipping, watching me over the rim. He doesn't ask me anything, and I appreciate that, because I have no words. We simply sit there and drink our coffee while he holds my free hand up against his chest as if to ground me. It does. It also reminds me I must survive this day and tomorrow and tomorrow and tomorrow all by myself, and I melt down once more.

Taking my cup from me, he sets it down next to his and folds me in his arms. "It's okay. Cry all the tears you want to. We've got time."

"I don't want to be always crying on you, Calvin," I wail. "You may not believe this, but usually I'm the one who helps others in their pain. I don't know why I'm losing it so often with you. I probably look terrible, and I haven't been out of my pajamas for almost a week now."

He quirks an eyebrow. "That's important because?"

"Silly." I sob-laugh. "Because I look like last week's leftovers and probably smell like them too. I'm embarrassed about it."

"Shhh, honey. No need to be embarrassed with me. I'm your friend, remember? You're going through a very rough stretch right now, so go easy on yourself, you hear?"

I swallow back the fresh wave of tears welling up me at his gentle kindness. "Okay." Taking another sip of my coffee, it's my turn to watch him over the rim, this wonderful thoughtful human who is literally rescuing me by his presence. I can't process the gift or the magic that is. I only know that he saved me last night. I don't believe I could have made it through those dark hours alone intact.

"Here's what I'm thinking, if you're up for it, and if you're not, I'll scuttle the idea. How about after we finish our coffee, you and I go for a little drive, simply to breathe the outside air and be out under the sky? If you don't want to dress, that's fine. We don't need to stop anywhere, or if we do, we can take your blanket along for a cloak."

"Where would we drive?" I ask, trying on the idea, checking in with my heart to see if it feels up for that.

"We could drive all the way to Montana if you want to or just stay local." He winks, and I'm startled at how my stomach insists on doing a little flip flop at that, even in the state I'm in.

"You should be careful about your winks, Mr. Robinson, sir," I say, feeling like smiling for the first time since I learned I truly lost Jimmy.

He wiggles both eyebrows at me and chuckles. "Duly noted, ma'am. Glad to know they can be effective."

I shake my head. "You're—" I was going to say impossible, and it doesn't fit. "You're wonderful." I say instead, tears springing up again.

A little more holding. A little more breathing in tandem until mine begins to mirror Cal's slow, calm in-and-out, and the emotion peaks and passes. "Did you mean it about wearing my pajamas? Because I can't face dressing right now, though I think maybe I can wash my face and slip my sandals on."

"I did mean it. Let me help it happen." He sets our empty cups down, and taking my hands, pulls me to my feet, steadying me against him, his warm strong arms wrapped around me. That's as far as I get for quite a while because holding is still what I need, I guess, and he somehow knows that. Cradling my head on his shoulder, he sways a bit, rocking me in his arms until I'm steady enough to stand on my own.

I draw a big breath. "Okay. Operation face wash is a go."

Cal keeps an arm around me as we walk, as if I'm an invalid leaving her hospital bed for the first time in ages. That's certainly what I feel like. He runs the water till it's hot, washes my face with the care he must have taken with his children when they were small, then leans in the doorway while I run my fingers through my hair and push and prod it into order. "I think I'm going to have to go without eyebrows today." I grimace.

"Eyebrows are overrated." He smiles his wonderful smile again. "Why don't I go locate your shoes while you finish up?"

★ ★ ★

It's a cool, misty morning as we set out. This time Cal not only finds my seatbelt for me, he leans across and buckles me in, tucks my blanket in around me and kisses me on the cheek. "There you go, my friend."

"Thank you, Cal," I say, tears standing in my eyes again. I think now I'm crying because tears have become my only response. He simply hands me a tissue and smiles. We drive through the stillness of the morning, out to the river bottoms where the land and the deer and the day all seem to be part of each other. Wandering in the woodlands, we traverse more country roads than I knew existed, stopping at a state park miles and miles from town for a pit stop. The air smells of pine and toasted grass, birdsong is all around, and I'm taking big, deep breaths as Calvin stands behind me, holding me against him within the protective circle of his arms, and letting the land's magic and his own rhythm reset me.

I wonder if he feels the moment I come to the surface, my nose above water for the first time since reading Jimmy's email. I know I do, because that's the moment I think that maybe, just maybe, I might eventually be okay. It feels like a lightening of the weight on my chest, or as if my heart, crushed and broken, has given one tentative beat, then another as it comes back online.

CHAPTER 22

"**D**id you have anyone who helped you—who rescued you like you're doing for me when your wife left you?" I ask Cal as we drive home. I'm holding his hand like the lifeline it is, enjoying his profile, and how his short-cropped salt-and-pepper curls go so perfectly with his warm brown skin and grizzled skim of a circle beard.

Taking a deep breath, he blows it out slowly and nods. "My brother came, and I don't know what I would have done without him."

I know how that feels. I squeeze his fingers, and he smiles, his eyes sad as he pulls my hand over to hold it against his chest. "Remembering all that, I'm thinking you need a bit more time before you're ready to fly solo again, lady, and here are my thoughts on that. I cleared my calendar for the next few days. We'll swing by my house so I can pick up some fresh clothes and sundries, and then I'm moving into your place until you're begging for some space of your own."

It's so unexpected; so kind and so perfectly what I need, that of course, I'm crying again. "You'd do that?" I ask once I can talk.

"It would be my privilege, Lady Jane." He holds my hand against his warm cheek now, his eyes on the road in between glances to read my face. "We'll figure out the details as we go. Right now, you need someone on site in case the waves rise too high again. I want to be that person for you."

"Okay." It's a weak and watery okay, but I think he can hear the relief behind my words. I pass the rest of the day in a stupor, really. Not talking. Not able to string thoughts together without losing the thread. Not reading. Not watching TV. I'm simply laying comatose on the couch, tucked up cozy with my favorite blanket and pillow, and Cal sits in the chair next to me where I can see him without needing to move.

He reads, slouched and comfortable in stocking feet, chin propped on one fist, one leg crossed over the other. If he catches me watching him, he meets my eyes and smiles, not speaking unless I do, and he doesn't watch me, an act I very much appreciate, even if I'm not reciprocating it.

Whenever I need to use the bathroom, he helps me down the hall, waiting by the door, and situating me on the couch again afterwards. I take a few sips of water when he offers them and at some point, he makes a sandwich for me, but I can't eat; the lump in my throat won't let anything pass. At least I'm not crying, though. As much. As long as I don't think about Jimmy and how he doesn't love me more than Peruvian archeology.

Not anymore.

As late afternoon gives way to evening shadows, Cal stands up and stretches, then crouches down beside me to smooth my hair back and kiss me on the cheek. "How are we doing?"

I smile up at him, the only real thought I have is that he smells very good, and I like that.

"When is the last time you ate anything to speak of, lady?"

"I had some chocolate yesterday. Or maybe it was the day before. I can't remember."

"I see. I get it. I do. Your stomach says it's going to reject anything you send down there, assuming your throat will let it pass. We're going to persuade them it's okay though, because you need to eat, honey, or it will make everything harder."

I shake my head. "I can't, Calvin, really."

"You leave it to your friend, Cal, okay? I'm slipping out for a few minutes. You lay here and rest easy, okay?"

"Okay." Like I've been doing anything else. I must drift off to sleep at some point, though, because I wake to the sound of the door opening.

"It's me, Eisel." Cal appears a few moments later with a bowl, a spoon, and a very determined look on his face. "Alright now. You're going to have to trust me on this one," he says as he assists me to a sitting position, wraps my blanket more snugly around me, and takes a seat to my left. "Here, turn a bit my way, chickabiddy. I'll feed you the way my bro did me and see how it goes."

Chicken soup. I don't know where he found it, but it tastes salty and good, and that takes me by surprise. I manage to swallow it, and he waits a beat before offering more. "Let's go with ten spoonfuls, Eisel J, and then if you want to, we'll take a break."

I nod, intent only on trying not to let the broth dribble down my chin as he spoons it in. Part of me is aware that in the right circumstances, this could be a very romantic moment. The other part of me is simply hoping not to look so completely and utterly in pieces that Cal will still want to spend time with me after this whole disaster, if it's not already way too late for that.

We do this soup routine once more before bedtime, and it's not quite so hard to swallow the second time around. "Thanks, Dr. Cal. I think you might have missed your calling." I say, leaning my head on his shoulder as he sets the bowl down.

He chuckles in that way I love, caramel-colored and rumbly. "I have hidden talents you know not of. Yet."

"Silly."

"Definitely."

As if I'm standing somewhere outside my body, I feel detached, past emotions, while at the same time, I'm aware of iron bands still constricting my chest so that it aches with a dull insistent throbbing. Not as intensely as yesterday, though, and I watch as Cal turns back the bed for me, covers me once I'm in, and kisses me on the cheek.

"Okay, Lady Jane. Here's what I'm thinking, and you tell me if it sounds okay with you; Firstly, I'll sit here and read until you fall asleep. Then I'll grab that quilt from the couch and curl up on top of your blankets over on the other side. That way if you need me in the night, all you have to do is reach over, and I'll wake up."

Perfect. You're perfect. I think I say it, but I guess I only think it and cry again, because Cal kneels down to my level, blots my tears with a tissue, and then lays his torso across mine, like a warm, masculine-smelling, weighted blanket to call my spirit back to my body. "There, there, honey. It's okay. I'll stay here with you as long as you need. It's okay. It's okay."

He begins singing over me again, his head propped on his elbow and staring off to somewhere at something I can't see as he strokes my hair. This time he croons "Down in the Valley," an old cowboy song I've always loved, and he follows up with others just as low and sweet until I drift off.

★ ★ ★

When I wake in the night, I find the pool of inner stillness from earlier has spread a little further, and the edges that it touches don't seem quite so brittle or sharp. In the moonlight, Cal is a mound under his quilt on the other side of the bed, face in the shadows, his hand within touching distance. Softly so as not to wake him, I slip mine into it simply to feel the warmth and brightness of another human being where not that long ago, all light had gone out.

I wake up to the aroma of bacon and coffee, and I'm almost affronted that it smells so good. After a quick shower and a new outfit—really only a glorified set of pajamas masquerading under the name of lounge wear—I follow my nose to the kitchen.

"Good morning, Dr. Calvin Lifesaver Robinson."

He smiles and comes around the island to envelope me in a long, gentle hug. "A very good morning to you, Miss Flatterer Extraordinaire."

I smile. "Just telling the truth, sir. It's my greatest weakness and also my superpower."

"Well, I like it fine, so you keep on keeping on. It's quite effective." That wink again. "I reckoned we couldn't go wrong with a little bacon and an English muffin toasted fine, and I think you must love blackberry jam, because that's all I can find in your fridge."

I smile. "True. Jimmy loves strawberry, but when he left, I threw the jar away." I pause to see if the thought, the mention of Jimmy will stab me, and I brace for it. It does hurt, but after the sadness, I find a bit of humor. "Can you believe I threw away a perfectly good jar of jam because I was pissed?"

"Makes sense to me."

"That's because you don't know yet that I'm one of those people who never throw away food if I can possibly help it. Starving children in China and a guilt-ridden childhood make sure of that." I grin as he holds out a slice of bacon for me to sample, taking the rest from his fingers. "I believe your chicken soup remedy has begun to affect a cure."

"I'm mighty glad to hear that, Eisel Jane. Mighty glad indeed."

"Of course, I would argue that chicken soup itself is only part of the equation," I add, meeting his gaze and pouring all my gratitude into the look I give him. "I do think the hand that fed it to me and kind heart that kept the night watch is what really made the difference."

His eyes glitter as he slides a cup of coffee and a plate my way. "I'm so happy it helped and that you're feeling a bit better, my friend. Remember, there's no rush. I wish I could say that it's smooth sailing from here on out. However, we both know things don't go that way in the real world. They swing up and down, backwards and forwards. Don't you fret it, though. You're going to make it through, and I'll be walking right alongside you to help that happen."

I think I've never met such a kind person, and I have no words. I only smile and nod and try not to cry. To distract myself, I change the subject. "If we were at my own little house in the country, we could take our breakfast out to the porch swing," I say as I savor the goodness of the well-toasted muffin, letting the salty, buttery richness and dark fruit sweetness flood my senses. "I feel bad that I left Dan to figure things out without me."

Cal nods. "Understandable. However, I talked to Dan a couple days ago, because we were both concerned about you after your text. He gave me an update on the house as well. The inside painting is done and outside repairs wrapped up Friday, plus the floor refinishers will be done and out of there by today."

I don't know whether to be embarrassed or flattered that Dan and Cal were discussing my emotional state. I decide the latter is preferable. "That's amazing. So theoretically, I could start moving in anytime from now on?"

"Sounded like that to me."

I feel a blip of excitement, and a sudden flurry of logistical thoughts—arranging for movers, changing my address, which items of furniture will go with me. Renting this house out. "Amazing. I didn't realize how close I was to checking that item off my bucket list," I say. "It feels quite fitting that you'd be here when that's taking place, seeing as you're the one who helped it happen."

"Speaking of your bucket list. I'm thinking that when you're ready, we need to keep working on the other item you mentioned.

Yes ma'am. I'm mighty interested in pursuing that at your earliest convenience."

Definitely blushing now.

★ ★ ★

Cal stays with me another three full days, lending his kindness, support, and strength as bit by bit, hour by hour, I pick up the pieces of my heart, sifting through the rubble for what remains. Nights are the worst, as they always have been for me. Knowing Cal is within reach keeps me from wandering lost in the darkness, and each morning when I wake, I feel more like myself. Still raw and wounded, yet more able to let my mind touch on Jimmy and how our marriage has really and truly ended without being swept out to sea with the grief of it all. Or not swept as far out, anyway. I can now find my way back to shore when that happens, and though I know there'll be times I'll be rolled under those waves again, I now believe I'll eventually be okay.

I can't answer Jimmy's email yet. Instead, I send him a short text. *I got your email. I'm so very sad about it all, and I will always miss you and all we shared. Thank you for still being my friend. I will always be yours as well.* Ironically, this text sends just fine and shows as delivered.

I could fill a book telling how I don't know what to do with the level of pain I feel over knowing that life together as we knew it— all its shortcomings, all its sweet joys—is over. How do you express such a thing in words anyway? I don't try. Maybe I can take a trip to Peru once I feel stabilized enough. Some day. Some year.

I call Scott and ask him to serve the divorce papers, because it's clear that things between Jimmy and I are over. Really and truly over, and delaying isn't going to change that reality. I cry a new river of tears after this call, held in the safety of Cal's warm embrace, yet afterward, I find a more solid ground beneath my feet for having crossed this line of demarcation.

Cal goes home the next day around eleven, texting now and then throughout the afternoon, checking in on me, then sleeping under his quilt on the other side of my bed as he has done since that first night. I don't care what the neighbors might think to see his black SUV drive up every evening and leave every morning. What I do is my own business and besides, I'll be leaving this neighborhood soon.

Each day, I fill my time with sorting through belongings, packing the ones I want to take to my new place, and queueing up movers for next week. Maybe Cal will go with me for a walkthrough this coming weekend. I'd love to see my own little home all fresh and waiting for me to inhabit it. I could never have known what a gift that item on my bucket list would be, but I'm flooded with gratefulness that I will not need to craft my future while living here at this house. It is too full of memories of Jimmy and our life together to ever rest easy in again.

I still text no one, but maybe next week I will. Or this weekend.

Finishing out the week this way, putting my past to rest item by item, within me peace spreads out hour by hour until I no longer feel the same searing pain when I think of life without Jimmy. Yes, it still hurts, aching like a broken bone—fragile, stabbing when bumped, yet healing bit by bit, and I find myself believing that one day, the break will be a mere white line proving that I have indeed made it through to the other side.

Five thirty on Friday, Cal arrives with a box of Kentucky Fried Chicken that we eat while watching *R.E.D.* with Bruce Willis, Morgan Freeman, and John Malkovich. I grin. "Cal, did you know that the first time I heard your voice, I could have sworn I'd dialed heaven by mistake and gotten an angel or even God? Morgan Freeman should be jealous," I say, watching Cal's face, my fingers entwined with his as we sit there. "You have such a lovely, irresistible voice."

Pursing his lips, he smiles, waggling his eyebrows at me. "Thank you for that compliment. I can't claim God status, that's for sure. However, I will say that is some excellent information right there, lady. You may be sure I'll use that to my advantage at your earliest convenience."

I can't help laughing at his banter, especially after he adds his signature wink and brushes a knuckle up my chin, setting me tingling. This is the first flirting he's engaged in since Jimmy's email, and I smile to find myself quite ready to slip back into that mode. Is this really me, the one who was thrashing in a black and bottomless underground river not all that ago? I think about that as we wash up the dishes afterwards, testing my emotional balance. I think I'm going to be okay. If so, I should let Cal sleep in his own bed, bless his heart. But at that prospect, the coming night looms before me like a long dark tunnel.

"Cal," I say as I dry the items he washes. "I hate to ask you, but would you please sleep with me again tonight? I know I need to get past this, but—" I look over at him, and he's ginning. "Whatever are you smiling about, Mr. Robinson?" I ask, mirroring in spite of myself.

"You." He lifts his hands from the soapy water and deposits a dab of suds on my nose. "You asked the perfect question and didn't even know it, you refreshing person, you." As I process that, I blush, especially as he adds the next sentence. "I would *love* to sleep with you, Eisel Jane. In fact, it would be my privilege and my very great pleasure to sleep with you every night, and you can take that any way you please, lady."

To mask my embarrassment and the surge of tingles I feel as the implication of his words hit home, in a classic teenager move despite my sixty-four years, I scoop up a handful of water and flick it full in his face, laughing as he startles.

"Oh, it's like that, is it?" He laughs and promptly returns the favor.

Yelping, I retaliate, then dodge around the island, ducking his next shower, laughing somewhat hysterically as my emotions come back online after being hijacked by sorrow.

Hands dripping, Cal chases me, and I circle the island, snagging a dishtowel as I go, throwing it at his face to slow him down, squealing as I evade his grab, and we're both laughing as I flick another handful of water at him, this time ice cold from the fridge dispenser as I pass it. Eyes twinkling, arms spread, Cal stalks me, and I back away, then make a break for it, only to have him pound after me.

Skidding around the corner, I meet him coming the other way. Cornered, breathless, I throw up my hands. "Truce!"

"Truce, is it?" He laughs, stepping close. "Then, come here, you." Gently and insistently, he draws me toward him, hands on my waist, staring down at me with complete focus until I'm flushed and trembling. Smiling, he shakes his head, and I smile back, suspended in this timeless moment as the rest of the world fades away. Still holding his eyes, I oh, so slowly reach up and stroke his cheek with the back of my hand, not hurrying. Savoring the warmth and wonder of this man who has become my friend on a level I have never experienced before. "Calvin."

Swallowing, he leans into my touch, eyes deep and soft, his voice a mere whisper as he responds. "Eisel."

We hold there for long sweet breaths, my hand still against his face. This is magic. This is romance. Man-woman, beyond friends, past flirting, and my body lights up in a whole new way as he turns and brushes his lips against my knuckles. Holding my breath, I sway toward him, electricity zipping through me as our bodies touch.

Pulling me against him, Cal reaches up and skims a finger along my hairline, watching me with such intensity it sends another rush through my core. I'm floating, registering how good he smells, how good he feels, and that enchantment wraps me deeper. "Cal," I breathe. I'm not thinking, not attempting to solve or fix or head any direction at all. I'm just here. Now. Completely caught in who he is, mesmerized, fully engaged.

One hand still on my waist, holding me against him, Cal trails his fingers down my face again, down my neck, down my arm, and takes my hand. Then with a smile as kind as sunlight, he hums the first notes of a song as he gazes into me. I'm sure he sees the moment I recognize just what that song is; I have no power to resist even if I wanted to as all the lyrics flood me in one swift download. The song is "I Can't Help Falling in Love with You," and the meaning and anticipation of the words sweep through me like a wind shear, leaving me weak in the knees, breathless, yielded.

"May I have this dance, lady?" His voice is as soft and plush as velvet as he moves us into position and snugs me closer against him. Like someone in a trance, captivated with the magic unfolding between us, I rest my other hand on his shoulder, and he swings me into the beginning steps, singing as we dance in a slow sensual body-melded swaying.

Tingling, biting my lip, I look up and meet his eyes. They're shining down at me, and beyond the words he sings, I see a question there as he starts the second verse. "Shall I stay—"

My heart, the one I thought was broken forever, the one that just buried its first and longest love, is ascending in full brightness. It feels like a miracle, and I fight back tears because I don't want to hijack that feeling or slip back into what must become the past. The way he sings those lyrics, they're not Elvis'. They're Cal's very own. With his heart in his eyes, he's asking me if I'm okay with him staying. Okay with him singing these words to me. Would it be too soon or too much or not welcome?

No, I discover. It's not too soon. Not too much. I blink up at him in slow motion. Does he really mean to tell me he's falling in love with me? Because I'd bet my new little old house he's saying just that, and I can't help but smile as I feel my answer rising.

As if he can't believe what is happening between us, he smiles back, his breath catching, his hot gaze holding me as we move. The longer he looks at me, the more I melt, captured, buzzing with all that's singing through me. Just when I think I can't sustain eye contact any longer, Cal pulls me in against his chest as he moves into the chorus, his body so warm and solid against mine, I gasp at the rightness and the hunger sweeping me.

He drops from leading me in the classic box pattern we've held like we're melded together and simply sways in place. I'm melted, swimming in the beauty and sweetness of the moment, feeling reborn and alive again in a tender, new way. Then as he holds me out from him just a bit, I see his eyes are filled with tears. They hang on his black lashes like stars and his lips look so soft. A smile tips their corners up as he begins the next verse, and with a whisper touch, he strokes my face, my neck, and I dissolve into his gaze. As he sees that, he gives a long, slow wink and grins as he swirls me out to the end of his arm, then tugs me back in so my face is only inches from his.

I've lost all contact with the shore, yet the ocean I'm on right now bears no resemblance to that thrashing, killing sea I just survived. I find Cal's dark brown gaze to bring myself back to center, and as he starts into the last stanza, our steps slow further, then stop.

Now he traces down my cheek, skims along my jawline, and floats his thumb across the rim of my lower lip with the lightest of touches while his fingers cup my face. I don't even care that he can probably feel my pulse racing under his fingertips. Then again, I don't know if he's thinking about that so much, because his gaze drops from mine to fixate on my lips. He's done this before;

this time feels different. He flicks his eyes up to mine again, and they're hot, his heart pounding against me.

His gaze drops again, slowly, as if he's trying not to but can't help it. Will he kiss me this time? I want him to. Oh yes, I very much want him to, more than ever before, like a deep hunger in me. All the times he refrained, all the butterfly touches that never crossed this barrier, they're piled up in my wanting like a logjam blocking a river in flood. Please, Cal, I think as I lift my face, lip caught between my teeth, longing for—oh, so desperate to feel his lips on mine, to taste him, to cross into that sacred bonded territory. Please?

He holds off, though, motionless except for his heart throbbing under my hands, now spread on his chest. Gazing up into his eyes, I'm fully enchanted. Trembling. We're so close, his breath warm on my face, and I'm completely enveloped in this still, wondrous moment. Another wave of desire sweeping me, I part my lips, ready for his.

Eyes focused, breath as fast and shallow as mine, he leans in, hovering above me, one hand cradling my head, the other warm on my back. I lift my chin, waiting to receive this kiss I realize I've been longing for for weeks, and I swallow in anticipation. We're so close, panting there, lips mere inches apart.

I sigh. Cal echoes, but he doesn't move.

Something must give before I die of need and wonder. Then in this moment, I realize it's me. I'm the one who says yes here. I'm the one who must choose, and to choose this is to choose him and him only, and he's waiting for my answer. The time has come.

I must be the one who initiates, the one to take this where I want to go. To choose Cal over every other man in the world, known or unknown. This life-altering truth is suddenly crystal clear and completely okay with me, because it's not merely my body responding to this lovely man. It's my heart. The very heart I thought was crushed beyond recovery I see now was really only caught in the undertow of grief for finally and completely owning the fact of what it had already lost. But this? This is completely other. It's perfect and right, and it feels like coming home.

I love him. Love him! I know this with absolute, life-giving certainty. With Cal, I feel safe and seen and adored and more—all the important boxes checked, and I know in this moment without a doubt that I do not want to go through life without this wonderful man.

So I smile up into those questioning dark eyes of his, my own half closed with the rush of affection and longing surging through me. I bring my lips up, up up until we're a breath apart, Cal and I, and there we stand, as still as starshine and moonlight and deep space until I can stand it no longer. I reach in the final distance to touch my lips to his.

Then he takes me down with him as he goes.

CHAPTER 23

In a story like this, there's always a wrap up, right? All those loose ends that need tidying so no one is left hanging. I'll do it quickly so as not to detract from the single stunning reality that I, Eisel Jane McCord, am currently and completely and thrillingly experiencing a great romance right now, and his name is Calvin Felix Robinson. We're sitting on my couch, a love song playing low in the background, and everything feels almost too perfect for me to take it in. I'm sailing as high as the moon.

Now about those loose ends. Kate can wait. She'll understand. She'll be thrilled for me once she hears my whole process, has known me for almost as long as Jimmy and I have been married, and she loves me, so nothing to dread there.

Dan Baker. He's such a lovely man, and I need to be so careful with his heart. He's been nothing except good to me, and while he's a cowboy, he's a straight-shooting, uncomplicated, and earnest one. I've enjoyed all the hikes we've taken, the sunsets on the bluffs, and conferring with him on the repairs he did on my house. A week or two after I told him about Cal, we transitioned from his version of a goodnight kiss to a long hug instead, because he let me know he hit his limit of investing without giving his heart completely away, and until I knew which way mine would choose, he needed to stop at that line.

It was hard at the time, yet now I'm glad. He's too special of a man to have his heart broken again, having buried a beloved wife, and I'm too fragile myself to survive disappointing someone else. I'm now doubly glad, because from here on out, there is only this wonderful, warm, wise man named Cal for me. I'll need to meet Dan and tell him and see if he's still okay with planning for a monthly burgers-on-the-bluffs catch up, because I really enjoy him as a person and a friend.

"Calvin," I say, though mightily distracted by the fact that he's stroking my arm up and down, so very softly. "I have to tell Dan. About us."

"Agreed, that does need to happen," he says, kissing me again, long and slow and deeply. "Talking with him during these last few days, I admire him more than ever. Also, I'm not about to share you with anyone."

"Silly," I say, tracing his lovely eyebrows with my finger and enjoying how he closes his eyes and purrs beneath my touch. Enjoying that quite a bit. "No worries there," I add. "Having three men in my life at the same time in the romantic realm was not only extremely confusing, but it was also never my intention. I simply needed the time you were so wise to ask me to give. Did you know then, somehow—did you have an inkling how it would turn out? Who I would choose?"

He shakes his head, and I think I see in his eyes all the days of uncertainty he's lived until now, and it melts me further.

"No, baby. I did not. I didn't dare assume or ask you about it either, because I know myself. I know I'd never be content with only part of your heart, and it wasn't mine to take. Only yours to give."

"You marvelous person, you," I say, skimming my thumb back and forth over his soft lips until he can't stand it any longer, and pulls my hand away to set those lips on mine again. "I also need to tell Maggie."

"For sure. How're you feeling about that?"

"Terrified." I kiss his eyes, his nose, his lips, so soft and answering then sigh and lean against him. "I'm sure she's taking this news about her dad pretty hard, and I haven't had it in me to try to comfort her. I'm afraid if I tell her my decision about you, she'll feel even more devastated and be hateful to you. That would break my heart again for the both of you. I'm also afraid she'll think you're catching me on the rebound or some such nonsense and try to sabotage us."

He clears his throat. "Not to worry, my lady. Not only am I impervious to sabotage and can have a remarkably thick skin when it comes to protecting someone I love, I'll have her know that I've been hoping for this scene or one very like it since I first walked you through that old house of yours."

"Really? I'm going to want to hear more about that," I say, tickling him under the chin, which is apparently code for "kiss me."

He smiles down at me as I recuperate. "Now before you go looking so adorable that I can't resist doing that all over again, I do have some thoughts about the timing, if you'd be interested in hearing them. Not saying you must do it this way, but for what it's worth."

"Yes, please," I say, stroking his neck from jaw to collarbone with the back of my finger simply to see him catch his breath and try to stay focused.

"I'm wondering how long my little truth teller can go before reaching maximum pressure to tell it like it is.

I grin. "I suppose that depends on what it is, and why I'd not be telling sooner than later."

"As I suspected." He folds me into a warm, safe hug, and I sigh at the comfort of our connection. "Remember when I asked you to promise to give your heart time to choose?"

"That advice saved me more than once, and I think I can safely say that my heart has now chosen. Chosen you, in case you need me to say that in words." That statement earns me a deep lingering kiss that sets my whole being on fire. "Yes, I choose you,

Calvin Robinson," I whisper once I can breathe again. "Also, and for the record, I love your kisses."

"I've been saving them up, waiting for this auspicious day, and I don't consider I've hardly gotten started on that little item." He nibbles my ear. "Okay, back to my thought, or should we do another round for good measure?"

"Another round, please, kind sir."

He's more than obliging, and the taste of him is magic as we bond deeper with every shared breath, fully immersed in this wonder. Eventually, he sighs and tries again. "On telling Maggie? I think this is another situation where time can be a gift, Eisel. A gift for Maggie, because I think she'll need time to process all that has happened between her dad and you before she learns about us. More than that, I'd really love to see you give your own sweet heart a bit more time to heal before you use it to heal others."

Nestling me into him, he holds me there, stroking my hair away from my face, looking into my eyes until I'm swimming in his deep brown gaze. "It's as if you've undergone open heart surgery and just starting on the road to recovery. As your doctor—I hope now, your favorite doctor—I prescribe that you treat that heart as you would if it was someone else's. Don't push it beyond what it feels able to bear. Be careful not to rip open stitches or scar it worse. Give it time."

I relax into him. "I have to admit that sounds lovely. It also feels selfish, especially when it comes to Maggie."

"Sweetheart," he says, sniffing my neck in one long indrawn breath, (and I'm feeling glad I added a little perfume after my shower this morning, a habit I've gotten into since that day he confirmed it was effective). "I understand. I do. However, if Maggie was in your place, what would you want her to do? Break her poor little heart again trying to help others make sense of something no one should have to face in the first place?"

I picture my sweet Maggie in my shoes (heaven forbid she ever is, though that is not the point here). Would I want her to be barely emerging from being almost swallowed by the black hole in the universe that opened up under her—to be just starting to smile and think and possibly feel the stir of life and purpose she was sure had been stolen forever—would I want her to stress that brave yet barely beating heart in order to make other less devastated, and honestly, less involved people feel better? Absolutely not.

"No." I sigh. "I wouldn't. I suppose I'd want to set an example of how to navigate loss, though that's a bit presumptuous at this time," I add with a laugh. "Because at this point, the only thing I know for sure that is that if someone doesn't have a friend like you to come alongside and simply be with them, grief may just swallow them whole, like mine was doing until you came."

"So may I ask another promise of you, lovely Eisel Jane?" Cal says, his feather-touch stroking my cheek, his eyes gazing into mine. "Would you promise to wait to tell Maggie about us until your own heart is stabilized?" His voice and his eyes go even softer, something I hadn't thought possible. "Promise that you'll wait until every time you think of Jimmy, it doesn't bleed sadness and regret? Until all the questions and all the answers have settled into a cohesive narrative you can live with? Talk to her about Jimmy and your feelings as you feel ready. That's most relevant to both of you, but don't mention me. Keep us a special secret until you're ready, okay?"

He lets that sit a bit, and as I think that over, it feels as if he's thrown me another lifeline, something I can use to guide my actions and decisions when confusion rules. So yes, I can wait to tell Maggie because I realize that he's completely right; I need time, and she needs time.

However—and this is a very important differentiation—I also know I have already crossed the valley of death, and I'm standing on the other side. Maybe on shaky legs. Maybe not ready to do more than I'm doing at this moment—hiding away with the one person who doesn't capital N Need me to be anything except who and what I am—yet as I gaze inward, I realize that the quietness inside myself has not only enlarged, it's grown to where I can't see the edges anymore. I feel—I feel fine. I feel good. I feel as if there will come a time when I will be able to share with Maggie about this special thing Cal and I curate between us, and I will not be afraid of any storms that could result.

There may even come a time, if Maggie can make that journey herself, that someday she'll be there watching this wonderful man and me, this new "us" stand under a lovers' arch and make our vows to each other. I hope so. One thing I know for sure, though—I know I'm going to cherish every moment from now to the end of my days for the wonder and the romance that I have found with Calvin Felix Robinson. That's not sad. That's very *very* glad.

"Look at me, sweetheart," he says, turning me in his arms until my legs are draped across his and my hands are clasped behind his neck while his arm encircles and supports me. "Before you answer me, I want you to be very clear on something, in case anyone ever questions why we delayed in telling people about us. I want you to know as certain as we're looking at each other right now, that if it wasn't for the terrible wounding you just weathered and the aftermath of that pain, I'd be wanting you to tell everyone. Now. Tonight." He cradles my face in his hand, smoothing my cheekbone so gently. "The truth is, I'm over the moon proud that you're choosing me. Of all the decisions you could make, I hardly dared hope for this." Tears glisten in his eyes and mine tear up in answer.

"In case you might wonder if somewhere behind it all, I don't want the news to come out about this lovely thing we're building between us, I promise you on my honor as a man and a lover, that nothing could be further from the truth. I want to tell everyone. I want to walk down main street with my arm around you and kiss you long and hard in front of everyone in broad daylight. Then look around to make sure everyone is watching and do it all over again."

"I appreciate the warning." I lift one eyebrow to tease him, which he then traces with a finger and trails down my cheek, down my neck, down my arm. I'm so very amazed to be here and now and experiencing the romance and wonder of belonging with him. Finally, I catch his hand and hold it still, because I know I'm only a breath away from completely losing connection with the earth, and I want to say one more thing while I still can.

"Too much?" he whispers, leaning in, brushing my lips with his, then drawing back a fraction. "You're so lovely, and the thought of all we will share has me wanting to move into that more sooner than later." His eyes twinkle into mine.

"No," I whisper. "Not too much, Cal, and I am very interested in that more as well, just so you know. Before we go there though, I just want to say that I promise." I cup his face in my hands and rest my forehead against his. "I promise I'll wait until I'm ready, and at that point, I'll gladly walk with you down Main Street and in the sight of every neighbor and child and dog, I will kiss you back."

Then I guess you'd say we practice for that coming occasion, and time stands still while the music plays, and everything around us begins to shimmer.

ABOUT THE AUTHOR

LESLIE J. WYATT crafts romance novels that celebrate love in later years. Born into Utah's high desert country, and raised in Montana's rugged beauty, she now resides in Northern California, where she creates immersive worlds filled with true colors, flawed but lovable characters, and wishes coming true.

A professional writer since 1997, Leslie's work spans romance, historical novels for young readers, and non-fiction. She has published over 1,000 pieces, including articles, profiles, and essays, in publications such as *WritersDigest.com* and *Romance Writers Report*. Leslie presents at literature festivals, writing conferences, workshops, writing-related podcasts and events. Find her online at lesliejwyatt.com, or on social media @lesliejwyatt and @artfortherestofus. When not writing, she enjoys camping with her husband and marveling at the countless stars in the night sky, finding inspiration for her next story in the beauty of the universe.

ACKNOWLEDGEMENTS

Acknowledgements for me are an equal mix of pleasure and panic—pleasure to thank all the wonderful people who played a part in making this book a reality—and panic in case I leave someone out. Just know that *I* know and so very much appreciate how you helped make this possible, even if I don't list you specifically.

To my marvelous first reader—where would I be without you? Your enthusiasm, grace, hair-splitting insights, and unflagging support made this journey joyful. I hope you never tire of being my first line of defense because your creativity and encouragement are invaluable.

To my Writing Buddy Forever, Emily McIntyre (emilymcintyre.com). Your challenge to "try something new" catapulted me into romance writing, and I need to invent a word more potent than "thanks," because that is lackluster for what I feel in this instance. But just for the record, THANK YOU!

A special shout out to Vicki DeArmon, publisher at Sibylline Press (and wearer of many other hats as well). Your insights on a cold October afternoon gave me fresh wind in my sails. I'm so grateful to have gotten to work with you on this book and for your kindness in the process.

All the wonderful folks at Sibylline Digital First have been amazing. It's truly delightful to hobnob with such professional, proactive, and creative humans as you are. You've restored my faith in the traditional publishing process and made me an avid fan of Sibylline Press and Sibylline Digital First,

To my incredible family—OMG, every one of you. I could fill pages with thanks, but for now, I want to say how much I appreciate your unwavering enthusiasm for my writing. Somehow your eyes never glaze over as I ramble about plots or characters, even when I realize halfway through I'm repeating myself. How can I not keep going, with all of you rooting for me?

And to my readers—you were in my mind and heart while I wrote *When I'm 64*. My hope is that something in this story encourages, comforts, and inspires you in your own journey. Never doubt that you carry something precious—the "who you are" in your essence—that is a treasure in this world.

BOOK GROUP QUESTIONS

1. Eisel ends up in a very different place from where she starts out in this story. How is this true of her inner world as well as her outer one?

2. Were there any moments or interactions that stood out to you as particularly memorable and what were they?

3. From Eisel's viewpoint, what was the underlying problem in the way Jimmy went about pursuing his dream in Peru and how could he have done that differently? Do you feel it would have made a difference in the ultimate outcome?

4. What missing element(s) contributed to Eisel's belief that she had never experienced a great romance despite her forty-three years with Jimmy? How valid do you think they are?

5. Jim, Dan and Cal are all lovely men in their own right. Which one did you hope Eisel would choose and why?

6. How does Eisel grow and change over the course of the story? Which of her conclusions resonated with you the most?

7. If you were to make an *Ingredients of Romance* list, what would be on it? Give an example of what each might look like in practical application.

8. Did the book evoke any strong emotions in you as a reader? If so, which scenes or moments resonated with you the most and why?

9. Did the book raise any social or ethical questions for you? If so, what were they, and how did you grapple with them as a reader?

10. Were there any messages or lessons that you took away from the story and how might they affect the future you?

Sibylline Press is proud to publish the brilliant work of women authors over 50. We are a woman-owned publishing company and, like our authors, represent women of a certain age.